ELEPHANT

JUICE

ELEPHANT

JUICE

Stephen J Cherrill

ISBN 9780648623519

 A catalogue record for this book is available from the National Library of Australia

ACKNOWLEDGEMENTS

To my friends who gave their time freely to read and critique several versions of *ELEPHANT JIUCE*, which enabled me to turn this book into a worthwhile read. I can't thank them enough. A big thank you to Sharon Priestley for her remarkable poem. Sandra Pustelnik, for her many words of encouragement. Cherrylin Twiner; Sandra Lee; Nicola Robertson; Dougall Potter; Marion Barker; Diane Thompson; Kerrie Hains; Lofty Roberts; Jean Halpin; Elizabeth Vicky Brauner for back cover author photograph; Erilyn Wedd for her cover design; and not forgetting the late Edwin, (Ted) Cherrill, my amazing Uncle. I would also like to thank a wonderful man, John Warren, who tirelessly helped me publish this book. His unending patience kept me on the right track. For that, I am eternally grateful.

Email: cherrill52@live.com

An arrow of anguish sears my soul

Tears constantly call as grief takes its toll

My eyes are unseeing, my senses are numb

as despair wins the battle, and I'm overcome.

The loss is not short, but forever and a day

For my child to leave before, a heavy price to pay

Cocooned in memories to help me get through

The jigsaw lies unfinished; it's not the same without you.

I cherish the moments that happened in the past

It breaks my heart, my darling; those memories were your last.

But still, I will remember, on your special day

The overwhelming love I felt when you lay in my arms.

To live this life without you is more than I can bear

But live I must, 'till I am dust, for life is never fair.

I gain some peace and comfort, from knowing you're in God's care

And pray the silken thread that binds us will one day guide me
there.

Sleep tight, my spirit child.

© *Sharon Priestly*

She held her hands like a beckoning Angel, eyes glistening with the warmth, affection, and unconditional love only a grandma has. I hesitated, but having accomplished my task, I knew it was time. The heavenly aroma of Sandalwood and Lavender surrounded me like a warm-scented breeze. As the light above intensified, love slipped over me like a silken cape and entered my soul as though by invitation.

"It's time." She whispered.

"I'm ready," I replied.

ONE

It was a bitterly cold, bone-chilling afternoon when you don't go outside unless you have to. Impervious to the cruelly cold afternoon, a man darted from a bush to a nearby alcove and took advantage of the swirling mist like a lion stalks its prey. With a cap pulled low over his eyes and a scarf wrapped around his mouth, the man paused in the alcove while his mark entered the Post Office.

She left the Post Office, and he held his foggy breath to avoid detection. Then he dashed to a nearby bush and waited while the young girl crossed the road. From behind a brick shed in what seemed like a well-rehearsed routine, the man darted behind a hedge when the girl entered the cemetery. He kept his distance, creeping and crouching, then by flattening himself against a stone monument, he knew that she was unaware that she was being followed. Deep inside the cemetery, mist hung like a grey sheet, sending shivers racing down her spine. The last slivers of daylight cast long shadows across the grass as she tramped along the familiar meandering gravel footpath; her footsteps broke the creepy silence. When the girl reached her destination, she knelt beside a grave and whispered a prayer. An unexpected sound startled her while she arranged the flowers in the granite vase. She glanced over her shoulder in time to see a blackbird rustling through last summer's spent leaves. Her relief was intense.

The man crouched behind a leaning headstone and held his breath when he thought he'd been discovered. Apprehensive, she spun around at the sound of a snapping twig. Then, the man leapt into view and glared at her while their foggy breath collided. She tried to scream, but her voice caught in her throat. Without warning, the man pounced and pushed her violently, sending her sprawling backwards onto the frost-covered grass. Her head struck the granite grave rail, then with no hesitation, her assailant leapt forward and pinned her to the ground with both knees and placed a hand across her mouth to silence her desperate call for help. She squirmed and flailed her arms about in a dazed and disorientated frenzy, but the man dodged her arms like a lean boxer. Every attempt to force him off failed as his hand tightened over her mouth. One moment, she was fighting for her freedom; now, she was fighting for her life. His spider-like fingers moved to her throat as blood from the back of her head soaked into the grass. Unable to breathe, consciousness slipped away, and she fell into a dark abyss...

TWO

Early November

The lid on the jigsaw puzzle showed the Red Arrows Display Team flying in formation over Buckingham Palace. I slotted one or two pieces into place, then drifted into a world filled with meaningless scenarios and the clatter of the dishwasher being loaded.

Summer was a distant memory, and my sixteenth birthday seemed ages ago. It may seem strange for a sixteen-year-old to share a jigsaw puzzle with her mum. But honestly, I love spending time with her. The 2000-piece puzzle will take a while to complete, so I hope she tells me stories of when she was a teenager. She says our time together prevents me from spending too much time on social media. *As if.*

I stared through the French window, and my eyes glazed over as I watched the thickening mist consume the garden. The world I'd descended into was filled with memories of my grandma as I pictured her flitting around her cottage, dusting and polishing and singing to whatever song was on the radio. I remember the aroma of lavender and cinnamon potpourri filling every room. When I was eight, Gran made me giggle when she told me her place was so small that she could stand in front of the sofa and dust the room without moving.

My senses told me I wasn't alone.

"Penny for them," a voice said, interrupting my daydream.

"Mm? Err? What?"

"Penny for your thoughts. You were miles away."

"Huh?" I said, dragging myself back to the now.

"You were daydreaming."

"Oh? Right. I was, wasn't I? I was thinking of Gran. I miss her." I said as she gently ran her fingers through my hair.

"I know you do, sweetheart. Me too. Life's not the same without her." We both reflected in the moment of silence.

"How's the jigsaw going? Is it an easy one?"
"No. Not in the slightest. There's too much red and brown. I've made some progress, but my mind keeps wandering."

"You were staring into space when I walked in," she said, tickling me.

"Mu-um!" I complained, pushing her arms away with my elbow. "You know I don't like you tickling me."

"Sorry. I couldn't resist. You look so sweet when you twiddle your hair around your fingers."

Mum sat in the chair next to me and mouthed 'elephant juice.' I mouthed it back in return. Why elephant juice? It was our little secret, and mouthing the words 'elephant juice' began when I was about seven, going on fifteen. (Mum joked about me being an old soul.) When you mouth 'Elephant Juice,' it looks like you are saying, 'I love you.' We've continued saying it since, and it's our private joke. Dad is aware of it but doesn't join in.

Mum bought the jigsaw puzzle at a local car boot sale because the picture reminded her of her first visit to London. She and a friend skipped school one day and caught a train to Paddington Station. They waited for hours outside Buckingham Palace, clinging to the black and gold gates after pushing through the crowd, camera at the ready, waiting for a glimpse of the Queen. The glow of excitement passed, and their anticipation dwindled. Her Majesty was a no-show. I'm pleased Mum shared her story, inspiring me to live in London after graduation.

We combed through the jigsaw pieces as the clock counted the minutes, and a blackbird sang its sweet song, announcing the end of the day. How does that poem go? 'The curfew tolls the knell of parting day…' something like that.

She gasped.

"Gosh! I forgot to tell you. Mrs Rousso phoned to tell me Isabella went straight to bed after walking Sandy."

"I'm not surprised. She knows that too much walking is exhausting for her. Do you think she'll ever be well?"

"Her heart isn't functioning correctly, and she needs a heart replacement."

"A heart replacement? Is she that ill?" I queried, not wanting the truth.

"Didn't you know?" She said and touched my arm. "Isabella was born with a congenital heart defect, and it's getting worse. Now she's at the stage where a heart transplant is her only option."

"I knew she was born with a heart problem because she's always been excused from gym lessons. I hadn't realised she was that bad and needed a heart transplant. I'll call in tomorrow on my way to the station."

"Where are you going?"

"I've arranged to meet Abigail in Swynbourne."

"Stay away from that gang that hangs around the Mall."

"They're nothing but trouble, so we always avoid them."

"Good. Getting back to Isabella. If I were you, I'd phone first. She may not be well enough for visitors."

"Wow! I'm shocked. I knew she was ill, but I hadn't realised she was that ill. She never talks about it unless asked, and even then, she brushes it off as if it's no big deal." I turned to Mum.

"When do you think a donor heart will become available?"

She cupped my hands and stared deep into my eyes.

"I have no idea, sweetheart. Many people carry NHS organ donor cards, so she may be fortunate enough to have received a heart in time. Her mama said Isabella's been on the transplant waiting list for more than two years but will probably jump the queue, given the circumstances. On a lighter note, she'll be able to live a near normal life after the transplant."

While I slotted several puzzle pieces in place, I considered what she said. I prayed that a heart would soon become available for Isabella, one that would fit in place as easily as the puzzle pieces.

THREE

My name is Charlotte Beatrice Dubois. Dad's parents were born in France, and Beatrice was his grandmother's name. I loathe the name because it reminded me of a children's book about talking rabbits. I never tell anyone my middle name, so I'm just plain Charlotte at school.

Dad taught me French when I was young, and thanks to him, I always got A+ at school. *He would have killed me if I hadn't.* Gran called me Lottie ever since I was a child. I remember I was in her kitchen when I stood on my tip-toes to grab the handle of a pan of boiling water on top of the stove. She yelled 'Lottie' in sheer panic. Her short, sharp tone made me leap away. She prevented a disaster and called me Lottie until she died almost two years ago. Abigail is my bestie at school and calls me Charlie. I'm not keen on being called Charlie, but her way of saying it makes it sound cool. My favourite food is Spaghetti Bolognese, and I like crisply ironed sheets, IKEA furniture, and the cool, smooth sensation of sliding my hand inside the sack of grass seed on the floor in front of the Post Office counter. I enjoy law, which will be my main subject at Uni. I have blonde hair, a pale olive complexion (from my dad's side), and eyes like a tropical blue ocean, which Abigail swears glow in the dark. I doubt that, but it's funny. I have a round face, characterised by soft, curved lines with the width and length in equal measures, creating a circular appearance. My lips are symmetrical and wouldn't look out of place on a big screen. Hollywood! I'm here.

Our village must be the most boring village, like, eveeerr. Nothing happens here to create excitement except when the annual fête is held in the summer. During that time, the population tripled, and the locals complained about cars being parked across their drives and on the footpath. It's chaos, but it gives them something to talk about. The refuse collectors call every Thursday morning to empty the wheelie bins, which is the highlight of the week for some as they watch from behind twitching curtains.

I spent my formative years at Ashmarsh Queen Anne County Primary School, where I learned to read and write and aspire to be the best person I can be. *That's what the School Vision Statement said.* My parents are Philippe and Katrina, and I named my adorable golden Labrador Sandy. He's so cute, and he melts the hearts of everyone he meets. Dad owns a silver BMW, and yes, he does use the indicators. *It's a family joke.* Mum recently purchased a BMW SUV with plenty of space in the back for Sandy.

Every time I walk past the Celtic cross on the village green opposite, I touch it and make a wish. Detective Chief Inspector Tim Cunningham, his wife Celine and two boys, James, 12, and Stephen, 14, live in a converted barn on the outskirts of Ashmarsh. Dad met DCI Tim Cunningham through work; our families are close friends. I like Tim because he treats me like an adult. He's hot, and I mean HOT. He's younger than my dad, but with a square jaw, streaky grey temples, full-length cashmere coat, trilby, and black Chrysler 300, he reminds me of an up-to-date version of an American gangster. Despite his appearance and deep smouldering voice, beneath his facade lies a gentle and loving family man.

Mum left her job when I was born, and with me grown up and time on her hands, she plays bridge with a group of local women, including Celine. *It's more of a gossip fest than anything else.* Dad is head of the Planning Department at Swynbourne City Council. He is used to dealing with difficult people, and it's my job as a teenager to make his life challenging. *I'm only joking.* I love Dad and Mum to the moon and back. Vanessa, or Ness, our maid, or 'head of domestic services,' as Dad calls her, cleans our cottage twice a week, and after she's cleaned my room, I can never find anything. I could clean it myself, but Ness is good at her job. Isabella lives with her mama and papa at 1 Church Lane, and she takes Sandy for a walk every other Saturday if she's well enough. She's always breathless and stops regularly when in need of a rest. She has lots of time off school but somehow manages to keep up with schoolwork. We're in the same class, and she's my equal bestie, alongside Abigail.

Isabella waits at the cemetery gates with Sandy while I take flowers to Gran's grave. She is superstitious and won't go into the cemetery ever since she heard the story of the man found dead early one morning. *How ironic? A body in a cemetery?* This body was positioned on top of a grave. It was years ago, but it bothers her immensely. About Gran. I miss her and talk to her whenever I take flowers to her grave. My only regret is not having the chance to have had one final conversation with her before she died.

"Meet me at Fairy Bridge in ten minutes."

"Okay. See you then." Isabella wheezed over the phone.

We call it 'fairy bridge' because when we were kids, we imagined fairies lived there and often took sweets and biscuits as gifts. Everything had gone on our next visit, making us believe in fairies even more.

The bridge quivered as I gazed dreamily over the handrail into the shallow, rippling waters. Isabella laboured towards me, and it was obvious she was struggling. She rested her arms on the rail to catch her breath, so I didn't speak because she would struggle to reply, and I didn't want that. She will talk when she's recovered.

Isabella needs very little encouragement to be out in the fresh air with me, who happens to be the owner of the cutest dog in the village. I recall the first time we met. It was after Mum had invited two friends over for a game of bridge. Mrs Rousso brought Isabella with her, and we occupied ourselves while the grownups played cards and talked over tea and biscuits. We got on well together, but even then, I noticed her breathing was very different. Although we became besties, I wasn't ready to share the old lady that visits me. I thought she might think I was silly. Then again, we believed in fairies, so I told her, and she became excited at the prospect of seeing a ghost. (This was before she had heard the story about the dead man in the cemetery.)

Isabella's thick, lush eyebrows are perfectly sculptured, and she has beautiful sweeping eyelashes and long ebony hair flowing down her back like a chocolate fondue. Her gorgeous skin tone is darker than mine, and sometimes I feel jealous, although I catch up with her in the summer months, and dare I say it, her bra size is much bigger than mine. Boys are attracted to her but are soon put off by her illness, and she can be a little immature at times, but I think that's because of how her papa treats her. She makes every word count when she speaks, probably due to her struggling to breathe. Her papa won't allow a dog in the house, so she 'borrows' Sandy. Her papa keeps her little girl by overprotecting her to the point of stifling her development. Perhaps he projects his fear onto her at the thought of losing her. One day, she will fly the coop, breaking his heart, but until that day comes, she will always be his dear bambino.

"Hi, Isabella. Not one of your better days!" I remarked when she began to relax.

"How did you guess?" She said, smiling thinly. "One day at a time. Today is an off day. I was pleased when you rang. Papa was driving me crazy."

"I missed you at school all week."

"I missed you too," she said, staring over the rail and instantly mesmerised by the chattering stream. "Papa keeps a close eye on me. He doesn't know I've slipped out, so I expect to be in trouble when I go home."

"He loves you so much that I doubt it. I take it you're not up to walking to the cemetery?"

"Not today. I'd rather stay on the bridge and drop Poo Sticks into the stream."

"Sounds like fun."

"I won't dare go into the cemetery because of the dead homeless man?"

"You mean the homeless man that slept in the cemetery one warm summer's night and was found dead in the morning?" I said creepily. "His hair turned white overnight, or so they say. He wasn't known to anyone, so his hair may have already been white. The coroner said he died of shock, and ever since then, the gates are always locked at night."

"Don't. I'd rather you didn't talk about it."

I apologised and hugged her.

"I was trying to be funny. Hey! I bet you would go into the cemetery if you had to. Like, if you were visiting a close relative or friend."

"Like, I'd have to think about it first. There's no reason for me to go in there for now."

"True," I said, pouting. She did have a point. No one goes into a cemetery without a valid reason.

We moved to the riverbank and sat swinging our legs while we talked. The ground was damp, but we didn't mind. Isabella asked me how school was, and then we talked about boys and all the usual stuff. She said she wished she was as active as I was. She agreed I wasn't sporty, but I got the gist.

"I should go. I need my oxygen," Isabella announced. Even on a weekend, she has schoolwork to catch up on, and her papa will no doubt hover over her until it's done. Somehow, I don't think she'll be doing much homework today. Her papa loves her but has built a wall of protection around himself. Paradoxically, her mama was the opposite. A typical, tentative Italian mother who fusses over me, calls me Bella and smothers me with kisses whenever I'm near her. She's a fantastic cook, but her scones are nowhere near as nice as grans were.

We thought her papa wouldn't be angry with her if I walked home with her. *He wouldn't dare.* We were right, and her papa greeted her with a warm welcome. When I phoned later, she told me he was being extra nice. *Big win.*

When you think about it, my monthly cramps are nothing compared to Isabella's daily struggle. She has been in and out of hospital from the day she was born. She jokes about spending more time in the hospital than at home. That is not strictly true, but I bet it feels that way. She wouldn't win a school attendance award, which rewards luck and punishes misfortune. No one ever said life was easy. Each breath for her is a battle, but she never complains. She won't give up. She has no choice.

FOUR

It was like swallowing a razor blade as the ice cream slipped down my throat. I was lying on a sun lounger next to Chris Hemsworth on Sunset Beach, California. We were sharing an ice cream when he cupped my chin and pulled me in closer. I closed my eyes as his lips brushed mine. Then, the moment I'd longed for was interrupted by a soft, rhythmic tune. Chris stopped what was one of the most amazing romantic gestures I've ever experienced. I opened my eyes to see why he had stopped, and the tranquil scene morphed into my dreary old room. With crusty, dry eyes, fire in my throat and a blocked nose, I realised it wasn't the ice cream hurting my throat but a good old-fashioned British cold. Oh no! This is the first cold I've had in years. It's Sunday, so I can spend all day in bed if I please.

The church clock struck eleven, awakening me. My pyjamas were soaked in sweat, my head was pounding, and I knew I had a temperature. My first thought was to message Abigail to tell her I wouldn't be meeting her at the Mall as previously arranged. I dressed slowly and sauntered downstairs, wondering what sarcasm I would get from Mum and Dad for staying in bed so late.

When I walked into the lounge, Mum and Dad were sat at either end of the sofa. Dad was reading the paper while Mum skimmed through the Sunday supplements. Sandy barged in, and once he'd been patted on the shoulders, he trotted to the French windows and sank onto the rug, warmed by the sun.

"Good afternoon, Charlotte," Mum said, dishing it up with a large spoonful of sarcasm and a big grin.

"Not now, Mum. I'm not in the mood."

"What's wrong?" She asked. "You're usually full of fun." She remarked while I flopped into the middle of the sofa, resting a cushion on my knees.

"I've got a cold." I croaked. "Anything interesting in the supplements?" I asked, diverting the attention away from me.

"Don't sit so close. I don't want your germs, thank you very much."

"Well, someone gave them to me, so I thought it rude not to," I said, sounding like a screeching donkey when I laughed.

"Oh, very funny," Mum said. Dad lowered the paper and looked at me.

"What about school tomorrow? Will you be well enough to go?"

I slapped the back of my hand against my forehead and fell in a heap across his lap.

"Well enough to go to school then." He said and grinned, then concealed himself behind the newspaper again.

"Mum?" Do you know where the thermometer is?"

She stretched out her arm and felt my forehead with the back of her hand.

"It's in the bathroom cabinet where we always keep it. You have a temperature."

"Then what use is a thermometer?" I queried, then slumped back into the sofa. "Thank you, nurse Dubois. I'll see how I am in the morning."

"I can drop you off at school tomorrow if you decide to go, although you may have to make your own way home," Dad said. I sighed.

"Public transport it is then," I announced, dreading the thought of travelling on the train with the way I was feeling. That's if I decide to go."

"Will Isabella be going to school tomorrow?" Mum asked me.

"I'm not sure. I'll phone her in the morning and check."

Sunday went so quickly, and I had achieved very little. My weekend was relaxing, apart from feeling ill, and by Monday morning, I felt less like I'd been hit by a bus. I had the sniffles, but I decided I was well enough to go to school, and true to his word, Dad gave me a lift.

By Friday, my nose was red and sore after constantly wiping it, and my lips were dry and flaky. Isabella didn't attend school all week, so I sat alone at the school gate checking Instagram while I waited for Dad. My phone flagged a message from Dad. He was sorry, but he'd been held up, and could I make my own way home. I thought about waiting, but it was sooo cold, and besides, I could be waiting for hours. I replied, saying his abandoned daughter would find her own way home. He understood my sarcasm because he sent me a laughing emoji.

First-formers were out of control and were running up and down the station platform. I was afraid one of them might fall onto the track until the station master came out of his office and lectured them on safety. The end of the platform disappeared as swirling fog crept in like a prowling cat, and I heard the announcement before I saw the train. First-formers scrambled on the moment the doors opened. I let them settle and sat by the window in the next carriage. A lady slumped into the seat next to me, and I moved closer to the window to avoid contact with her chubby arms. The fog made it impossible to see out the window, and I could see a perfect reflection of the carriage interior and my red nose glowing like a beacon. I amused myself by playing a game to make the journey go quicker. I chose the reflection of someone in the window and then tried to locate them in the carriage. My face flushed, and I quickly looked away when a man caught me watching him. Fortunately, he got off the train at the next station and spared my embarrassment.

When I arrived home, I hung my coat in the boot room, removed my boots, and kept my scarf around my neck despite the warmth and cosiness of the cottage. Sandy burst in from the kitchen when I collapsed onto the sofa. He nudged my knee for attention, so I ruffled his coat while he rewarded me by tugging and gnawing on my scarf.

"Let go, little monster," I teased. Did you miss me, ay?" I asked, kissing his nose.

I heard noises coming from the kitchen.

"Hi, Mum," I shouted, hoping she would hear me above Sandy's growls.

"Is that you, Charlotte?"

"Who else calls you, Mum?" I yelled. The phone rang, and she began talking softly, but I couldn't hear what she was saying. It went silent two minutes later, and then she shouted something, which I didn't quite hear.

"Be there in a minute," I yelled, yanking my scarf from Sandy's drooling canines. My phone was beeping and telling me the battery was low, so I promised myself I would charge it later while simultaneously wondering if Mum summoning me to the kitchen had anything to do with my untidy room, even though Ness had tidied it the other day. *Forewarned is forearmed.*

When I entered the kitchen, Mum was stirring a pan on the AGA. She had her back to me and spoke without turning.

"Be a love and lay the table for me, please." *Does she have eyes in the back of her head?* She caught me by surprise. What? No untidy bedroom rant? Mum has conveniently forgotten how much I do around the cottage. I must remember when she next has a go at me. I rinsed my hands under the tap and began setting the table.

"Dinner smells good. What time are we eating?"

"As soon as your father is home."

"Aww! He could be hours. I'm starving. Are there any crisps?" I asked, heading for the cupboard.

"Don't spoil your appetite. I've made your favourite: Spaghetti Bolognese."

"Mm. Yummy. My favourite." I replied, not paying particular attention.

About to broach a delicate subject, she was gaining momentum. How did I know? Because she wipes her hands on her apron many times. Maybe I'm wrong, and I am in for a telling-off.

"Thanks for setting the table, Charlotte. Sit down. I want to talk to you." *Uh-oh! Here we go.*

"Look. If it's about my room, will you please ask Ness not to touch my things? I can never find anything after she's tidied up. I've asked her, but she ignores my request."

Again, she wiped her hands on her apron and took a deep breath. *You're not getting a divorce, are you?*

"It's not about your room, darling, and yes, I will speak to Ness."

"What have I done wrong now?" I fretted.

"You haven't done anything wrong." She said, sitting next to me at the table. "Mrs Rousso phoned to say Isabella is very sick and in bed. Her doctor says she's reached the point where a heart transplant is the only way forward. They could fit a temporary artificial heart until a suitable donor heart becomes available, but that could mean a long hospital stay, which could last for months."

"What? You mean she needs a heart transplant, like, right now and may have to rely on an artificial heart until a donor heart is available. Will she die if she doesn't receive an artificial heart?" I asked, already knowing the answer.

"Look, Charlotte. It's a lot to take in. I wanted to keep it from you, but she's your best friend, and I'm sure you would prefer my honesty." She clasped my hands, and her face softened with empathy. "The artificial heart will give her heart a rest, then it's a waiting game."

"Not really a game, is it?" I said, knowing it was only an expression. "Poor Isabella. We have two kidneys and two lungs. Why don't we have two hearts? Dr Who has two hearts."

"If only Dr Who was real. She knew one day this would come, but she had put it to the back of her mind until now."

"She can't die. She won't die. She's my bestie, and I've known her almost my entire life." I said, staring at the wooden floor. "I don't want to think about it."

"Her outlook isn't good. I'm sorry to be so direct, but there's no other way to put it. 'Espérer le meilleur et se préparer au pire.' Expect the best. Prepare for the worst, as your mémère on your father's side used to say."

"I know what it means. Isabella would hate being in hospital for weeks, or months, even. Isn't there anything we can do?" I added, playing with the knife and fork on the table while Mum's words made their way to the part of my brain that dealt with injustices. "When will a heart become available?"

"There's no way of knowing. There could be a phone call tonight, tomorrow, or in a week. No one knows, not even the specialist. It's not like they have spare hearts waiting in storage. Maybe one day, we will have special medical beds to heal people's ailments in minutes or to grow a new heart in days. Until that technology is publicly accessible, she could be waiting a long time before a suitable heart is available. I know you care deeply for her, Charlotte, and I'm so sorry."

I leaned my head on her shoulder, then sat upright when a thought dawned on me.

"Isn't it ironic? One family's hopes rest on another family's tragedy, and someone must die for a heart to become available." I said gloomily, my words catching in my throat. "I know this may sound awful, but I pray to God a heart becomes available before it's too late."

Mum turned when she heard clicking claws in the hallway. Sandy paraded into the kitchen and rested his muzzle on her lap. She stroked his ears, and her face lost all expression. Her thoughts were more than likely that of Mrs Roussos and how devastated, she would be if she lost her teenage daughter.

"People don't die to have organs removed for a donor. They agreed to donate their organs if their life ends prematurely," She stated.

"Yes. I'm aware of that."

"I know you are. This is as hard for me as it is for you. Isabella is like a second daughter to me."

"I'm sorry. I know you care about her. I can't get my head around the fact that it's as though people on a transplant list are waiting for a death so they can live. It sounds selfish when expressed in that way."

FIVE

A short yelp sprang from behind the kitchen door. Sandy was in his basket and pricked his ears when the garage door whirred open. Briefcase in hand, Dad hurried along the hallway to the kitchen, then stared at us with questioning eyes.

"Have you both been crying?" He asked. I laughed nervously. It's all I had. Then I said. "How can you tell?" With a dose of irony.

"Oh! It's just a wild guess. Nothing to do with your red, puffy eyes."

"We've been talking about Isabella."

"What about her?" He asked with concern. He kissed Mum and then me on both cheeks.

"Isabella is in urgent need of a heart transplant," I announced. He sat next to Mum with a deep-furrowed look of concern.

"That's awful. I'm so sorry. She often deteriorates in winter but is fine by spring."

"It's only November; she won't live that long if nothing is done."

"Mum!" I protested.

"Sorry, Charlotte, but there's no sense in beating about the bush. No one knows when a heart will become available. It's a tragedy."

"When did you last see Isabella?" Dad interjected.

"Two days ago," I said, recalling the day she had to go home from Fairy Bridge because she needed her oxygen. "We were going to do our homework together, but her mama asked me to leave. I hope she's gonna be all right."

"Going to be alright," Mum said, correcting me. "I wish you would use correct grammar the way you were taught. We don't spend money on private education for you to talk that way. Don't they teach correct grammar at your school?"

"Mm-mm," I said, not paying attention. I had a lot on my mind. In the ensuing silence, I envisaged us thinking of the dire consequences of Isabella not receiving a heart in time.

"It's a terrible time for her Mama and Papa." Mum eventually said, sending a cold shiver rippling down my spine.

"Is there nothing we can do?" I asked, feeling Mum's warm hand on mine. She gazed at me, then brushed my hair from my forehead. Her eyes spoke volumes, but her lips remained silent, then she said.

"We'll be able to think clearly after we've eaten."

I offered to help Mum, but she declined. While she served dinner, Dad asked me how I was feeling.

"Much better, thanks, Dad. My cold has almost gone, although my nose is still blocked."

"You look better than you did last Sunday."

"Gee 'tanks, Dad," I said in my best American gangster accent. He laughed, and then my phone beeped, telling me the battery was low. *Not again!*

My phone required a new battery, and I could buy one quite easily. Isabella needed a new heart, but it wasn't as simple as picking a battery off a shelf. This may be a poor metaphor, but Isabella needed a heart replacement within days, or, Heaven forbid, she may have to have an artificial heart, which would involve a lengthy hospital stay.

SIX

Saturday morning

The double-glazing was no match for last night's cruel frost. It was bitterly cold outside, and condensation had run down the window and collected in pools on the windowsill. I clawed my way back to consciousness. I knew it was foggy outside because of the light pouring into my room, even with the curtains drawn. I sipped water from the glass on my bedside table, and then I was annoyed with myself for not charging my phone before I jumped into bed last night.

When I threw back the duvet and swung my legs to the floor, the fog had burned away. I placed my phone on the charger cradle (better late than never) and ran to the bathroom. Mum and Dad used their ensuite while I had the family bathroom to myself. Yes, the family bathroom is outdated and hideously pink. I feel embarrassed when visitors use the toilet.

I padded downstairs in my pyjamas and favourite bunny slippers. Mum and Dad were in the kitchen and stopped talking when I walked in. All eyes were on me.

"Morning." I croaked. Sandy climbed from his basket and clung to my side like a lost sheep as I went to the cupboard for a clean glass.

"Good morning, Charlotte. You sound a bit croaky?" Dad remarked.

"I'm alright. Better than I've been all week." I croaked again; then I sensed Mum's eyes burning into me.

"Why aren't you wearing your dressing gown? It won't keep you warm hanging on the back of the bedroom door." I know she means well. "Has someone turned up the heating? It's hot in here." I said, closing the cupboard door, filling my glass with water, and sliding into the seat next to Dad.

"You may still have a temperature," Mum said, then asked me what I would like for breakfast.

"Nothing, thanks. I'm off food. I can't taste anything."

"You need to eat! Have a bowl of cornflakes. They will make you feel better."

"I know. Feed a cold, starve a fever." I mocked.

"Cheeky monkey," she said, then smiled. Mum couldn't be angry at me for long.

"N importe quoi." (Whatever). I replied and brushed my hair behind my ear. I didn't have the energy to argue. "I'll have a small portion of cornflakes if it makes you happy."

"It's not for my benefit, Charlotte." She affirmed, and I watched her eyes flick to Dad for support.

"Don't drag me into it," he said, leaving the kitchen. I helped myself to a bowl of cornflakes, sat down, and stared vacantly into the bowl.

"I had a dream about Isabella last night. It was very odd. She'd gone through a heart transplant operation but was sad for some unknown reason. You would think she would be happy having received a new heart, wouldn't you? Anyway. It was only a dream. I expect she'll be jumping for joy when it eventually happens."

"I expect Isabella's been playing on your mind after our recent conversation," Dad said, explaining my odd dream.

"We're going out for the day. Would you like to come?" Mum asked while I stared despondently at my cornflakes, growing soggier by the minute.

"Err, no, thanks. I want to relax today. I'm too tired to do anything, although I'll walk down to the cemetery and replace the flowers on Gran's grave. The frost will have ruined the ones from last weekend."

"What about the rest of your day?" *Oh, here we go again.* I can run my own life, but Mum tries to organise mine.

"I just said I'm taking it easy." *That sounded harsh.*

"Don't be disrespectful."

"I'm a teenager. Aren't I supposed to be moody?" I lightened up when Mum shot me a hard stare.

"I'll catch up with friends on the phone, then perhaps I'll listen to some music, and then I'll phone Isabella to see how she is.

I might take a long soak in a bubble bath. I dunno. I don't have any plans. I want to relax for once."

She pursed her lips. *Here we go again—another lecture on the vernacular. Brace yourself, Charlotte.*

"Since you're staying home, will you be a treasure and clean Sandy's mess from the back lawn?" *Dodged one lecture straight into another.* I pouted.

"Mum. Can't it wait? I said I don't have the energy. Why won't you leave me alone?" My words came out louder than intended, which was when Dad walked in. *Just my luck.*

"Charlotte!" He snapped. "Don't speak to your mother in that tone. Have some respect."

"I'm sorry," I said, thinking his jumping down my throat was his French side showing, or was I being a grouch? "I'll do it tomorrow. I promise. Today is my chillax day."

"Chillax? I don't know where you get those words from. I'm sure you make them up." She said while unloading the dishwasher. I've asked Ness to leave your room as it is…" She stopped herself. *Saved.*

Mum set the dishwasher in motion, then sat next to me after putting the clean crockery away.

"We'll be calling into town on the way home. Is there anything you need?" She asked, smoothing the troubled waters. Mum disliked conflict. I wonder if her parents were strict when she was a child, although I knew them better than that. I also don't like conflict, so I must take after her. As for Dad? He enjoys a lively debate. I would imagine Isabella wished she had someone like him to fight for her and put her at the top of the transplant list. I chewed my cheek and gazed at the oak beams above me.

"I need an antiperspirant. I like the one with a tick on the side, but Mrs Barnes doesn't always have it in stock."

"Ok, and how are you for sanitary pads?"

"Mum!" I complained, blushing with embarrassment. "Not in front of Dad!"

"Don't mind me with your ladies' talk."

"Sorry, Charlotte. I should have been more discreet."

She was on her back foot, so I tried one of Abigail's techniques.

"I'd love a new phone, if you're feeling generous?"

"What's wrong with that one?" She said, pointing to my shabby phone on the table.

"Since you asked. There have been two new models since this one. It needs charging every night, and the screen is cracked."

"You should have looked after your phone. If you spent more time with your friends and less on the phone, it wouldn't need charging so often. Why don't you socialise more on a weekend?"

"I do," I protested. "I help the neighbours and visit them most weekends. One minute, you tell me to keep my phone with me, and the next, you're complaining I use it too much. Make up your mind."

"Charlotte!" Dad scalded in his rich, velvety French accent. My name sounds lovely the way he says it.

"Sorry," I said, sensing his glare. "Anyway, I have many friends at school."

"I know, but when did you last bring anyone home to meet us? The guest rooms are always ready if they want to stay the night."

"What, and use the hideous pink bathroom? I like my life as it is, thank you very much." I said, scraping the last morsel of cornflakes from the bowl. "I'm fine. There'll be plenty of time to socialise when I've graduated."

When Dad left the kitchen again, there was a short pause. Then Mum said, "Okay. I know you like your independence, but I worry about you. I only want what's best for you."

"I know that Mum and I appreciate it. I'm sixteen and no longer a child. I need to follow my own path and make mistakes along the way. That's how we grow and learn."

"It's hard to accept how fast you've grown into a young lady. I love you, and I still want to keep you safe."

"I know you do, and I love you too. Trust me if you want to show how much you love me. I will make mistakes, but you've taught me right from wrong, so hopefully, my mistakes won't be that big a deal."

Mum has forgotten what it is like being a teenager.

"All right! As a treat, you and I will go shopping in Swynbourne next weekend. How does that sound?"

"Aw, Mum. That's fantastic. Can I buy a new phone when we're there?"

"We'll see. You and I will have a girly day in Swynbourne. We could go for a facial."

I beamed at the thought. Mum will treat me like an adult, and I can't wait for the weekend. She put my breakfast bowl next to the sink, and her expression changed.

"Keep your wits about you while you're in the cemetery. Since the new housing estate was built in Carter's field, you never know who's lurking around the village. A young girl alone in the cemetery isn't safe." She cautioned."

"I'll be all right. I'll have Sandy with me."

"Not today. We're taking him to Riddlington Park Lake for a walk."

"Whose dog is he?" I snapped, claiming ownership.

"He is your responsibility, but we like to take him with us occasionally. You are invited. But since you don't want to come, you will have time to — chillax." She counter-argued. *Oops! That came back to bite me.* I tossed my hair from my eyes.

"I don't get a chance to walk him on the weekend when Isabella has him."

"Your agreement was for her to walk him every other weekend when she can. She loves taking him for a walk."

"I know she does, and honestly, I don't mind sharing him," I said, attempting to remove the sting from my words. "He raises her spirit." Then I thought for a moment. "She does have the best of both worlds, doesn't she? A dog to walk and play with, and no responsibilities." *That sounded fair.*

"I'll be okay in the cemetery. Gran will protect me."

"I'm sure she will. Be careful, though. Be alert, and take your phone with you," she cautioned, "and don't forget to dress warm before you go out. Are you okay? You seem a little tetchy."

"That time of the month, I expect," I said, half joking. "Seriously though, I'm a little run-down," I said as an excuse.

"I hope you'll soon become your normal self again. I love you but don't like you when you're irritable."

I mouthed, 'Elephant Juice.' She smiled, returned the fun gesture, and left the kitchen just as Dad walked in. *It's like Heathrow Airport in here.*

"See you later, sweetheart. Enjoy your day. Your chores can wait." He said, then winked and kissed me on both cheeks. "Do you need money for flowers?" He asked, and before I could reply, he'd already pressed a ten-pound note into my palm.

"Thanks, Dad. Can I keep the change?" He winked and disappeared into the garage with Sandy following him, claws clicking rhythmically on the laminate floor.

"Bye, Dad," I shouted. "Drive carefully. I have a strange feeling about today."

SEVEN

Sandy stared wistfully from the back of the SUV as I waved goodbye. I must have been crazy to stand in the doorway wearing my flimsy pyjamas. Mum was right. I should have worn my dressing gown.

It was a luxury for me to be alone at home. I had no privacy other than closing my bedroom door or taking a bath or shower. I love being with my parents, but I needed some alone time to pamper myself today. *Sanctuary.*

Peace at last, or so I imagined. Our cottage is anything but silent, and I swear I could hear her ancient timbers breathe in a clumsy improvised symphony of creaks and cracks. The cottage's whimsical characteristics didn't bother me during the summer months, but today, they sounded creepy. I ran upstairs to take a bath. My thoughts turned to Isabella as my image vanished in the steamy bathroom mirror.

The odd sensation I experienced earlier had stayed with me, and I hoped my foamy bath would dispel it. I like a shower but always love to soak in a bubble bath. Why? Because lying beneath a layer of foam is where I wash away my cares and put my mind's chatter on hold. Mum allowed me to use the ensuite, but it felt wrong. The family bathroom suite may be an awful pink, but it is my sanctuary, and I look forward to another soak in the bath next weekend before we go into town.

When the bath was full, I finally climbed in after removing my precious locket to hang it on the back of the chair. I inhaled the lavender fragrance, turned up the volume of my iPod, slid beneath the bubbles, and was whisked away to some far-off land while listening to my favourite music. I rested a foot on the cold tap and closed my eyes to the sound of foamy bubbles popping rapidly. Little Mix blasted from the iPod speaker, smothering the scramble of fizzing in my ears.

My fingers and toes were like wrinkled prunes when I emerged from my long soak. I dried myself and stared at the deep crevices in my fingers before applying a gorgeously perfumed moisturiser. Now rejuvenated, I dressed and realised I could breathe through my nose again, crediting the lavender oil.

My mobile phone was still not fully charged, so I ran downstairs and lay on the sofa to chat with Isabella on the landline while filing my nails.

"How are you?"

"Fine."

"You're not fine. The weather's fine. How are you, like, really?"

"Not one of my better days. — Can we change the subject?"

"I know you dislike discussing your health, but I care. I worry about you, too."

"I know you do, but I'm okay, really. Anyway. What're you up to?"

"Just chilling. Mum and Dad have taken Sandy in the car, so I have the cottage all to myself. Bliss. Are you ever alone at home?"

"Never. I go to my room, but Mum always interrupts by bringing me food and drinks. I know she means well, but surely, she must know I need privacy."

"That'd be right. I hope I'm not like that when I have a family."

"You're a lot like your Mum."

"Oh, no! Don't say that." I said, giggling. "Why don't you come over? I'll be popping across to the cemetery later. I'd love your company."

"Err. No, thanks. The cold air will start me coughing, so I'd better stay home. Besides, you know I won't go into the cemetery."

"The story of the dead homeless man is an urban myth."

"Papa is superstitious. He believes the story, and so do I."

After we'd chatted for what seemed like hours, I told her I'd better make tracks because I didn't want to be late going to the cemetery. It was already growing dark.

The mist was closing quickly, and frost clung to rooftops like a glistening carpet. All this made the decision to leave the warmth of the cottage more difficult. I promised Gran I'd take flowers to her grave, and I wasn't going to let her down. You know what it's like when you don't feel like doing something and it takes every ounce of self-will to do it? Well, that's how I feel.

The weather forecast said it would be a hard frost tonight, and I intend to be home before dark. Not because Mum told me to, but because I don't want to spend the night in the cemetery if Old Jake locks the gates while I'm still inside.

'Dress warm before you leave the cottage.' Mum said, and I did as I was told for once by wearing several layers of clothing. I checked I was wearing my locket before stepping outside.

Despite the watery sun trying hard to filter through the grey mist, Jack Frost's cruel fingers clawed at my lungs, causing my chest to burn and my nose to become blocked again.

The pavement was slippery underfoot as I walked quickly to the Post Office. The lane was deserted, and it felt like I was the only one brave enough to venture out today. The thought of walking past Norman Taylor's house made my skin crawl. He's bound to be sat in his window, watching me walk past. He always does. With my head held high and eyes looking straight ahead, I marched defiantly past his gate and focused on the crimson post box in the distance.

I had no idea if Norman was watching me as I marched past his house, but I relaxed once I was safely in the post office. The brass doorbell jingled as I stepped inside. The shop was colder than it was outside. Mrs Barnes magically appeared from behind the green curtain. She loved a good chat and had a unique way of keeping customers engaged to extract information from them before they even realised it. The Post Office was tired and long overdue for a makeover. It was the only shop for miles and was convenient if we needed anything in a hurry. Mrs Barnes was the heart of the business. Her husband, Earnest, was the Postmaster until cutbacks and centralisation closed the Post Office side of the business. Nowadays, he usually stays in the back room, hidden from the public eye behind an old, thick green curtain.

"Hi, Mrs Barnes. How are you today?" I asked, banging my gloves together to return the circulation to my fingers even though I hadn't walked far.

"Hello, Charlotte, my dear. I can't complain." She wheezed. "Today's been quiet. Folk — don't want to venture out in the cold." She said, catching her breath. "I don't blame them. — There's nothing better — than sitting by the fire — on a cold weekend — and watching a bit of telly. Have you got a cold, my dear?"

"I'm getting over the worst," I replied, avoiding her investigative mind.

"Would you like a pack of — honey menthol sweets?"

I declined the menthol sweets and purchased some fresh dahlias for Gran. Mrs Barnes wrapped them in silver paper with pink stripes and bundled them with pink ribbon.

"You don't look too well yourself, Mrs Barnes. Are you okay?"

"Don't you worry about me, love? The doctor told me if I didn't lose weight, — I would suffer a heart attack or stroke. — I told him I was too old to diet." She said, laughing. "I'm not a lettuce and celery person. I like fish and chips too much."

Her reply surprised me.

"You should listen to your doctor."

"We have to die at some time," she replied.

"Don't say that. The village would miss you. I'd miss you."

"Don't you worry, my dear? I'm not going anywhere just yet." She said and winked.

The shop was more of a hobby to her than a business, and she and Mr Barnes should have retired long ago. It's an Aladdin's cave of merchandise and hasn't changed since I was a child. Boxes of candles lined a sturdy wooden shelf, and the heady aroma of soap and washing powder, the earthy smell of potatoes and the woody scent of broom heads gave the shop a unique odour, so different to a supermarket. It is as cluttered today as when I wasn't tall enough to reach the counter. Mrs Barnes turned away, so I removed a glove and slid my hand into the sack of grass seed in front of the counter.

"The flowers will be for your grandma — I expect?"

"That's right," I replied, quickly withdrawing my hand from the seed sack as she turned.

"I like to keep her grave looking tidy."

"Mind you, don't dawdle. Old Jake will be — locking those gates soon." She said, with more than a hint of motherly advice. She means well, but I can take care of myself.

"I won't. He always rings the bell to warn people he's about to close the gates. It's cold outside, so I won't stay long."

"Is Sandy with you?"

"No. Mum and Dad have taken him to Riddlington Park Lake." I said, realising I had been drawn into a conversation I didn't have time for. "I must go, Mrs Barnes. It's almost dark, and Old Jake will be locking those gates before long." I paid for the flowers and held out my hand for the change.

"All right, my dear. Cheerio." She said, handing me my change. My foamy bath hadn't dispelled the strange feeling I had earlier, and it was still with me as I stashed the flowers inside my jacket before stepping back outside.

EIGHT

Saturday. November 24th

Charlotte hunched her shoulders in defiance of the cold. She looked left and right, then crossed the lane. Old Jake often locks the cemetery gates early on cold autumn evenings, but they were wide open when she slipped through and crunched her way along the familiar gravel path. An unsettling stillness troubled her as magpies cackled from tall trees, a stark reminder that she was alone. Waves of fear made her breath falter. Her quickened pace matched her pounding heart, and Charlotte realised that being in the cemetery at this hour wasn't one of her best ideas. The further into the cemetery she went, the meaner the frost became, and she shuddered at the sudden drop in temperature. Headstones on either side glistened with frost as she progressed with uncertainty, heightened by the recent reminder of the myth of the homeless man. The promise of leaving flowers on her gran's grave was the only thing preventing her from fleeing. She tensed. A ghostly mist surrounded her and isolated her from the world. She could easily have found her way through the cemetery with her eyes closed, but panic set in as the mist disorientated her. She was lost until she recognised a familiar obelisk in front of her, then she knew her gran's grave was close, and at that point, she felt the familiar tickling sensation in her hair.

"Is that you, Gran?" She asked, hoping it was.

Last week's flowers hung limp down the sides of the vase, and she knelt to remove them. She unwrapped the fresh flowers and arranged them neatly in the vase.

"That's better." She whispered. Her body tensed as she glanced uneasily over her shoulder. '*A girl wandering around a cemetery alone isn't safe...*' Her mum's words echoed, and she laughed nervously. A sound she wasn't expecting had her glancing over her shoulder, but her fears were soon allayed when she saw a blackbird foraging amongst the leafy mulch. She laughed uneasily again, and as she leaned back on her heels to admire the flowers, her hackles raised faster than a speeding arrow. She jerked her head around as a dark figure appeared through the mist and stood so close she could hear them breathing. She scrambled to her feet in horror, and the fearful figure remained silent, leering at her while she gathered her jumbled thoughts. Terrified, Charlotte tried to scream, but her voice failed. Upon realising that this menacing figure was within arm's reach, she froze on the spot. She held her breath as they stared at each other in hostile silence. The figure's bulging eyes ogled every inch of her trembling torso, and she felt naked. Vulnerable, helpless, and frozen with fear, their foggy breath mingled. Without warning, the man pushed her violently and sent her hurtling backwards. A sickening crack rang out as her head struck the unyielding grave surrounding. Dazed and confused, bright lights flashed before her eyes and blurred her vision, and searing pain shot through her skull to muddle her already confused thoughts. Her mind was begging for answers as blood from the wound soaked into the grass. *In God's name, please don't let me die!*

The dark figure pinned her to the ground and clamped a hand tightly over her mouth, then slowly and deliberately, his spider-like fingers slid to her throat.

Balanced on the edge of an abyss, this was the fight of her life. She struggled before her senses abandoned her, and she was weakened. Darkness swallowed her. She was too weak to fight back, and as she descended into nothingness, the man's contorted face became deeply embedded in her mind.

NINE

One cottage within a short walk from the Post Office stood out from the rest, and in that cottage lived an oddball of a man called Norman Taylor. Due to his lack of personal hygiene and domestic skills, he and his home stank with an unholy aroma, not unlike the stench coming from the nearby dairy farm. His nickname was Stinker Taylor at school, which later became Creepy Norman, owing to his lack of social skills. It was unkind to call him names, but children can be like that. The stone cottage, bought from the council during the Thatcher years when his parents were relatively well off, now, through lack of maintenance, was in desperate need of repair.

His parents died within two weeks of each other, which pleased him, but then it dawned on him that he would have to manage alone for the first time. His wretched life was all he knew, and the family lived in a poor and pitiful state due to years of unfortunate circumstances. His parents' autocratic regime had stifled his growth, and he despised them from a very early age, and for good reason. His mother beat him daily, and on warm summer nights, screams and yells emanating from an open window could be heard across the village. The cottage was a mess. Rooms were piled high with rubbish, and old furniture sagged under the weight of magazines and discarded items. He barely spoke to anyone in the village and grunted when buying newspapers or cigarettes from the Post Office. He walked with a downward stoop from a lack of self-esteem or shame. He shaved maybe once a week, his greasy, shoulder-length hair protruded from beneath his cap, and his unique appearance frightened children. Norman craved love and attention like every child, but as an adult, he spurned help whenever offered.

Confined by the rusty cage of childhood, he learned to be rebellious and deceptive. No matter what behaviour he displayed as a child, a scalding or beating from his mother was his reward, and on those occasions, it felt like he existed. He thought his mother tormented him for being born, while all other times, he may as well have been invisible. He detested his parents, the house, and his life; what life he had. He preferred the bullying at school to being home with his parents, and each night after school, the thought of returning home was his idea of hell. When he was late home from school, his mother lay in wait by the gate, arms folded squarely across her chest, lips pursed, face wrinkled with rage. He knew what was coming and retreated to his headspace. And after his mother had worked out her anger, she sent him to bed without nourishment.

His inimitable odour may have earned him the nickname 'Stinker Taylor' at school, but he didn't care. It wasn't nearly as bad as the abuse he received at home. Through his formative years of ill-treatment, coupled with resentment and fear fed by negative attention, he had a giant chip on his shoulder. Norman was a damaged man. He displayed all the hallmarks of child abuse and neglect and thought the world owed him a living.

TEN

Saturday: November 24th

The chain clasp loosened during the frenzy, and the locket catapulted into the air. It landed on the ground, inches away, but those inches may as well have been a giant chasm as it and its owner lay forever parted. The man's bony fingers clawed along the frosty grass towards the locket. Cupped in his grubby hand, he closed his eyes and raised the locket to his lips. He opened his eyes when he realised how vulnerable he was kneeling astride an unconscious girl in the vast emptiness of a cemetery. He admired the locket, then slipped it into his jeans pocket.

The mist began to swallow the distant gates. Alone and exposed, apprehension overwhelmed his troubled thoughts. Through narrowed eyes, he searched for an escape route as the mist and failing light closed in. He had one final look at Charlotte's lifeless body, then flints scattered in every direction as he ran, puffing and wheezing through years of smoking, like a man twice his age.

Relief struck him when he and the trophy locket reached the gates. The church and cemetery were dark, and only a streetlamp threatened to expose him. The light barely penetrated the mist, and he felt almost invisible. He was resting against a stone pillar to catch his breath when a car came towards him, headlights illuminating the lane in shimmering, dancing light. He darted behind the stone gate support and watched a well-dressed man put a suitcase into the car's boot and clamber into the back. The vehicle turned in the lane and drove away, leaving the man in a dark, unsettling silence. He scrambled across the road and ran breathlessly towards the Post Office, laboured efforts deeply engrained in his forehead.

ELEVEN

Saturday: 8:40 pm

Pain and confusion ebbed as peace and calm swept over me. The excruciating pain in my head had diminished, and I was left with a dull headache. The ringing in my ears had stopped, and there wasn't a whisper. Not a sound. Nothing. I slowly opened my eyes and glanced at my surroundings. I was shocked when I realised I was sitting on the stone flags outside the church doorway. *'This can't be real.'* The black and featureless sky caught my attention, filling my mind with questions with impossible answers. *'This is a dream, and I'm asleep on the sofa or at the dining table.'* The hands on the church clock said eight-forty. That's *impossible. It was close to three-thirty when I bought flowers from the Post Office.*

I struggled to recall past events and piece things together, and that was when I realised I had company. Someone, or something, touched my shoulder and addressed me in a soft, angelic tone.

"Don't be afraid, Lottie." The voice coached. 'You're at peace, now." I turned and was astonished to see a slender female standing before me, surrounded by a soft white glow. Gran was the only one who ever called me Lottie.

"Gran! I-I-I don't-understand." I said, barely able to form a meaningful sentence. "You're here. Y-y-you're alive! I can see you."

"Yes, you can see me. You are in spirit, and I've come to take you to the light."

"That can't be right. I'm sixteen, and my life has barely begun. I don't understand."

She welcomed me with a hug.

"There is no denying it. You are in the spirit world, and it's time to follow me into the light," she said, running her fingers through my hair. I gazed at her translucent form, then rested my head on her shoulder and slid my arm around her waist.

"I'm confused. Why are you here? Don't get me wrong. I am pleased to see you, but how can I be in spirit when I was placing flowers on your grave only a moment ago?" She cradled my head and stroked my hair as she used to when I was a child. "A grubby man crept up behind me, and when I faced him, he pushed me…" I gabbled, "…I fell backwards and hit my head. Then I couldn't breathe, and I was terrified when everything went black. Gran! Don't let go of me."

We remained in that position until my awareness settled on an object in the distance. I released my grip on Gran and rushed to the object lying between two graves. Suddenly, everything had meaning when I stood beside a young female lying motionless on her back. I knelt by her side and touched her shoulder. By the thick frost layer on her clothes, she must have been here for quite some time. I'm no doctor, but her slow, shallow breathing suggested she was close to death. I stared at her familiar clothing, then jumped to my feet. Gran had joined me.

"Nooo! It can't be! It's me. I'm in Spirit." I wailed. Gran held me.

"I tried to break the news gently. Now you know that you are in spirit, it's time to leave. Shhh! Shhh! It will be okay."

"Shush? How can I shush when I'm looking at my own body?"

"Stay calm, Lottie. Everything will happen in the way it's supposed to. It cannot be altered."

"I can't shush. Aren't I allowed to be upset? I'm too young to die. I won't go with you to the light. I can't."

I paused when I realised I was behaving like a spoilt child.

"I'm sorry. I didn't mean to shout. Can't you make this nightmare go away? I want to go home to Mum and Dad."

My mind was in turmoil, but I knew Gran was right. I knelt, then wept alongside my half-frozen self.

I stared at my superfluous body after I'd calmed down.

"I'm so sorry, Charlotte, I said to my earthly form. "It's my fault. I should have taken more care of you. This is a tragedy. I had so much living to do before I even considered dying. It's grossly unfair." I said and turned to Gran. "How will they cope without me? I'm their only child. Isn't there anything you can do? Anything?" I begged. My entangled thoughts were attacking me from every angle. "It's a dream. It will all be over when I wake up. I know it."

Gran knew I needed more time to let reality sink in, so she stepped away and left me with my thoughts. With anger welling inside, I stared at my motionless form, but those thoughts were quickly replaced with feelings of revenge.

"My physical body is still breathing, so clinically, I'm not dead. Quick! We must do something. We need help." I asserted. She prevented me from falling as my knees collapsed beneath me.

"It's too late, Lottie. I'm here to guide you to the light. We must leave."

"My body is breathing; therefore, it's alive. I can't leave now. Not yet, anyway." I said stubbornly.

"True, but look what you've become. Take my hand. We must leave at once."

I hesitated, then stepped away from my body.

"What will happen if I do regain consciousness?"

"That's not possible. You've been separated from your body for far too long. You can never return because your soul will no longer recognise your body."

"Can't I at least try? I've read about near-death experiences where people die and then return to their physical bodies."

"It does happen, but it's your time. You are in spirit, and I'm here to lead you to Paradise."

"Where there's life, there's hope," I said in desperation.

"There are greater forces at work. Greater than you will ever imagine."

"So, what you're saying is, I have no choice?"

"Correct. It is the way."

My chest barely moved beneath my jacket, but my eyes showed signs of life.

"Part of me wants to leave, but the other part knows I'm not ready. I know the man who attacked me, and I must share that vital information with Mum and Dad; otherwise, no one will ever know. I can't leave and let them go through this awful tragedy alone."

Gran beckoned me, and her smile was like gentle waves lapping over a sandy beach. The ache in my stomach was the same ache I had when it was time for me to choose my fundamental GCSE subjects and the ones in which I excelled. I have argued against things I don't like doing all my life, and no one could ever force me. It got me into heaps of trouble at school and home. I am my own person, I suppose. That's what growing up is all about. Stand by your truth, assert yourself, and push boundaries. Not to just exist, but to march through history and leave a mark. Mum said I was stubborn, but I told her I was 'finding myself.' We are so alike.

My choice was unbearable. My ego was telling me to stay and help have my attacker arrested, and my true self knew Gran was right, and I had to leave. I couldn't stay. Unless…"

TWELVE

Years of heavy smoking had taken its toll on Norman's health. Running from the cemetery had been a bad idea, and he almost collapsed with exhaustion when he opened his gate. He dragged himself along the path and finally landed on his doorstep. Coughing and wheezing like an old steam engine, he searched for the key. The door flew open, and he fell to his knees, fighting for his breath in the hallway. With every ounce of strength he could gather, he clawed his way upstairs, collapsed onto his bed and curled into a tight ball. His heart raced, his breathing rattled, and his chest burned while he battled to slow his breathing.

It took him over an hour to recover. By now, his face was less crimson and had returned to its normal pasty white. He stripped, dropped his clothes on the rug, and searched for the locket. With his eyes tightly closed, he formed an image of its previous owner, and with a devilish grin, he placed the locket on his cluttered dressing table.

A chronic recluse, he sidled through the village and verbally abused anyone who looked at him or dared to speak to him. He was rarely seen without a cigarette in his mouth, spat frequently, and avoided villagers whenever possible. Devoid of all compassion, resentment gnawed at his insides like a raging ball of hatred burning in his belly. His upbringing was traumatic, but being anti-social and bitter was by choice — a choice made long ago.

Eight-year-old Norman Taylor set fire to his stuffed teddy in his bedroom because it was a gift from his mother. It meant nothing to him; he loathed that teddy and all it represented. He hated it, and destroying it was his revenge. As the teddy burned at an alarming rate, at least he had the presence of mind to throw it into the fireplace to avoid setting fire to his bedroom or burning down the cottage.

Children have no comprehension of why their parents abuse them. It's all they have ever known, and they believe that every family behaves similarly. There was no love from the day he was born, and as he grew, he cried when he saw other mothers show their children love and affection. Why was he not loved? He hadn't asked to be born. He needed to feel loved, not starved, abused, and beaten black and blue. Hatred grew like the pressure inside a volcano, and one day, that volcano would erupt and spit out hate and revenge at anyone within easy reach. He truly believed he must be a bad person if his mother mistreated him, and it was all his fault.

Mentally scarred by the ones who ought to love him, he realised he was unlovable and created a defence mechanism to protect himself from being hurt. The resentment, if not vented, would manifest into one or many medical conditions. Life was grim for a love-starved child, and he wound up in the school sick room most days, complaining of a headache or an upset stomach. Destined to spread hate and seek revenge on the world would only end in disaster; after a lifetime of 'if onlys and what ifs,' Norman was steeped in guilt and paranoia.

🐘

Naked as the day he was born, he shivered in the unheated bedroom, wishing he had another teddy or something equally combustible to burn on the fire to warm the room. He searched the drawers for clean clothes and decided three layers would stave off the cruel cold air. Norman picked up the locket from the dresser, held it in his palm and drifted off into wistful oblivion. He slid the locket into his pocket and peered from the window, hoping no one had seen him. Satisfied no one had, he scooped the bundle of clothing from the floor, thundered downstairs, and ran into the garden, collecting a pile of old newspapers on the way. He built a fire on the apology of a lawn, grunting as he bent over, then stepped back to watch roaring flames climb into the air. Guy Fawkes' Night had been and gone, but he didn't care; this was urgent.

After he'd nourished the hungry fire with his tainted clothes, he stepped back and admired his handiwork. Sparks, like miniature stars, tiny packages of guilt, clambered into the air from the bosom of the fire, taking with them purging embers from within the flames. Guilt was released, but would that release be only temporary?

Warmed by the fire, he relaxed as the clothes burned to oblivion. A flash of fear had him diving into his pocket for the locket, now glinting in the flickering flames as the chain hung loosely through his fingers. Gripped by a deep-seated fear that ran through his mind, his judgement was tainting. Should he destroy the locket in the fire or keep it? There was no question that Charlotte's body would be discovered. But how would they know it was he who had caused her death? Self-preservation was at the forefront, and he no longer cared for Charlotte. Devoured by the flames, his clothes shrivelled and glowed a warm apricot hue. Those clothes would have put him at the crime scene, but now they were gone forever. He smirked. His view was that he had outsmarted the police.

THIRTEEN

Saturday: 9:25 pm

The night's frost created a halo around the pale moon. With my earth body close by, Gran turned away and stared at the sky. Shortly after, I heard her whisper, 'Amen,' and then she turned to me.

"I have spoken with the Devine Council, and they have agreed to permit you to stay. This is only temporary; you must understand, and I will be your guide until you have earned my trust. But be warned. You must not interfere with others' lives…" she cautioned, "…your actions may have far-reaching consequences."

My mouth gaped while her words sank in. *I have been granted permission to stay. How awesome.*

"Thanks, Gran. That's amazing. You make it sound so terrible, but I'm excited anyway. I promise I won't interfere with anyone's life. Thanks again, Gran, it means so much to me. Everything has happened so quickly, and I am struggling to keep up. I haven't had time to think things through, but I know I still have work to do on earth." I said, guilt rising as if I'd manipulated her. *If you don't ask, you don't get.*

By now, my parents will be frantic and worried. I want to go to the cottage and be with them if possible."

"Of course, we can go to your parents. But only if you're sure you're ready. Be prepared, as it may be a traumatic experience for you."

"I'm ready," I said, unsure whether I was. Reluctant to leave my earthly body alone in this dark, eerie cemetery, I had one last look before we trudged towards the cemetery gates.

"Can't we vanish and reappear in the cottage like on TV?" I said, half joking.

Gran smiled.

"I know you're joking, and you can do that, but not until you've been to the light. Until then, you are bound by the village's limits unless you leave on available transport."

"No change there, then. And I thought it would be fun in spirit."

"There will be plenty of time for fun. But you must take one step at a time. You always were in a hurry."

We walked the familiar path that had loyally led me to Gran's grave for two years. This is crazy, and I don't understand what's happening. The gates were locked, but we passed through with ease. *This is so cool. Imagine having that skill as a living human being.*

I wasn't used to walking in spirit and wasn't making as much progress as Gran. It was the same motion as before, but my body wouldn't do as it was told. My feet slid along the ground, and I had to concentrate on my actions.

We neared the cottage after passing the Celtic cross, with no time to make a wish tonight.

When we arrived, Mum and Dad were in the kitchen, discussing how late I was. The bright kitchen lights hurt my eyes, and I found it difficult to adjust to my new existence. I panicked, knowing that they had no idea where I was or what had happened to me.

"This is awful, Gran. Mum — Dad. It's Charlotte. Don't worry about me being late. I'm okay; well, sort of."

"Stop!" Gran said in a loud whisper. "You may frighten them. They won't be expecting you in your new form."

"Oh my gosh! Sorry. I wasn't thinking. It breaks my heart knowing that they might never see or hear me again."

"I said it wouldn't be easy. We are vibrating at different frequencies, and our voices are beyond their audible capability."

Gran explained the intricacies of frequency vibration and how the five human senses represent only a tiny percentage of the entire frequency spectrum. I understood most of it, and luckily, I paid attention in science class.

"Will it help if I step closer?"

"Probably not. They would have reacted by now if they had heard you. Look at your body. You are pure light. There aren't many people that can see or hear us.

I was disappointed and relieved at the same time. If they were able to hear me, I could have told them who attacked me and where to find me. That was my intention, but they may have been terrified if they could hear me. I didn't think it through.

"Did you ever communicate with Mum when you first entered spirit?"

"I tried. But then I realised it wasn't necessary. Your mother can't hear me, but I know I'll always be in her thoughts."

"You have visited before, then?" I said, sounding more like an accusation.

"I often sat in my old rocking chair and watched you wrestle Sandy on the kitchen floor."

Sandy was so quiet I'd forgotten he was here. I went to his basket to say hello, wondering if he could hear me. I was surprised when he sat up and tilted his head.

"I'm sure he's aware I'm here, although he hasn't given me away. I was rather hoping he would." Gran continued.

"I was there each time you visited my grave and listened to every word you said. I smiled when you apologised for forgetting to replenish the flowers occasionally."

My cheeks burned with embarrassment. Had I made a fool of myself? Gran pushed away from the Welsh dresser and made herself at home in her old rocking chair.

"Don't be too concerned about your parents. Initially, it will be painful, of course. But they will come through the other side, eventually. 'Time is a great healer,' your grandfather used to say. Your mum healed over my passing, as you had, and so will they with your passing."

"Isn't it too soon to pass it off that lightly? They don't even know I'm hurt."

"I'm sorry. I didn't mean to trivialise their pain, but there's nothing we can do to change anything. The story will unfold in its own time."

"When will they know what's happened to me?"

"I don't have all the answers. They were expecting you home hours ago, and I'm surprised they aren't already searching the village for you."

"What if they find me?"

"The cemetery gates are locked, so that's not possible."

"It's frustrating not being able to tell them who attacked me. What if I contact the police?"

"And how do you propose to do that?"

"I could contact the clairvoyants the police use," I said excitedly.

"Do you know where she lives? It will be daylight before you find her address."

I felt deflated and wondered what I could do to help.

"Events will unfold exactly how they're intended and in the right order," Gran said wisely. I glanced at Sandy again. I'm sure he can sense I'm here.

FOURTEEN

10:17 pm

"Charlotte is usually home by now. I wonder where she is?" Philippe commented and checked the clock for the fourth time in as many minutes. "Did she say anything about visiting a friend's house today?"

Katrina played with her necklace.

"No. Nothing. She said she would have an easy day. I'm becoming quite anxious. It's foggy outside, and the village isn't as safe as it used to be. I'll try her phone again."

She dialled Charlotte's number, and faint music came from outside the room. She followed the tune to the foot of the stairs, now louder than before, and ran upstairs to Charlotte's room. Her phone was on the charger, playing its merry tune. She hung up and went back to the lounge.

"I told her to take her mobile when she went out. It's still charging in her room.

"She must have forgotten it when she went out," Philippe said in Charlotte's defence. "I imagine she forgot it was on charge. She said it needed charging every night."

"You don't know our daughter. It's late, and she shouldn't be out now that the nights are drawing in, especially when it's foggy. I'll phone and see if she's with Isabella."

"Wouldn't she have called if she knew she would be late? Call her anyway. Then, at least, we can rule that out."

"Isabella might know where she could be if she's not with her."

She twiddled with her necklace while dialling Mrs Rousso's phone.

"Yes, yes…uh-huh! You're with her now? I'm pleased she's comfortable. Thank you. Give her our love, won't you? Bye, Mr Rousso." Mum palmed her mouth.

"What is it?"

"That was Mr Rousso. He said how sorry he was, but he hadn't seen Charlotte all day. Isabella was unwell and hadn't left the house. Mrs Rousso is too upset to talk on the phone."

"Is Isabella all right?"

"She's not improving, and they may have to call a doctor."

"That's not good,"

Philippe put Isabella to the back of his mind. His priority was his daughter. Katrina examined her shaking hands as the colour drained from her face.

"I wonder if she's with Mrs Smyth? You know how they love to chat."

"Mrs Smyth is always in bed by eight-thirty when the nights grow longer, and it's gone ten."

"She won't mind my calling her when I explain why."

The phone rang for what seemed like forever until Mrs Smyth said a puzzled, 'Hello?' She confirmed Charlotte was not with her and said she hadn't seen her all week.

Philippe tapped his foot, and Katrina drummed her fingers on the sofa arm.

"Let's go to the cemetery to see if she's there. If she isn't, then we should call Tim. He'll know what to do."

"The cemetery gates will be locked, so there's not much point. She probably caught a train into Swynbourne or could be with another neighbour. I can't think of anywhere else she might be."

"She said she was too tired to go anywhere other than the cemetery. I'm sick with worry, Philippe. She may not be at the cemetery, but we can't be certain. God forbid. I'll never forgive myself if anything has happened to her." Katrina fretted.

"Don't even think about it." He said he, too, feared the worst. "Charlotte can take care of herself, and I'm sure she'll have a good reason for being late."

"I hope you're right, Philippe." She said, peering through the curtain as the fog gripped the night.

"Look. I'm sure Charlotte is safe. You'll see. We brought her up to be respectful, but she does push the boundaries now and again."

"Oh, come on, Philippe. This is more than her pushing boundaries. Do you ever sense when something is wrong?"

"Not really."

"Well, I do, and I think every mother on the planet does. I'm trusting my instincts. Come on. Put your coat and shoes on; we're going to the cemetery while we can still find our way in the fog."

"But the gates will be locked."

"I know, and that's what worries me." She said, leaping to her feet. It was easier for her to do something rather than sit at home and do nothing. Philippe unhooked Sandy's lead from the back of the kitchen door.

"Leave him. He'll be alright. We won't be long. I'll leave a note in case Charlotte arrives home before we do. She'll know we're not far away when she sees Sandy."

Philippe took the powerful torch from the kitchen drawer.

"She'll be fine. You know how she gets talking and loses all track of time." He said, trying to soften the situation.

'Out looking for you. Phone when you get home. Love, Mum xx,' she wrote on a post-it. Katrina stepped out into the cold night air, pulled her collar around her neck and rummaged in her handbag when her phone beeped.

"I thought that was Charlotte. My phone needs charging. I'm as bad as her, aren't I?" She said and laughed, which sounded more like a sob.

"Let's hope the battery lasts until we get home. Have you got your phone with you?"

"No. It's in the car." He said, turning towards the garage.

"Leave it for now. Let's get to the cemetery before the fog closes in."

They approached the uninviting churchyard, which would incite fear in anyone who dared venture in at night, especially if they knew about the legend of the homeless man. The church floodlights made it easier to find their way, but the moment they reached the gates, the lights turned off, and they were plunged into darkness. Katrina screamed, and Philippe shone the torch on her, then at the cemetery gates.

"I was right. The gates are locked…" he said, eyeing the chain and padlock barring their way, "…and as far as I know, this is the only entrance."

"We need the keys. Old Jake won't mind if we wake him and have him unlock the gates."

Her eyes widened.

"Even if we had the keys, I wouldn't dare go in there. Not now the floodlights are turned off. No one would dare go in there after dark. You know the story about the homeless man. Oh, my goodness! My baby! She could be alone in there!"

"I wouldn't hesitate if I knew Charlotte was in there for certain." He said, rattling the massive iron gates, disturbing the thick layer of frosty spikes. His voice echoed across the empty void.

"Char-lotte. Char-lotte." He yelled, shaking the gates with each syllable. They stood motionless, each holding their breath while listening for a distant reply, the tiniest hint of sound, or an indication that Charlotte was there. That didn't happen.

"She's not there, Philippe." She wailed.

"Listen," he hissed, gripping the cold ironwork with a gloved hand while shining the torch as far as the beam could go. He peered into the misty darkness for a sign, a whisper of hope. Katrina stifled her emotions and glanced through the gates at the frost-covered ground.

"If she had come to the gates and they were locked, wouldn't her footprints show in the frost? If I were her, I would wait by the gates until someone passed." Philippe was too busy shining the torch through the gates and kept his thoughts to himself.

Katrina's mind drifted to her teen years when she waited with a school friend outside Buckingham Palace gates to see the Queen. Fear gripped her when she snapped back to the now and realised she wasn't outside Buckingham Palace but peering through the local cemetery gates, searching for her daughter. It dawned on her that her daughter couldn't be in there. Not the sensible child she'd taught to be strong and mindful of her surroundings. There must be some other explanation.

Philippe cocked an ear, listening for a clue. Katrina stared at her phone, desperate for a call from Charlotte, and her heart sank when it turned itself off with a decisive beep.

"We'd better get home. My phone has died, and Charlotte won't be able to contact me if she calls. She's smart enough to come to the gates if she *was* in there. It's pointless staying out here in the cold. It's freezing. Let's go home and phone Tim before we get lost in the fog." Katrina said, turning her back on the gates separating them from the horrifying truth.

Back at the cottage, Katrina struggled to insert the key into the lock. Philippe helped her open the door, and she ran to the kitchen.

"Charlotte? Charlotte? Are you home?" She called but was met with silence. Sandy didn't move when the hall light illuminated the note on the corkboard, exactly where she'd pinned it less than fifteen minutes ago. She used the counter for support and folded her arms to prevent her hands from shaking.

"Something's wrong, Philippe. I know it." She fretted. He lifted the wall phone from its cradle to phone Tim.

FIFTEEN

11:24 pm

The black Chrysler circling the grass island sent flickering shadows dancing across the kitchen wall. Tim climbed out of the car, buttoned his Leonard Hughes coat, knocked on the door and walked in.

"Hello, Tim, Philippe said gratefully. "I know it's late, so thanks for coming out. Come through to the kitchen. It's warmer in there."

Tim removed his hat and followed Philippe to the kitchen. Philippe offered him a seat, but he said he preferred to stand.

"Sorry to drag you out on such a cold evening, Tim. As I mentioned on the phone, we're concerned about Charlotte. She should have been home hours ago, and usually phones if she will be late."

"Don't apologise. I'm as concerned as you are. How's Katrina taking it?"

"She's worried, naturally. She'll be down in a minute."

The sound of the toilet flushing above their heads was awkward. Katrina walked into the kitchen, sat at the table next to Philippe, and forced a smile.

"Hello, Katrina. I know this is stressful for you, but I'm sure Charlotte is safe and well and will contact you before morning."

"I do hope you're right, Tim," Katrina said.

"I have my business hat on tonight, so I must ask you a few questions—first, a word of reassurance. Most missing teens are found safe and well within twenty-four hours of them being reported missing. Meanwhile, we are doing everything we can to find Charlotte."

"There's been no word from her," Katrina said, frowning. "No phone call, and her friend's in hospital, so she's not with her. I'm so worried, Tim. She's only ever spent time away from home on holiday."

"What time is she usually home?" Tim enquired. Katrina glanced at the clock.

"She usually gets home well before ten, earlier in winter. I know it's not a school night, but she's never been this late without contacting us to say where she is."

"She said she would be going to her gran's grave, and I gave her money to buy flowers," Philippe added.

"Uh-huh. That will be your mother, Katrina?"

"Yes. Her name is Evelyn Turner." She said, and Cunningham wrote it down.

"What clothes was she wearing when she left the cottage?"

"We don't know because she was in her pyjamas when we left, but she lives in her jeans at this time of year. Her Khaki jacket is not here, and her woolly hat, scarf, and red woollen gloves are not in their usual place."

"Do you have a recent photo?" Katrina took the photo frame from the Welsh Dresser, slid out the photo and handed it to Tim.

"Does she have a boyfriend?" Cunningham asked and unbuttoned his coat.

"Not as far as I know. Has she mentioned anyone to you?" She asked, and Philippe shook his head.

"Most of her friends are female, and I always joked about boys distracting her from school work."

"You're right, Katrina. What about any distinguishing marks? A birthmark, scars, or tattoos, for instance?"

"No scars or birthmark, and I'm sure she doesn't have a tattoo. Mind you, you never know these days, do you? Teenagers sometimes have tattoos in places parents never see. I believe she's too sensible to defile her body." Katrina said proudly.

"I take it you've called her mobile?"

"That was the first thing we did. She left her phone in her room."

"Why?"

"It was on charge, and she may have forgotten it. It needs charging every night."

"That's not important for now, Katrina," Philippe said.

"I know, but I…" Katrina's voice tailed off.

"Do you think she may have run away?" Was Tim's next question.

"She has no reason to. All the comforts of home are here, and besides, we love her and have a good relationship. I'm certain she would have taken some of her belongings and wouldn't leave without taking Sandy."

"I know you both love her very much."

"Is there a possibility she may have been kidnapped?" Philippe added.

"Philippe! We're not mega-rich. Why would anyone want to kidnap our daughter?"

"With no phone call or demands, nothing suggests she's been kidnapped. Has she any health issues we should be concerned about?"

"None. She's rarely sick, although she is recovering from a cold."

"Does she have social media accounts?"

"Yes. Facebook, Instagram, and Tumblr. There may be others, but I can't keep pace. Her laptop is in her room with her phone." Katrina said.

"Can I take a look?"

Katrina took Cunningham to Charlotte's room. He ducked down on entering the odd-shaped room and noticed the phone on the charger. Her laptop was balancing on a chair arm, and he had to smile at the poster-covered walls. Katrina gathered Charlotte's clothes from the floor, folded them neatly and laid them on a chair.

"We weren't expecting visitors." She said, embarrassed.

"Okay, Katrina. Thanks. I'll have her social media accounts and phone searched for clues and photos. They may reveal her whereabouts."

"Of course. Do what you must, Tim. I can't stand the waiting and not knowing."

"Those can wait 'til morning. Hopefully, she'll turn up before then. We don't usually treat a person as missing for the first twenty-four hours unless serious matters relate to their safety and welfare. She's a family friend, so I'll prioritise it since she's so young."

"I'm concerned for her safety," Katrina said, arms folded tightly across her chest. She led the way back downstairs. Philippe offered Cunningham a hot drink.

"No, thanks, Philippe. I'd better press on. Everything that can be done is being done to find Charlotte. We're checking CCTV footage at the train station, and a team are searching the village as we speak. Get some rest, and I'll update you when we have any news."

"We can't rest until we know Charlotte is safe. She may be injured for all we know." Katrina said, her eyes filling with tears. Philippe squeezed her shoulder, but she pulled away.

"Perhaps she caught a train into Swynbourne to meet a friend."

"Maybe. Look, Katrina. At this stage, we're unsure if she visited the cemetery. She may have caught an earlier train or the bus into Swynbourne." Philippe reasoned. Katrina wasn't convinced, and the burden of a mother's concern twisted her expression. Cunningham shifted on his feet, ran his fingers over the rim of his hat and edged towards the door.

"One other point before you leave, Tim. We went to the cemetery earlier, but the gates were locked." Katrina said. "Search the cemetery first, I implore you. I know she's there."

"Okay, Katrina. I promise it will be the first place we look."

"You should have a hot drink before you leave. It's a bitterly cold night."

"No. Really. I'm fine, thanks. I need to get the team organised."

Philippe walked Cunningham to the door.

"Take my advice, Philippe, and get some rest. We've got it from here. I promise I'll contact you the moment I have any news."

"Can't we help with the search?"

"You'll be of more help to us if you stay here in case Charlotte returns or phones. Call me if she does contact you."

Cunningham drove off into a sea of flashing blue lights. Philippe returned to the kitchen and caught Katrina clutching the empty photo frame.

"I'm sure Charlotte is safe." He said, wrapping his muscly arms around her. "It's after midnight. Come on. Let's go and lie on the bed."

"We should be helping with the search instead of waiting here for any news. I won't rest until she's home." She said, holding the photo frame tight to her chest.

"At least we can relax if we do as Tim asks. He's doing all he can to find Charlotte, and it's no longer our responsibility. He dotes on her. You do know that, don't you? Come on." He said, leading her by the arm. "There's nothing we can do for the time being. At least if we lie down, we'll be comfortable and may fall asleep."

"I doubt it."

Would they ever get any sleep with all that chatter bouncing around in their heads? Their relentless internal dialogue would surely sour their dreams even if they fell asleep.

Katrina glanced in the bedroom mirror; her eyes reddened with tears, and her hair was as straggly as a rag doll. They watched blue lights flash across the ceiling from the comfort of the bed, a blatant reminder of the search for their missing daughter. Katrina rolled onto her side with a tear-soaked hanky in her palm.

"Over 'ere Sarge." A distant voice yelled urgently.

SIXTEEN

Sunday: 12:29 am

His phone sounded urgent for some reason, so he answered it with a degree of apprehension.

"…okay. Thanks." It took a moment to gather his thoughts. "I'm on my way."

The call from Woody was not what Cunningham wanted to hear. He knew instinctively that something was amiss. A lack of sleep, the bitter cold, and searching the village for his friend's daughter all took their toll. He would have preferred to be at home with his wife rather than outdoors in the middle of the night. Frozen to the bone, he wished he'd taken Philippe's offer of a hot drink before venturing into the cold night; he parked that thought. Not because he had put his needs on hold and would do the same for any missing child, but because Charlotte was a close family friend.

Instead of wasting time waiting in his car for the key to open the cemetery gates, he searched the remote end of the village while some of his men searched the surrounding area. He intended to work his way back to the church, but entry to the cemetery had been gained quicker than anyone had anticipated. The call from

Woodcroft had him running across the village and into Church Lane, where he was almost run over by an ambulance, leaving the village in a hurry. A constable at the cemetery gates waved him through.

As the sole keyholder, old Jake was woken from an alcohol-induced stupor to unlock the gates. The stench of whiskey and cigarettes lingered on his breath as he waited in the police car.

"Le'me out. I wanna a piss." He demanded. The female officer had one ear on her radio and the other on Jake.

"Can't it wait?"

"No, it bloody well can't. I need a piss, NOW."

"Don't you dare pee in the car?" she shouted. "Go and pee in the bushes if you must. Old Jake leapt from the car.

"Make sure you come back; we're not done with you yet. Close the door. You're letting in the cold."

His Cashmere coat failed to keep him warm due to a lack of sleep or Woody's nightmarish phone call. He yanked his collar up and joined a small group searching the cemetery grounds with powerful lights. Cunningham recognised Woodcroft in the shadows and went over to him.

"What have we got, Woody?"

"Two officers found an unconscious female lying here." He said and pointed to a frost-free area of grass cordoned off with tape. "Pretty girl. Early teens, I would say. She was hypothermic, so paramedics whisked her away. I didn't get a chance to see her. She had no ID on her as far as I know."

"You didn't get a good look at her, then?"

"Unfortunately, not. One of the paramedics said the girl suffered substantial blood loss from a head injury and signs of a Basilar Skull Fracture. Her upper clothing had been disturbed, but that may have been the medics. I noticed bruising around her throat and signs of a struggle but no obvious signs of a sexual assault. I instructed the team to search the area for anything that could have been used as a weapon."

"Well done, Woody. You gleaned plenty of vital information, considering you only saw her briefly. Any idea of the time the alleged attack took place?"

"Too early to say, Guv. Frost on her clothing suggests she's been here for quite some time." Woody's lips thinned. "She was clinging to life when they took her away, and to be honest, most people would have died after being exposed to the cold like that. She's certainly a fighter."

"Mm," Cunningham said, quietly making mental notes. "Were there any footprints or drag marks?"

"There are faint scuff marks in the gravel and grass over there," he said, pointing, "but nothing obvious. She left a red woollen glove here, so, on balance, this appears to be the primary scene. We're checking for other exits. But for now, we believe there's only one way in and out of the cemetery. I'll ask the gate guy." Woody said. "Are you implying that she was attacked elsewhere and dumped here? Why would anyone go to that much trouble?"

"Just a thought, Woody. Who knows how a felon's mind works?"

"It seems odd that she was here. Teenagers, especially females, wouldn't normally be alone in a cemetery after dark."

"Paramedics said she was hypothermic, so she must have entered here before the gates were locked," Cunningham added.

"Unless she climbed over the gate, or there is another way in, Guv."

"Judging by their height, she would have had to be damn keen to have climbed over the gates. We're barking up the wrong tree, Woody. When I spoke to the missing teen's parents earlier, they said their daughter planned to leave flowers on her grandmother's grave yesterday afternoon. She may have arranged to meet someone here, although I can think of better places to meet."

"I agree. Especially when it's so damn cold. We haven't much to go on, and the heavy frost hasn't helped."

"Forensic will uncover something, I guarantee. Any footprints leading from the scene?"

"No old footprints. The frost is thick, as you know."

"Well, whoever did this didn't float out of here," Cunningham said with a hint of annoyance. "Footprints would have been lost when uniforms' size nines stomped all over the scene, I suppose."

Woodcroft's eyebrows shot up.

"Only fresh footprints from the two constables who made the discovery and both paramedics. That's why we have avoided walking on the pathway."

"Standard procedure," Cunningham replied, then stared at the frost-free area where the teen was found. He mentally noted the dark patch of blood in the frost and the fresh flowers on the adjacent grave. He then illuminated the headstone with his phone torch. 'Evelyn Turner.' Katrina's mother. He remembered Philippe telling him that he had given Charlotte money to buy flowers for her gran's grave, and he made a mental note of the fresh flowers, wrapping paper, and pink ribbon. With that information, he dismissed the idea of the attack having taken place elsewhere.

"I'll have forensics extend the crime scene. Meanwhile, no one goes near the area without my authority. This may turn out to be a murder enquiry." He walked away, leaving Woody in charge.

Cunningham was reasonably confident that the girl in the cemetery was Charlotte.

SEVENTEEN

An unusual stream of traffic wound its way along the lane. It stopped at the church car park. The traffic noise disturbed Mum and Dad while they lay on the bed waiting for a phone call from me or DCI Cunningham. Gran and I stood at the end of the bed, watching Mum and Dad gaze at the ceiling. The noise outside was reduced to a low hum, and it was quiet enough to hear Jack Frost playing a tune on the phone wires. A distant thought sent shivers down her spine when Mum sat up to remove her necklace. Dad saw it.

"What was that?"

"Nothing, really. A thought flashed through my mind, but it's gone now. It'll probably come back when I'm least expecting it."

"Was it important?"

"I don't know. It's completely left me."

"Did you get any sleep?"

"No, I don't think so. How about you?"

"Not really. I tried, but I kept thinking about Charlotte."

"I feel terribly guilty. We should be helping with the search instead of lying here, waiting for any news."

"Tim said we were more useful staying here should Charlotte come home or contact us. There's a whole team searching the area, so there's no need for us to be out there with them."

Mum glanced at her phone, standing to attention on the charger. She desperately hoped for a missed call or message, but the only flashing lights were coming from the other side of the window.

"I would have preferred to have helped. She is our daughter, after all."

"I would like to do my bit too, but Tim has a vested interest, and we know he will do everything he can to find Charlotte."

"I hope they searched the cemetery first. I don't want to be pessimistic, but I have a bad feeling about it."

Gran got comfortable in the wicker chair next to the cast iron fireplace, and I sat on the edge of the bed. To give them their privacy, we decided to go downstairs, and when we did, Sandy was asleep in his basket.

When Sandy was a fluffy ball of fun, I sneaked him into my room at night and let him sleep on my bed. Mum and Dad must have been aware, but they never let on. I pictured him running around in circles in the back garden, and then I was snapped from my dream when I heard Dad treading softly on the stairs. I glanced at the microwave clock: 2.30 a.m.

Cunningham arrived at the cottage in his Chrysler, then knocked and waited. Mum was already in the hallway and let him in. He slowly and deliberately removed his gloves; her motherly instincts told her it wasn't good news.

"Have you found Charlotte?" She asked, wishing the answer to be a resounding 'Yes.'

"Where's Philippe?"

"He's in the kitchen."

Dad stirred his tea and left the spoon in the sink as they walked in.

"Have you found Charlotte?" He asked, propping himself up against the counter.

"We're not sure, although I can tell you that a young girl was found in the village earlier and was rushed to Swynbourne Hospital."

"Oh, my goodness. Is it Charlotte?" Mum quizzed.

"It's possible, but the girl's face was so swollen, making it difficult to identify her. She's unconscious and unable to give her name and had nothing on her in the form of identification."

"Unconscious? Why? What happened?"

"That's what we need to find out. A crime scene has been set up, so we'll have more information as time progresses."

"Where was she found?"

"In the cemetery."

"Our cemetery?"

Cunningham nodded gently when a pained expression distorted Katrina's face.

"I was right, Philippe. I knew she was in the cemetery: I sensed it. We were so close. If we had gained access, then she may not have been unconscious. Why would she be in there after dark?"

"That's a good question. We don't have all the answers at this stage and are unsure if it is Charlotte. I would like you to come with me to the hospital to try to identify her."

"Are there any other missing teens in the area?"

"None."

"Then why are we still here? It must be Charlotte. Even if it's not her, a young girl shouldn't be alone in hospital." She said, leaping from the chair.

"Was the girl drunk or drugged?" Dad asked.

"I can't say any more until we know her identity."

"We have a right to know."

"Look, Philippe. It's natural to be upset, but don't get ahead of yourself. We need to find out if it is Charlotte first, then we can take it from there."

Gran and I watched the story unfold. Mum's lips formed a thin smile while she put on her coat, but even though the news had given her hope, her eyes showed only sorrow. All three climbed silently into Tim's car.

"It's too painful to watch, Gran. They believe I'm alive, and there's hope, but we both know I'm in spirit."

"You must not interfere," Gran warned. "It's important for them to go through this. Be patient, and you'll understand once you enter the light."

"Not too soon, I hope."

"It can't be avoided. Have you thought about what you will do with your extra time?"

"I have, but I haven't devised a plan yet. Mum and Dad can't see or hear me, which rules out that idea. What are the chances of me recovering and re-entering my body?"

"Remember. You've been separated from your body far too long. It will no longer recognise your soul."

"That's unfair. I'm determined to stay until my case is solved."

"Determined. Just like your mother." Gran said with a smile.

"I don't like being told what to do. There's nothing wrong with that."

"As long as we don't infringe on the rights of others. Listen. This is very important."

"I'm listening."

"Your parents will need time to adjust when they find out it is you in hospital. That's where you can help."

I decided to concentrate my efforts on Cunningham, but I had no idea what my plan was.

EIGHTEEN

1:52 am

Mrs Barnes leapt out of bed after a loud banging on the shop door woke her. She shuffled downstairs, wondering who was knocking at this hour.

"Go away. We're closed." She shouted until she recognised the tall, dark figure of DC Woodcroft standing in the doorway. He apologised for waking her, explaining his reason for being there. She took him through to the living area. Woodcroft stood in front of the fire and warmed himself by its last glowing embers.

Mrs Barnes listened to Woodcroft and then described the clothes Charlotte wore that afternoon while he took notes. She was visibly shaken by the news that she may have been the last person to see Charlotte before the attack if, indeed, it was her.

"Charlotte is like a daughter to DCI Cunningham. Whoever the girl is, she will recover, won't she?"

"I have no idea at this stage. Until someone identifies the girl, we won't know whether it is Charlotte. Don't be too concerned for now, Mrs Barnes."

"But I am concerned. It must be her. It's too much of a coincidence not to be." She said, expressing her fears.

"As I said. We won't know for sure until she's been identified."

Mrs Barnes shuddered as the room grew colder with each chilling thought.

"Charlotte popped in to buy flowers. I always wrap them in paper and tie them with ribbon." She said, reaching out to poke the fire into life. "She often buys flowers — on a Saturday." She wheezed.

"Did Charlotte say anything about meeting someone?"

"Not to me. — As far as I know — she went to the cemetery alone. — She didn't have Sandy with her — either."

"No. Sandy's at home." Woodcroft's phone vibrated in his pocket. He answered the call.

"Okay — thanks for letting me know."

Woodcroft stared at the glowing fire, its embers burning silently, as did his apprehension.

With the odds of the girl in the cemetery being Charlotte, he had never met her but struggled to keep his emotions on hold. He recalled the number of times Cunningham's children were ill or injured. On the day of Harry and Meghan's wedding, his eldest son, Stephen, suffered a mild concussion when he fell from a swing, a day Cunningham would remember for all the wrong reasons. Stephen's concussion paled into insignificance compared to what he'd just learned of the mystery girls' condition. His phone rang again when he was mulling over his words about the girl being a fighter.

"I'll let you get back to bed, Mrs Barnes. You've been very helpful, and once again, I apologise for disturbing you at this hour."

NINETEEN

Sunday: 3:31 am

The only way for Charlotte to leave the village in the middle of the night was for her to hitch a ride in Cunningham's car. Barely a word was spoken during the trip to Swynbourne Hospital, and the subsequent silence had a myriad of uncertainties screaming full volume inside Katrina's mind. Is it her beloved daughter lying unconscious in hospital, or is it another doting parent's child? If it's not Charlotte, then who is she? Someone's daughter is missing, and they will be experiencing the same heart-rending emotions. And if the girl is Charlotte....? The relief of finding their daughter would be fleeting, and with many questions left unanswered, refusal to accept the truth would surely ensue.

City traffic was light, but that did nothing to calm the knot twisting Katrina's stomach. The hospital loomed against a dark backdrop as Cunningham turned sharply right into the car park. Gran and Charlotte followed them to the A&E department. Cunningham showed his warrant card to the receptionist, and she jabbed the keyboard, then announced a 'Jane Doe' had recently been transferred to the Intensive Care Unit.' (ICU.)

The potent odour of antiseptic met them as they entered the ICU. A nurse aide escorted them to the girl's cubicle, and it took Katrina only a fraction of a second to recognise her daughter before running to her bedside.

"Oh, God! What have they done to my baby? She said, in a guttural bellow. "It's your mother, Charlotte. Can you hear me?"

She whispered 'Elephant Juice,' more than she had ever meant it before. It came from the heart and was more needed than their private joke. She stared at Charlotte's motionless form. "She looks so — so helpless, Philippe." She pressed Charlotte's limp hand to her cheek, then kissed it. Letting the hand go, she stepped back and palmed her mouth. "No-o-o-o. You don't deserve this! Not my baby! Who could have done this to you?"

"I'll get a nurse." The aide said, sweeping the curtains around the bed.

Charlotte's arms lay limply by her sides. Wires and tubes drooped from her and terminated at a variety of medical equipment. Katrina gazed across the void. She squeezed Charlotte's hand and sent every ounce of her love to heal her daughter. She closed her eyes to escape reality and used the time to rest them. Overwhelmed with anxiety and disbelief, she sank to her knees and pressed Charlotte's hand to her cheek again. The bed shook with every deep-seated sob as tears dripped onto the space blanket, faithfully following her daughter's slim form. Tubes and wires blurred in her peripheral vision as she focused on Charlotte. Her mind was elsewhere when Philippe placed a reassuring hand on her shoulder.

She stared relentlessly at her daughter, her head filled with whys and if-onlys.

Proof of identity was confirmed, and Cunningham left Charlotte's bedside to speak to a doctor. He phoned Woody to tell him the sad news that the girl in the cemetery was Charlotte.

Every unfamiliar sound, echo, and movement grew louder with each minute. The pungent odour of antiseptic caught Katrina's attention, as did the regimental sucking and blowing of the respirator, which reminded her of a scene from a sci-fi film. But this wasn't the sound stage of a futuristic spaceship. This was real, happening here and now. Other patients in the ICU were also in comas, some induced, others not, and all dependent on the multidisciplinary team for their well-being.

"Oh! Sorry," a nurse said as she drew back the curtain. She closed the gap, and Katrina and Philippe were again encapsulated in their private world. They wished the curtain was a steel fence, allowing them to be alone with their daughter. *Leave us alone by our daughter's side so we may nurse her back to health and say all those things we should have told her every day.*

The privacy gave them time to come to terms with a situation no parent should ever have to endure. The nurse returned and disrupted their privacy.

"My name is Amy, and I'm the head nurse of the ICU. I understand this is your daughter.

"Yes. Her name is Charlotte." She sniffled. "I'm Katrina, and this is Philippe, my husband."

"Thank goodness you're here. We have everything under control, so please don't worry. We can pull her notes from Medical Records now that we know her identity."

"Will she be all right?" Katrina asked, fighting back her salty tears. Philippe stared at the bandage wrapped around Charlotte's head and the bruising to her throat.

"Charlotte had been exposed to the cold for an extended period. She was hypothermic when she was brought in, and we are slowly raising her core temperature. She's deeply unconscious and unable to breathe for herself, so a machine is helping her breathe. A subarachnoid bleed, a bleed in the lining of the brain, is causing pressure and swelling. We don't know the extent of the damage yet, but we will after her MRI scan. When we get the results, we can take measures to reduce the swelling and prevent further damage. Time is of the essence."

Katrina nodded, but the only word that stood out was the singular word, unconscious. That word sent shock waves through her aching heart.

"When will she regain consciousness?" she asked, staring at the tube spoiling Charlotte's lip contour.

"I can't answer that until we receive the scan results. Talk to her while you wait. She can hear you." Amy said, resting a caring hand on Katrina's shoulder.

"Thank you. Wild horses couldn't drag me away from our daughter." She said and meant it. Amy scooped the curtain aside with the grace of a dancer and left.

"She looks so peaceful, Philippe. Like when she was a baby."

Katrina had spoken to Charlotte about the endless times she'd watched her whilst she slept as a child.

The machine accurately meted out each breath, and her chest rose and fell in perfect synchronisation. It was a dance, a melody, conducted by a metronome lacking empathy. It was keeping her daughter alive, and that was all that mattered.

Cunningham was talking with the doctor in charge of the ICU. He handed her his business card and asked her to call him if Charlotte's condition had altered. Charlotte had been identified, and now there was work to be done. The following 24 hours would be crucial to the investigation.

"I'm so sorry. She's in safe hands, so relax and let the nurses do their job. I must go now. I'll call you later." Cunningham said. Not only did he have to leave to continue his investigation, but he needed to escape, to scream silently at the horror and injustice of what he was witnessing.

TWENTY

5:15 am

Her mama had a vital role, and she was slapping her back to dislodge mucus, robbing her daughter of air. She removed her daughter's sweat-soaked pyjamas and helped her into dry ones. Her mama, who was like a swan, calm on the surface but paddling frantically beneath, meticulously carried out her well-practised routine. She refilled the nebuliser, and Papa called the on-call GP, who arranged transport for Isabella to be admitted to the hospital. Hospital visits have been a regular occurrence for Isabella from the day she was born.

"Is — my night-bag — ready?" She gasped.

"Do not worry, Isabella. We done this many times." She said in broken English. The nebuliser was attached, and Isabella forced a smile through the oxygen mask.

Two critical-care paramedics wheeled Isabella to the ambulance and stabilised her before the ride to Swynbourne General Hospital.

"Ashmarsh has kept us busy tonight." One of the paramedics said.

"How so?" Said Mrs Rousso.

"This is our second trip to the village tonight."

"I saw lights in the night. What happened?"

"We rushed a teenager to A&E after she was found unconscious in the cemetery. She was still unconscious when we left, and we haven't been back to the hospital to enquire about her condition."

"Mother of Mary! Was the poor child local?"

"Can't say. We didn't get a name."

TWENTY-ONE

8:00 am

Deep-seated anxiety churned his stomach as he watched the early morning news on TV. *'A young female was found unconscious in Ashmarsh cemetery and was rushed to hospital in the early hours. Police believe she's a local girl and described her condition as critical.'*

He fretted over the news. He lit another cigarette and considered his options. Norman Taylor realised the underlying ache in his stomach was not anxiety but fire in his belly. He had concocted a vague idea and would see it through. There was no ambiguity. It had to be done. But executing his plan wouldn't be an easy task.

He clambered aboard the day's first train and walked from the station to Swynbourne General. He slouched along the featureless corridor and ignored any unwelcome attention. With limited reading skills, he understood two vowels and a consonant and followed the signs.

The entrance to the Intensive Care Unit (ICU) was in an alcove, and a proximity card reader adjacent to sturdy doors barred his way. Pft! Modern technology! Problem number one. His attention was caught by a smoke-glassed dome protruding from the ceiling. Cameras were watching his every move, and his heart sank. Problem number two. He couldn't believe how electronic surveillance had infiltrated everyday life and realised it might take a while for him to gain entry undetected. A nurse approached the ICU, and he thought he could sneak in behind her back.

"Can I help you?" She enquired.

"Nope. Waiting for a mate." He replied, hands in pockets and staring at the floor. She swiped her card and entered the ICU, but Norman wasn't quick enough, and the door closed in his face, leaving him stranded in the corridor.

Mum and Dad sat on either side of my bed. Their anticipation and internal dialogue drowned out the clunking and hissing of my life support. *('When will she wake? Who did this to her? How long do MRI scan results take to interpret?')* Numerous questions added to the uncertainty. Mum held my hand and gazed at my swollen face. By sending subconscious thoughts for me to return, she was willing for me to awaken from this hellish nightmare. And because skin contact made it more bearable for Dad, he stroked my arm. It had been a long night, and I needed a change of scenery.

When I stepped into the corridor, the last person I expected to see was Norman Taylor. Why was he here, and why was he waiting outside the ICU? He's got a nerve. He knows I'm here and probably isn't here to wish me a speedy recovery. It dawned on me why he was here. I must warn someone.

Norman wasn't close enough to the door to dash through when it opened again and wasn't prepared for what was about to happen. Mum also decided to take a break and stepped into the corridor. Had she seen Norman, she would have easily recognised him, but he saw her first and hid beside a crimson crash trolley. I knew he wasn't here to wish me a speedy recovery, and this was an excellent opportunity to warn her.

"Mum! Norman is hiding behind the red trolley," I yelled at the top of my voice. When Norman peered over the top of the trolley, Mum was the only other person in the corridor at the time, and he knew it wasn't her voice he'd heard. He squatted behind the trolley until her clicking heels faded, then sneaked back to the ICU entrance.

It wasn't long before the door opened again, and he instinctively grabbed the handle when a nurse rushed out. He was about to walk in but hadn't considered the nurse's awareness.

"And where do you think you're going?"

"Er, er, I-I'm visiting me niece."

"What's her name."

"Charlotte Dubois."

"You'll have to go back to reception. You can't just walk in here without permission."

The nurse closed the door, leaving Norman stranded in the corridor for the second time — problem number four.

Arbitrariness: *Noun. 'The quality of being based on chance rather than being planned or based on reason.'* That was Norman's modus operandi. Although manipulative, he was also prone to stupidity, and his idea turned out to be a knee-jerk reaction with no chance of success. If he could gain entry, how would he have accomplished his task? Perhaps he would have tried to turn off my life support. It made sense to me. I'm the only witness able to identify him, and his ill-conceived idea was flawed and destined to fail.

His heightened awareness moved to a new level when he realised the chances of being seen were huge. The nurse may have alerted security, and it was only a matter of time before they came looking for him. He'd spent far too long outside the ICU and knew he was being monitored. Pimple-like cameras are attached to the ceiling. Unblinking spider's eyes: arachnoid surveillance. His plan was far too risky. His every action would have been caught on camera had he gained entry. Hopes crushed, he made his way to the main entrance only to find two overweight security men standing near the exit, radios screeching in indistinct dialogue. Somehow, he slipped through the door unseen, then concealed himself alongside an ambulance when Cunningham walked in through the hospital entrance.

"Trouble?" Cunningham asked.

"Aw! Yeah! Nah! Some weird bloke loitering around the ICU. Probably up to no good."

"What did he look like."

"Yay, big..." the guard responded, then held his hand shoulder height, "...and scruffy."

"I expect he's gone by now," Cunningham said, moving swiftly on.

Cunningham may have put two-and-two together had he spotted Norman outside ICU. But that hadn't happened, and I was left wondering how to help have Norman arrested. I guess I am as guilty as Norman at Arbitrariness.

TWENTY-TWO

Sunday: 9:15 am

After stepping into the cold morning air for a break, Katrina returned to her daughter's side as a nurse wrote Charlotte's core temperature on a chart.

"Is Charlotte any warmer?" Katrina asked Amy.

"Yes. She's slowly returning to normal."

"That's positive news, but will she regain consciousness?"

"The doctor will see you later. She's been quite clear on Charlotte's condition."

"She could be wrong. She looks like she's sleeping." Katrina said, not wanting to sound confrontational while clinging desperately to hope. She prayed for her daughter's condition to be temporary and for her to regain consciousness after her brain swelling reduced.

While they were enjoying a walk with Sandy, Charlotte had been viciously attacked in the cemetery and left for dead. How could that have happened? Her sturdy heart was keeping her body alive, but a significant part of her brain was starved of oxygen for far too long. Nurse Amy comforted Katrina, something she'd done many times, but not to the parents of a sixteen-year-old. Her meagre words wouldn't come close to easing the vice-like knot twisting Katrina's insides. Philippe tried to make sense of the situation while staring out the window at the crowded car park. Amy's chin blanched when she spoke.

"Why not go to the family room? There's more privacy in there."

Amy led the way. All three stepped inside, and Amy closed the door to the outside world, which was collapsing by the minute.

"I am so sorry, Mrs and Mrs Dubois. The doctor has been called away, but she has been very clear from the start. There's nothing more we can do for Charlotte, as her scan results are irrefutable. She won't regain consciousness, and it's only the machines keeping her body alive."

"What shall we do? Wait to see what happens, or do we give our permission to turn off her life support? I can't bear to leave. There must be a glimmer of hope, surely?"

Amy shook her head.

"There's not even a minimal chance that Charlotte will ever recover. I'm sorry, and this may sound awful, but Charlotte is clinically brain-dead, confirmed by the neurologist."

Amy explained the dreadful situation to Philippe and Katrina in plain English. Katrina understood but didn't want to. She nodded in all the right places. Philippe was also in denial and wouldn't take no for an answer. Katrina didn't want to think about letting go of her precious daughter. Although she lacked medical knowledge, the extent of Charlotte's brain injury was all too obvious. At a crossroads, she didn't know which way to turn and relied on Philippe's support.

"Charlotte had an NHS Organ Donor Card in her pocket. I know this may sound a little premature, but would you consider allowing the procurement of her organs and tissues? It was her wish."

"We can't make that decision now."

"That's okay. Take all the time you need."

"Thank you, Amy. I want to return to her bedside."

Desperate for a response, Katrina squeezed Charlotte's hand, hoping to sense the twitch of a finger, the flicker of an eyelid, or any sign of life to prove the doctors wrong. She'd heard stories of people waking from long-term comas, and her only wish was for her daughter to awaken, not in weeks or years, but today — now. There's always hope, but hope was dwindling into a speck beyond her reach. Although she held her daughter's warm hand, a gap existed between them, widening by the hour. And Katrina wept quietly when she realised her daughter would never return. Philippe gripped the end of the bed tightly, turning his knuckles white. Words failed Katrina as her vision blurred. Philippe massaged her shoulders to relieve the heartache. He felt fragile but had to remain strong for his wife's sake.

'Charlotte is clinically brain-dead.' The neurologist had said. 'There was no choice but to turn off the ventilator.'

They stayed by Charlotte's bedside while the spirits of Charlotte and Gran watched from the end of the bed. Then, without warning, Charlotte's spirit body began to glow brightly.

This ribbon of glowing light streamed up to the ceiling and rotated, then burst into a rainbow of colours.

TWENTY-THREE

9:55 am

I'd experienced numerous oddities in the spirit world, but I could barely comprehend what was happening to me. My weightless body grew heavy, and I knew I was lying on my back, covered by the lightest of space blankets. I could not move, but my hearing and awareness were sharp and clear. Initially, I was confused, but I knew exactly where I was. As my awareness improved, the warmth of my hand in Mum's sent waves of joy surging through my heart. The sensation was pure love, and I was no longer afraid. I hoped against all odds that I would survive and open my eyes to see the look on her face when I started to breathe for myself. My throat hurt from the plastic tube helping me breathe, and I wanted a nurse to remove it. For the first time in hours, I felt blood rushing through my veins. Every vessel in my body pulsated with my heartbeat, and my chest rose and sank to the machine's rhythm. Although motionless and unable to open my eyes, heightened hearing and awareness helped me form mental pictures of my surroundings. The room grew darker when a shadow crept across my face. Warm lips pressed against my forehead, and I instantly knew it was Mum by her perfume and peppermint breath. She whispered, 'Elephant juice,' and with a combination of joy and sadness, her shadow fell away.

"We love you so much. Don't leave us," she pleaded, squeezing my hand. The sound of furniture dragging across the floor caught my attention. Dad had moved his chair closer.

"Be strong, Charlotte. Come back to us. We need you." She said, eyes blurred with tears. Then it was Dad's turn to kiss and hold the hand of the daughter he doted on, who, in his opinion, had touched the hearts of many. His grip was firm, as though trying to pull me back to the real world, something he knew was impossible. I was determined to stay in my body and live. I repeated the Lord's Prayer, but greater forces were at work. The decision had already been made. When Dad said, 'I love you, sweetheart,' a gentle force lifted my soul from my body, and I returned to the foot of the bed. Gran was there, waiting for me.

"That was simply amazing, Gran, and so unexpected. What a wonderful experience to feel her hand's softness and my heart beating. Did you do that?"

"No. It wasn't my doing. I can't take credit for that, Lottie, but I saw what happened. In case you didn't hear, they both said they loved you."

"I heard them, but I couldn't see them."

"You must have wanted that so badly. You made that happen."

"Really? So, we can create amazing events in spirit if we want them badly enough." I said, lowering my gaze. "Then It's decided. I will go to Paradise, but only when I'm ready."

Gran gave me a knowing look. Although I was pleased to return to my body for one last time and enjoyed the experience, I was left wondering what my next move would be.

TWENTY-FOUR

Approaching mid-day.

The hospital restaurant was deserted. There were only two customers besides Cunningham, too absorbed in conversation to notice him. His coffee grew cold as he dwelled on Charlotte's condition. He prayed for her to wake from her coma, but experience told him that it would take more than a miracle for her to recover from her extensive brain injury. Katrina and Philippe clung to a hint of hope, or was it denial? He was counting on the bacon sandwich and a second cup of coffee to overcome his fatigue. His mobile rang, and he answered it after wiping crumbs from his lips.

"Any news on Charlotte?" Woody enquired.

"The situation is rather grim, Woody. Charlotte has deteriorated, and she probably won't make it." He said, with a catch in his throat. "I'm working, but I'm also here to support them," he said, glancing at the time.

The caffeine fix didn't last long, and Cunningham reached the point of exhaustion. His eyes closed involuntarily, and he needed to close them long enough to be able to think straight. He sat in his car and rested his eyes for a few minutes. Almost an hour later, he was woken by a motorbike's loud exhaust in the car park. Partially refreshed, he returned to the ICU and found Charlotte's bed had been stripped, and the machines had been taken away. He dashed to the nurse's station.

"Hi, Amy. Charlotte's bed is empty. Has she been taken elsewhere?"

"I'm so sorry, inspector. Were you not informed?" She said, voice quivering. "Charlotte passed away nearly an hour ago."

"I specifically asked the doctor to call me if Charlotte deteriorated. Why wasn't I contacted?" He snapped.

"I'm sorry, inspector. It must have slipped the doctor's mind when she went off duty."

"Sorry. Please forgive me. That was insensitive of me. It must have been a huge shock to everyone."

"It was, for all concerned. Charlotte passed at 13:37. With only a short window before irreversible damage occurred, her parents permitted procurement of her tissues and organs. It was a difficult choice. They said their last goodbyes before Charlotte was taken to theatre. She's still in theatre as far as I know."

"Are Mr and Mrs Duval here?"

"Yes. They're in the family room." She said, pointing through the door and to the left.

Cunningham was annoyed because he wasn't by Charlotte's side when she passed. He put his thoughts on hold and then went to the family room. He paused at the door to compose himself, then walked in and went to Katrina to comfort her. Both she and Philippe explained the past events.

"I'm so sorry I wasn't there when Charlotte passed. I'll run you home when you're ready. There's no rush." Cunningham said. He left them to decide while he phoned his wife, Celine if only to hear her voice.

The leather creaked as he gripped the steering wheel. Cunningham was in shock, and it was too painful to talk to them about leaving their daughter behind, even though the cord binding mother and daughter could never be broken. The quiet drive home separated them from the pain and anguish of having to let go. Cunningham was family, and he was unable to find the words to console grieving parents. The hardest part of loving someone is letting go; they weren't prepared. Cunningham checked the rear-view mirror. Katrina was resting her head on Philippe's shoulder, and a tiny tear, a telling silver ball of secrets, rolled down her cheek and whispered its sorrow. She stared blankly out the side window as the scenery flashed past in a non-stop blur.

"Who would want to harm a 16-year-old girl?" Philippe blurted out.

"I'll do whatever I can to find out," Cunningham assured.

TWENTY-FIVE

3:27 pm

The cottage towered above them as Cunningham drove slowly into their drive. They used to call it home, but now, the cottage seemed to be a pile of cold, meaningless stone resembling a convenient dwelling. The hedge was decorated with many flowers, and a blue teddy was tied lovingly to the gate. Anne from next door ran unsteadily in high heels across the drive and waited for Katrina to climb from the car.

Cunningham said goodbye and left, and when Katrina opened the front door, she heard, saw, and felt the emptiness. Anne followed them inside, and Sandy ran towards them from the kitchen.

"I'm sorry I didn't answer your calls, Anne. My phone went flat, and I didn't get a chance to charge it."

"That's okay, Katrina. I watched the news on TV this morning; that's why I called you." Anne replied. Katrina smiled humbly.

"I would rather have kept the news quiet, but the media always seem to find out." She fretted.

"Then you'll know that some coward left Charlotte bleeding and unconscious in the cemetery. She would have been there all night had the police not found her." Philippe said. Katrina sat on the sofa with her coat draped across her knees.

"Charlotte was late home last night. We went to the cemetery to look for her because I strongly suspected she was there. I sensed it. She needed me, and I wasn't there. I let her down, and I feel awful."

"Shh. Don't torture yourself, Katrina." Anne comforted. "You couldn't possibly have known she was in the cemetery."

"But I did; that's why I feel awful. We couldn't gain access to the cemetery because the gates were locked. And when we reported Charlotte missing, I asked Tim Cunningham to search there first."

Anne rubbed Katrina's shoulder. "How could you have possibly known she was in the cemetery?"

"I just knew. Oh! Anne. How will I ever forgive myself?"

"Don't do that, Katrina. You did everything a mother could have done."

"If we had been able to access the cemetery, then maybe she wouldn't have been alone for so long."

"Is Charlotte alright?" Anne asked guardedly.

Katrina shook her head. "Her injuries were too severe."

"You mean…?"

Katrina stared into middle distance. "Yes. We were by her side when she slipped away."

"Oh my Gosh! I'm so sorry. I can't begin to imagine how you must feel."

Katrina's lips moved, but there were no swords. Philippe filled the awkward silence.

"Charlotte was unconscious when she arrived at the hospital. A machine was helping her breathe, and she had deteriorated by the time we arrived. Brain swelling caused soft tissue injury, and the doctor said parts of her brain were starved of oxygen for too long. An EEG showed virtually no brain activity, and an MRI scan confirmed the extent of the damage." He said, as though reading from a script. "The neurologist assured us she wouldn't regain consciousness, and there was nothing more they could do. He was sympathetic but blunt. Oh! God. She was warm to the touch and looked as though she was sleeping. I can't believe she's gone." He said and sighed a shuddering breath.

Philippe and Katrina wrapped themselves in each other's arms, and Anne stared at them in total disbelief. Katrina eventually summoned the courage to speak.

"We talked about turning off her life support, but the decision was made for us. I think Charlotte saved us from making that decision." Katrina said, staring at her trembling hands. "From now on, whenever I look in her room, I'll imagine her propped up on her pillows, laptop balanced on her knees, and wearing headphones while listening to her favourite music. I can't bear the thought of an empty room."

With that statement, three adults cried openly.

"Why did she have to leave us." Katrina wailed. "She will be deeply missed."

The day Charlotte was born, Katrina screamed like an injured fox and probably wanted to scream like that now. Philippe stared at Sandy. Sandy stared back, head tilted inquisitively, without comprehending what was happening. Anne leapt from her chair.

"I'll put the kettle on..." she said, dabbing her eyes, "...you look after Katrina."

It was customary in Ashmarsh to draw the curtains following a death, a mark of respect. Ann filled the kettle, then flitted around the cottage to close the curtains. She went to lower the kitchen blind and noticed two stationary vans in the lane, with satellite dishes pointing skywards and a small crowd holding microphones, standing at the gate. Drooling at the mouth like hungry animals, cameras at the ready, the media waited for a story from grieving parents to instantly flash across the globe. Information travels fast in today's high-tech world, but could the Duval's cope with this unwanted attention?

TWENTY-SIX

Ann drew the curtains facing the front, making the cottage look gloomier. Mum and Dad were assured of their much-deserved privacy, and the lounge at the back of the cottage gave them the space they needed to escape from long lenses and pushy media personnel. The pain of dealing with their loss was more than anyone could cope with, but having their grief beamed instantly around the world was much worse.

"I want to hug them, but it wouldn't be the same, not at all like when I returned to my body in hospital."

"Cherish that moment," Gran said. "You'll understand how the spirit world functions when you return."

"Return? I can't recall ever being there before. Aren't you mistaken?"

"Not at all. As spirits, we have been visiting Earth for millennia. Our frequency is lowered to enable us to function in the third dimension, and when we shuffle off our mortal coil, we return home where we truly belong."

"So, life on Earth for spirits is like a holiday, minus the luggage."

"You could say that, although many spirits would disagree. Life can be difficult in a three-dimensional world."

"I'll agree, even though I wasn't here for very long."

"This wasn't your first visit, Charlotte. When we arrive, there are lessons to be learned, tears to shed, and hearts that become broken, and when we return home, it feels like we have been through a washing machine on a full cycle. Some may return to learn more about life as a human being. All these experiences increase our frequency until we no longer need to reincarnate."

"Why can't I remember being here before?"

"Our Earth memories are wiped before we return, although some memories bleed through, especially in our pre-teen years."

"I have so much to learn. What about Mum and Dad, though? I want to tell them how much I love them. Why can't they hear me?"

"Your world has changed, so be careful what you wish for." She said, with a hint of warning. I smiled, then sat on the sofa arm next to Mum and ran my fingers through her hair. She flinched.

"I'm sure she sensed my touch. Look! Her arms are breaking out in goose pimples."

"You may be right, Lottie. Human skin is sensitive to the lightest of touch. Some may sense a passed loved one's touch, but they have no idea why. Do you recall a tickling sensation in your hair whenever you were by my graveside?"

"Yes. Yes. I do. Every time, Gran, like something crawled through my hair. Was that you?"

She winked. "Guilty as charged."

"That's awesome. I knew it! You were with me, after all. I told Mum, but she dismissed it and said it was only my imagination."

"It was the only way I could show you how much I loved you. You have that same ability." I clung to Gran's every word, hugged Mum and Dad in turn, and then spoke to them.

"There are no guarantees that you will ever come to terms with my loss. I am here, but not in the way you're used to. Don't cry over my loss, but celebrate my life. We had sixteen wonderful years together, and I know I wasn't perfect, but I love you both with all my heart, and I always will." I whispered, 'Elephant juice.' And even though my voice was unheard, I felt better having said it.

Ann got up to leave. She wanted to give Mum and Dad privacy. She slipped through a narrow gap in the adjoining hedge to avoid prying media eyes from the lane. As Mum watched Ann leave from the French window, I noticed a small object in her hand. It was a bottle with a rounded top and a white tick on its front, and sitting on the coffee table was a neat white box with a silver Apple logo on the lid. I sighed when it dawned on me that I would never come home again, not in the true sense. She knew I wouldn't return, and I bet she wished she could talk to me on the phone about the new boutique clothes shop opening in Swynbourne or if I liked her latest perfume. There are no phones in spirit, but spirits can be contacted, and I'll try anything I can to get a message to anyone who can hear me.

The following morning, Gran said she would stay at the cottage with my Mum. I decided to leave her and visit Isabella.

It was unusual for their house to be empty. There was always someone at home; then I remember Mum mentioning that Isabella was very sick and was admitted to hospital during the night. I could have visited her while I was there if I'd remembered.

I climbed into the back of a delivery van, one I knew was heading into Swynbourne, and when I arrived at the hospital, the main corridor was crowded, not with living people, but lost souls. Some acknowledged me, while others mooched around like sleepwalkers.

Was my bestie receiving the care she needed? She wasn't in the Cardiac Ward, but after an extensive search of all the relevant wards, my last call was to the Paediatric Intensive Care Unit. (PICU). I walked into the PICU, and Isabella's mama and papa sat on either side of her bed. Isabella's appearance took me by surprise. Tubes, pipes, and wires attached to her body snaked their way to machines and monitors like the ones I was connected to recently. Did I look like that when I was in ICU? Her Papa had his eyes closed, and her mama stroked Isabella's hair as it flowed across the pillow like raven's feathers. She whispered something to Isabella, and I wasn't sure if it was English. Isabella was calm as she slept in her Paddington Bear gown, and I wondered how much pain she was in due to the intrusive staples running down the centre of her chest. Her eyes slowly opened when I stroked her hand and kissed her on the forehead, and it was as though she was gazing directly into my eyes. A faint smile crept across her face, then her heavy eyes closed.

The abundance of get-well cards surrounding her bed was a giveaway, and I was delighted because Isabella had been given the gift of a new heart. It meant a human life had been lost for her to have received a donor's heart, but that was the last thing on my mind. She'd been saved, and that's all that mattered. *If a suitable heart hadn't been available in time, she would have certainly died.* That thought sent chills running through me.

Many of her cards were from school friends and heart-themed, while the remainder were from family wishing her a speedy recovery. Joy washed over me, and I couldn't wait to tell Gran the fantastic news. I returned to the train station and clambered aboard the train.

Back at the cottage, Gran was sat with Mum. I told her the news, but she wasn't as pleased as I'd thought she would be. Then I looked at Mum, playing with her necklace. Her facial expression was alarming. Her forehead was deeply furrowed, and her eyes were devoid of expression as though she wasn't coping well.

TWENTY-SEVEN

Vinyl floor coverings softened every footstep when medical staff moved across the floor in a well-orchestrated routine. All beds in the PICU were occupied, and the next twenty-four hours were critical for one special young lady.

Isabella's mama and papa surrounded her bed after she had returned from theatre and were with her post-surgery when she first opened her eyes. Potent post-op analgesia made her illusional and had her wondering what was real and what wasn't. She stared into middle distance and smiled just before a nurse opened her right eye and shone a pen torch into it.

"Wake up, sweetheart. Open your eyes for me, Isabella. Your operation is over; you'll be pleased to know."

The nurse unfastened the front of Isabella's gown and listened to her chest with a cold stethoscope.

"Breath in." Isabella did as she was told.

"And out. Again. You can do better than that."

Isabella breathed in deeply and slowly, and her face was a picture when she realised how easy it was to breathe despite the soreness.

"Excellent. Well done." The nurse said. "Physio will have you sitting in a chair for twenty minutes tomorrow, and the day after, they'll have you on your feet for a short while."

"Really? My chest is so sore." She said in a hoarse whisper. "What if my staples break?"

"Trust me, they won't. The sooner you're up and about, the sooner you can go home."

"Will I make a full recovery?"

"Of course. But only if you do as you're told." The nurse said, with a hint of motherly warmth.

"Be good, and you'll be home with Mama and Papa." Her mama said, patting Isabella's hand.

Isabella looked tired, and the nurse asked her parents to leave so she could rest.

"The cardiologist said you are responding well after your operation, young lady. Your stats are normal, and you'll be home in no time at the rate you're progressing." She said, smoothing the bedsheet. "Now, put that away. You need to rest."

"But I need my phone to message Charlotte. I'm sure she doesn't know I've had an operation."

"You'll have plenty of time for social media tomorrow. But for now, you need lots of rest. Is Charlotte a close friend?"

"She's been my bestie, like, forever. She's kind and allows me to walk her dog every other Saturday." She took a deep breath. "Ow! that hurt. She lends me her clothes and sometimes lets me keep them, and I'm like, they're like new, and she says…"

"Shh, shh. That's enough talking for now. Save your breath. Like I said, you need to rest."

"My throat's dry. May I have some water, please?"

Isabella sipped water from the glass, and the nurse fussed over her like she would her daughter. Now resting quietly, she became aware of a stranger's heart beating in her chest. She remembered having a conversation with the surgeon while being prepared for her operation and not getting too excited in case the donor's heart wasn't a suitable match. Thankfully, it was.

How grateful she was to have received a heart. Someone's son or daughter had been snatched from them, giving Isabella the chance of a new life.

TWENTY-EIGHT

Katrina was staring at a recent photograph of Charlotte when Philippe returned to the kitchen. She was struggling with her loss and was prone to prolonged episodes of staring into space and frequent crying. It had only been a week since Charlotte's death, and Katrina wasn't coping. Philippe wanted to take her to a doctor, but she said she was okay and would get through it without any medication.

The Chrysler's hot engine ticked down when Cunningham knocked and walked into the cottage. Katrina was in the bedroom and heard voices coming from the kitchen below. She came downstairs and sat on the wooden stool next to the AGA.

"Hi, Tim," Katrina said. "Is there any news?"

"None, yet. I was passing and wanted to see how you both were."

"It's not easy. Life seems so empty."

"It's early days yet, Katrina. It's only natural to feel sad. No one is expecting you to be your normal self so soon after your loss. If it helps, my family is feeling it too. I can't even begin to understand how awful it must be for both of you."

"Thanks for being such a good friend, Tim. We're taking one day at a time." Philippe said.

"I'm sure your loss will be much easier when we find Charlotte's attacker."

"I agree. Are you making any progress?" Asked Katrina.

"A little. I spoke with the coroner earlier, and he agreed with the neurologist on the cause of death. Forensics have detected saliva on Charlotte's scarf, and it's being tested for DNA. There were no fingerprints at the scene, but we'll conduct further tests."

Philippe fumbled for words. "Was she… did they…?"

"The attack wasn't sexual, if that's what you are suggesting, Philippe. Her upper clothing was disturbed, which may have happened during a struggle or by paramedics during their initial assessment. We will be questioning them."

Philippe sat at the table and nervously swept spilt grains of sugar into a small pile with a finger.

"Thank God she wasn't raped. Did she suffer?"

"When she fell backwards and hit her head, it happened so fast that I doubt she would have suffered. It was suggested that she may have known her attacker, so my investigation will include all males within a ten-mile radius of the village. And if that doesn't reveal anything, we'll widen our area and gender."

"Gender? Could her attacker have been female?"

"It's a possibility."

"Initially, you said Charlotte was struck with a blunt weapon. Now, you're saying she struck her head. Does that mean there was no weapon?"

"Yes. Initially, we thought a weapon was used, but we now know that isn't the case."

"Then how did she sustain a horrendous head injury?"

"As I said, Charlotte fell backwards and struck her head on a nearby grave rail."

Katrina couldn't bear it any longer and ran upstairs. She threw herself on the bed and repeatedly punched the pillow. Cunningham toyed with the rim of his hat.

"I apologise, Philippe. I'm sorry. Katrina doesn't seem to be coping well. I tried to be delicate. Would you like me to leave?"

"No. No. Of course not, Tim. Katrina needs time to grieve." There was a pause, and then Philippe leaned forward. "I'm curious."

"I can give you the facts if you prefer."

"You know I'm not good at expressing my feelings, Tim. Katrina says I'm uncaring, but I must be the strong one. You know — a shoulder to cry on. That's how it is…"

"It's okay, Philippe. We all grieve in our own way. Take some advice from a friend. Don't keep it inside. Feelings have a way of leaking out in unexpected ways if we don't deal with them at the time. Forget the macho image. It's okay to cry. You'll feel better for it, believe me."

"I cried last week. Anyway. Can we continue?"

"Okay. But I won't go into too much detail. Just the facts."

"Before you do. What caused Charlotte to fall backwards? Did she stumble, or was she pushed?"

"She may have been pushed forcefully for her to sustain such an injury. Usually, when a person falls backwards, they automatically put out an arm to lessen their fall. They often sustain an arm or wrist injury, but there were no such injuries, not even a bruised elbow. If she was pushed, the push was unexpected, and she was incapable of protecting herself from the fall."

"Charlotte may have fallen backwards so quickly that she had no time to save herself from falling. It sounds like it was a brutal push."

"Evidence would suggest that, and the coroner mentioned that in his report. There was money in her purse, so the motive wasn't robbery. It seems to have been a motiveless attack. Opportunistic, perhaps. We're unclear this early in our investigations."

"You mentioned earlier the possibility of the attacker being female. Would a female be capable of such a violent attack?"

"Girls can get jealous. It may have been a warning that went horribly wrong. We don't have all the answers yet, but we will." Tim said reassuringly.

"We'll be taking DNA samples from every male in the district, including you, Philippe. I know Katrina can vouch for you, but we must be thorough. Standard practice."

"Of course. Look. I want my daughter's attacker caught more than anyone, and I'll continue to assist in bringing that lowlife to account until I take my dying breath."

"I understand," Cunningham said, then paused. "The sooner we apprehend the culprit, the sooner you will have closure. I'll keep you informed of any developments."

"We'd much rather hear it from you, Tim. I prefer facts rather than second guessing."

"Leave the whys and wherefores to me, Philippe. Anyway, I must fly. I'll call you later. Cunningham left with one question on his mind. Was Charlotte's attacker known to her?

TWENTY-NINE

Table Mountain was named long before the Romans ever occupied Britain. The top is as flat as a table and appears to have been deliberately levelled off. Some say it is a giant tree stump, and the Gods chopped it down so that they could sit there and eat. No records in the history books suggest that, but the story may have some truth.

The climb to the top is challenging, but when you eventually reach the top, you are rewarded with an unspoilt view of a sweeping patchwork of greens, browns, and yellows. Mum and Dad took me to the top for the first time when I was young. Mum said. I let go of her hand and ran towards the edge. She almost had a fit and caught me before I ran over the edge. After that, she held my hand tightly until it was time to leave.

I remember the joy of my first experience of Table Mountain, which washed over me today when we climbed to the top and sat on a picnic bench. I plucked a blade of grass and watched the morning mist slowly reveal the sweeping landscape beneath. This is how I imagine Heaven will be.

Time on Earth is different for spirits, and Earth hours are mere moments to us. That's what Gran told me. As time stole the day, I watched the sun traverse the sky as I rekindled the last few days' events. I settled on the grass and turned to her.

"I've been thinking. Will Mum and Dad ever come to terms with my loss?"

"Of course, but that will take time."

"I hope they do. Barely a day went by without me thinking of you when you passed. I often wondered what you did during your day. What's Heaven like?" I asked, excited to know the details.

"I have no idea because I haven't yet been there."

"What? Then where have you been for the past two years?"

Before answering, Gran reached forward and brushed my hair from my face.

"Hades. I live in Hades, the Garden of Paradise, or Summerland. That's because we won't enter the Kingdom of Heaven until the Day of Judgment."

"Wow! I didn't know that. What is the Garden of Paradise like?"

"Heaven includes the Heavenly city and is where God resides. It's not a place but an experience. The Garden of Paradise is similar; you can manifest your every desire there. Dreams, wishes and childhood aspirations become your reality." She said, eyes widening with passion. "Paradise has exquisite gardens with vivid colours never seen on earth, all displayed beneath perpetual daylight. It's like living inside a colourful painting. Spirits have a higher frequency and glow brightly. Angelic music plays continually, and the pitch-perfect frequencies become you."

"It sounds wonderful, Gran, and I almost want to go there now, but… what about poverty and suffering?"

"There is no pain, disability, or poverty. Loved ones, together with their pets, live in harmony. Acres of grass glow an emerald green under a cobalt blue sky, and warm showers help flora and fauna flourish. Since the Lord provides abundance, no soul ever suffers or goes without."

"It sounds amazing. Do you often visit Earth?"

"Occasionally. I was with you through the good times and the bad and sent love and healing light to guide you when you were at your lowest."

"You did that for me, Gran? I sensed you were there. Anyway. I'm looking forward to entering Paradise, but for now, I can't leave, at least not until my attacker is caught."

"The path will unfold of its own accord and in its own time. It's not always about you, Lottie."

"Mm." Sometimes it feels that way.

We chatted until the sun was about to dip below the horizon, and that's when I noticed bright stars appear like silver specks on an indigo platter.

"Can you see that star, Gran?" I said, pointing to the brightest, most prominent star low in the sky. "After you passed, I was convinced it was you. But now I know it's false because you're here, and the star is still there."

"I can be both, Lottie."

"How do you mean?"

"Spirits are ubiquitous. We are the stars, the planets, and the universe. As spirits, we are all part of the eternal light and can be in numerous places simultaneously."

"Really? That blows my mind."

She grasped my hand.

"It may be difficult to understand for now, but eventually, you will understand."

"I Love your wisdom. I love you, full stop."

"And I Love you too, Lottie."

I laughed, which came out more like a snort.

"What's so amusing?"

"Oh. Nothing. I'm thrilled, although I keep wondering how I can help have my attacker caught. It's like being mute and not knowing how to sign. I can't communicate, so how can I get a message to someone? Anyone."

"Relax. All in good time. You have been granted permission to stay for a reason."

"I can't see how. You said yourself that the path will unfold in its own time." I sighed, then sat on the picnic bench and crossed my legs. "Nobody witnessed the event. There are no clues, and as far as I know, there are no security cameras in the area." My heart sank. "There's not much I can do, Gran."

"Be patient. It will come to you when you least expect it."

"I hope so. I should let go of the past and leave him to live a life of guilt. If I do, he may learn life's lessons. But then again…"

THIRTY

Ever since I was attacked, it wasn't unusual to see police cars in the village. So, when I saw a police car parked outside Norman Taylor's house, no one paid attention to it, not even the Thursday wheelie bin watchers.

Two police constables searched through piles of magazines and papers, taking up most of the floor space. After they'd made room on the sofa to sit, the male officer took notes while the female asked questions. The female constable momentarily pinched her nose to avoid the stench.

"…so, you're saying, Mr Taylor, you were at home all day the day Charlotte Duval was attacked. Is that correct?"

"Yeah. I told yer,' I 'ad a cold." He said, in a voice lacking vocal prosody.

Norman glanced over his shoulder when he heard someone call his name. He dismissed the voice and turned his attention back to the officer.

"Is there anyone willing to confirm your story?"

"Story? Cheek. It's not a Damn story. It's the truth. I was on me own all day and never saw no one."

When he heard his name called a second time, Norman gazed at the police, wondering if they had heard the voice. They seemed completely unaware.

"You have no firm alibi, so we'll have to take your word on that."

Norman shrugged.

"I might not 'ave an alibi, but that don't make me a liar."

"We have to be certain. What were you doing all day?"

"Mmm. Let me think. Watched the box, mostly, and slept in that chair."

"What did you watch on TV?"

"I dunno. Can't remember. The usual Sat'dy rubbish."

"You were seen in Church Lane late Saturday afternoon. What have you got to say about that?"

"'hoever said that is lying. It wasn't me. I told yer. I stayed 'ome all weekend."

"You've made a remarkable recovery." She remarked.

"Must've been a twenty-four-hour bug or summats." Norman stuttered.

"A twenty-four-hour bug lasting two days! You don't seem very certain. We may need to question you further, Mr Taylor. We will require a DNA sample from you. My office will phone to make an appointment."

"I don't 'ave a phone."

"Then go to the nearest police station, or a health practitioner can visit you. Which would you prefer?"

"I'm not going into Swynbourne just fer that. The 'ealth practner..., or whatever you call it, can come 'ere."

"Right. I'll make the arrangements, and you'll be contacted by post." She said, rising from the sofa. "Thank you for your time, Mr Taylor. We'll see ourselves out."

Norman closed the door and, through eyes that knew only hate, watched them leave from behind the thinned curtains. Norman returned to the room, pulled the locket and chain from his jeans pocket, pressed it to his lips, held it in his palm, and grinned a yellow, toothy grin. He blanched when a female voice said his name for the third time.

Cunningham had his suspicions about Norman Taylor. Those suspicions began long ago when a group of young lads, including Norman, played in the village stream. A five-year-old boy allegedly fell into the stream and drowned, and the police diving team later recovered his body. There were no witnesses, and Norman Taylor, being the eldest of the group, was looked upon with suspicion after he went missing for twenty-four hours. When questioned by police, each lad declared their innocence, and their recollections of events were sketchy and guarded. The coroner recorded, 'death by misadventure.' Cunningham recently retrieved the old file from archives, and after studying it, the seeds of suspicion flourished.

THIRTY-ONE

While Sandy was asleep in his basket, I remembered a comedy hypnotist show Mum and Dad treated me to last year. The hypnotist chose four members from the audience, hypnotised them, and they got up to perform hilarious antics on stage. The show was hysterical, and I'll never forget it. What if I could hypnotise Sandy? Not make him do tricks or anything, but plant a suggestion in his mind. That might work.

I knelt by Sandy's basket.

"Sandy," I whispered. "The next time you see Norman Taylor, the scruffy guy from down the lane, I want you to snap and growl at him, but don't harm him. Do that for me, and I'll love you forever." *I do anyway, but what else could I say?*

Sandy watched Mum go to the fridge, hoping for a treat before settling for a nap. Disappointed, he yawned, stretched, circled the kitchen table twice, and then curled up in his basket. She turned off the dripping tap, then stared through the kitchen window, eyes misty with tears. When I put an arm on her shoulder to reassure her, her recoil was barely noticeable. She was already edgy when a magpie hopped onto the windowsill and made her jump. Its ebony eyes latched on me, or had it seen its reflection in the glass? She laughed when it flew off; that was the first time I'd heard her laugh in days. I wonder if she's forgiven the magpie for taking the earring from the garden table last summer.

Although our cottage had been modernised over the years, it maintained much of its former character. Our cottage began life as a row of three cottages and was knocked into one in the early 1970s, long before I was born. Iron meat hooks protrude from the low ceiling where a larder once stood, and dark oak beams starkly contrast against the white ceiling. Most of the upper floors are uneven, and entering my room felt like stepping down into a secret fairy grotto. My bedroom floor slopes towards the window, where marbles and round objects can always be found. When I was seven, Dad lifted me onto his shoulders to show me the Roman numerals carved into the oak beams in the kitchen. I told Isabella that the Romans had built our cottage, and when I mentioned it to Dad, he teased me and said that the cottage was nowhere near that old. I liked it when Dad teased me. It was always in good humour, and my efforts at teasing him always failed. How would he tease me now if he knew I was in spirit? Perhaps he'd poke fun at me because I can pass through walls. Maybe not, but I regret that he will never tease me again.

A warm fuzzy feeling swept over me when Mum touched my photo and mouthed, 'Elephant Juice.' I mouthed it back out of habit, I suppose.

"You would have closure if you knew who attacked me in the cemetery," I said, then noticed a card tucked under the glass fruit bowl on the pine table.

'In Loving Memory of Charlotte Beatrice Duval...' it read in black, high relief lettering... *(did they have to publish my middle name?)* ...and a photo of me wearing my school uniform. I'm pleased I couldn't read the entire card because it seemed so sad, so final, and I'm not looking forward to my funeral at all.

THIRTY-TWO

Mid-December

My Christening was held at The Church of St Mary's in Ashmarsh. That was over sixteen years ago, so it's only natural for my funeral service to be held there. Ordinarily, the car park was full of potholes, but frozen puddles made it appear level for once. The village stream was reduced to a mere trickle, and fog hovered in the valley like a milky lake. The car bearing my coffin led the way, and Mum and Dad walked behind it as it was only a short distance from our cottage to the church. Media lights lit the usually dark church entrance as the Reverend Nigel Goodfellow greeted mourners personally. Gran went on ahead and suffered Mrs Barnes' enthusiastic organ playing. An upsurge of anxiety hit me when Mum and Dad followed my coffin, being wheeled through the wooden door on a chrome trolly. I quickly joined Gran on the front pew.

"I so, don't want to be here," I told her.

"You don't have to stay."

"I'll leave when everyone is here."

That said, it was standing room only as Mum and Dad sat on the front pew, their hands linked together in support. Dad wore a dark suit and tie, black shoes, a white shirt, and the cufflinks I gave him for his last birthday. Mum wore a dark, full-length coat, low-heeled shoes, a modest black hat with a veil, and a black Louis Vuitton handbag. There were no visible tears, but in her heart, it was raining.

"Abigail's here, and so are my classmates, but I can't see Isabella or her mama and papa."

"I haven't seen them either. Perhaps Isabella isn't well enough to attend."

"I hope she's all right. I couldn't have gone through what she has had to suffer." Gran smiled and drew me in closer.

The low winter sun shone through the stained-glass windows and bathed the church in a kaleidoscope of colours, and the century-worn floor shone like summer corn. The Reverend Nigel Goodfellow prepared himself to speak from the pulpit, and although the congregation fell silent, the building was less than quiet. Locked into the ancient masonry and timbers, stories performed a sonnet to the ears of both Christian worshipers and mourners. Uttered vows and promises, goodbyes, and songs of praise to the Lord are forever preserved in the sacred stonework. Dampened thoughts and internal dialogue screamed painful reminders of a daughter taken too soon. The internal chatter will fade, and their pain will be consigned to the cobwebby corners of their minds and replaced with joy and laughter. Their sorrows will diminish, but fond memories of sixteen wonderful years together will never fade.

Gran led me outside to distance myself from my funeral and to prevent me from dwelling on my sorrow. The part of the service we stayed for was uplifting and a joyful celebration of my life. From outside, we could hear my school choir singing.

Many mourners filed along the narrow footpath to the village hall after my burial,

"I don't think I'll ever get used to being ignored, Gran."

"There won't be time. You have very little time left." She said, with a hint of a warning. Her words made me realise I'd better hurry and find a way to help the police find my attacker before I leave. When my burial was over, we joined family and friends in the hall.

"What a beautiful service," Tim said to Mum, and she smiled.

"Thanks, Tim. The vicar did a wonderful job."

"Indeed. The service was appropriate."

"Charlotte never let death upset her when my mother, her gran, was alive, but all that changed when my mother died." She said, ignoring the lump in her throat. She asked Cunningham if he would like a drink.

"No, thanks, Katrina. I shouldn't really be here. I have so much work to do," he said and laughed. "There's no rest for the wicked."

"You're not wicked, Tim."

He laughed. "I know. It's just... I may as well tell you now. We received the results from the saliva sample taken from Charlotte's scarf. Forensics said it was of canine origin."

"That will be Sandy, more than likely." She said, eyes lit with joy. "Sandy chewed her scarf regularly. He was the love of her life, and she spoiled him."

"You can't help it, can you? Spoil them, I mean. I suspected it to be Sandy's saliva. We'll need to swab him for comparison; the offender may have had a dog."

"Mmm. I didn't think of that."

"Forensics will phone to make an appointment." He said, turning towards the exit, then quickly spinning around. "I'm sorry to ask at this untimely moment, but I have a question. Was anything missing from Charlotte's possessions when they were returned? A watch, a bracelet?"

"Not that I recall, Tim. She didn't carry much with her, did she, Philippe?"

"Uh-uh. I can't think of anything. She only took her purse and phone with her, other than on a school day."

"If you remember anything, no matter how insignificant, call me." He said, settling his trilby on his head.

My funeral gave Mum and Dad the closure they needed, and I hoped they wouldn't have a setback when my attacker was finally caught.

THIRTY-THREE

Light snow flurries didn't prevent the lorry driver from delivering a twenty-five-foot spruce. He unloaded it onto the village green. The tree was later decorated with tinsel, hundreds of colourful fairy lights, and giant baubles.

Each Christmas, Philippe decorated the fir tree in the front garden. Charlotte jumped joyfully as he balanced precariously on the step ladder to place the magnificent fairy on top. Every Christmas since her loss was stolen from them like a broken dream, and Christmas wouldn't be Christmas without Katrina's mother.

As Christmas approached, Katrina and Philippe weren't excited about the celebrations. Their joy had been drained. Christmas cards lay unopened on the hall table, and decorations and the glittery fairy that had spent weeks at the top of the fir tree remained in a box in the garage.

A further snowfall made Ashmarsh look like a picture postcard. The roads became impassable, cutting the village off from the main road. The snow finally eased mid-afternoon, and Katrina leapt at the opportunity to take Sandy for a walk.

Laughter filled the lane as the young children built snowmen, reminding Katrina of the time Philippe built a snowman for Charlotte when she was their age.

When she returned to the cottage an hour later, cheeks glowing from the fresh air, she heard voices in the lounge. Philippe was watching 'It's a Wonderful Life' on the TV, starring James Stewart as George Bailey, wishing he'd never been born. Although sad, the film conveyed that we are all connected and have an impact on other's lives. Our lives would be so different without family and friends. There was a parallel between George Bailey and Charlotte, and Katrina wondered if Charlotte would have had a similar experience to George Bailey if she had been able to return. Thankfully, Clarence Goodbody, Angel, second class, restored George Bailey's old life. It was only a film, but unfortunately for Katrina, Charlotte's life could never be restored.

A single candle burned in the window, and the glowing log fire sent flickering shadows dancing across their faces.

"Would you like a Hobnob biscuit with a cup of tea?" Katrina asked Philippe.

"No, thanks. Maybe later. Listen. Can you hear the silence? The snow deadens every sound, and there's little to no traffic. That would be how the village was years ago." Philippe's attempt at small talk was failing.

"How about a glass of Sherry?" He asked. She shook her head. It wasn't fortified wine she needed to warm her insides, but only her daughter's laughter could send waves of joy to warm her heart. A corner had been turned since the funeral, but with long, cold winter nights, their happiness was dwindling. A pair of magpies foraged amongst the snow-covered garden. 'Two for joy' — not today.

People often isolate themselves when they need friends most. It's as though they crave company yet enjoy solitude. It's a battle, a dance between two worlds. The inner voice craves isolation while simultaneously begging for attention—the need for someone to share their grief. Pushing friends away creates inner uncertainties, and people berate themselves for self-absorption, an unintended consequence — trickery of their own making.

The day was still. Birds were silent, and peace hung heavy in the air from unspoken words. They may be sharing the same thoughts, and unspoken words have meaning. They treasured each other's company, yet Katrina wished the phone would ring, or there was a knock on the door from a neighbour. Then, as if by magic, there was a gentle tap tapping on the door. Mrs Harper, a retired headmistress from the village, had ventured through the snow to bring them her warm wishes. She didn't want to come inside and stood chatting in the doorway.

"Have you considered buying a bench in Charlotte's honour?" Mrs Harper suggested. "I'm sure there's a nice spot somewhere in the cemetery if the vicar will allow it, Which I'm sure he will."

"What a good idea, Mrs Harper," Katrina said, attempting to sound enthusiastic. "I'm sure the vicar will agree. I'll discuss it with Philippe first, then speak with the vicar."

"There are many old and tired benches dotted around the cemetery. A new bench will breathe new life into the cemetery." Mrs Harper said, nervously knocking snow from her boots when she realised it was a poor sentence choice.

"There's no need to spend your money on a bench. I'll organise a collection, and you and Mrs Barnes can raise money by selling your lovely cakes if you feel up to it. The bench will be a gift from the village to the village."

"What a lovely idea. I'll mention it to Mrs Barnes when I next see her."

"Charlotte was always fun to be around. She's dearly missed, and I'm sure everyone will be more than generous." She said softly, knowing words couldn't describe how sorry she was for broaching the subject so soon after her daughter's funeral.

"Maybe we could start a crowdfund on Facebook."

"A crowd what?"

"It's…, never mind. Mrs Barnes and I will bake cakes while you organise a collection."

"I'm pleased you're keen on the idea. What a wonderful tribute to Charlotte. Leave it with me. I'll persuade the vicar; he listens to me." She said, with a wink.

"Let me talk it over with Philippe first."

"All right. Phone and let me know. Have a lovely day."

She waved as she left, cut across the snow-covered lawn, and almost collided with the stone statue in the centre.

"I'm alright." She said, waving without looking back. Katrina waited until the sound of her Wellington boots slapping on her calves faded, then went inside to talk to Philippe about the bench.

THIRTY-FOUR

A lone snowplough cleared the roads and created access and egress for the village. Reduced visibility on the motorway made driving treacherous, and as a lorry started to overtake him, the name 'Charlotte' appeared in his door mirror. Charlotte was forever in Cunningham's thoughts, and to see her name hand-painted on the front of a lorry had caught him off guard. He adored his sons, but Charlotte was the daughter he longed for. Spray from all twenty-two wheels of the overtaking lorry activated the Chrysler's automatic wipers. They appeared to be speaking to him as they flip-flopped across the screen. *Nor-man. Nor-man.* Every stroke repeated the same message. *Nor-man. Nor-man.* Were the wipers mocking him, or was it a message from his guides? Norman's name wouldn't go away, and it still haunted him when he reached the station car park.

It was a damp and overcast afternoon, and as he entered the Swynbourne police station, every light burned brightly.

He had only been in his office briefly when Woodcroft breezed in. He waited while Cunningham read an A4-sized sheet of paper.

"What's that you're reading, Gov?"

"Woody! I didn't hear you come in. I've just read the report from the two officers questioning Norman Taylor recently." He said, laying the report down.

"Leave your coat on, Woody. We're going for a ride."

"Righty-o. Where're we going?"

"To bring in that weasel, Taylor. He won't have that smug look when I've finished with him."

Bothered by a peculiar notion, his car wiper blades mocked him again as he drove back to Ashmarsh. One question was on his mind. Was Taylor being dishonest?

Norman Taylor sat in the back of the Chrysler as it whispered along twisting, narrow lanes. They were heading back to Swynbourne, and Cunningham's face contorted with repulsion at the foul odour coming from the back seat.

On arrival, they passed through security and trundled along a corridor until they reached a reeded glass door. Cunningham pointed to a room.

"Wait in there, Taylor. We won't be long." Cunningham said sharply, closing the door and leaving Norman alone to dwell on his thoughts. Norman attempted to read graffiti etched into the walls to pass the time but failed due to poor reading skills. He inspected every corner of the featureless room and stiffened when a shadowy figure loomed in the doorway.

"This way." A burly sergeant ordered, with a voice like rolling thunder. The sergeant led Norman along a narrow corridor to a smaller, gloomier room.

"Wait here. DCI Cunningham will be with you shortly." He boomed.

Interview Room 1, it said on the door. Things were becoming serious. He no longer had a fire in his belly but a gnawing in his gut.

Cunningham and Woodcroft had gone back to their office to discuss Norman Taylor.

"There's not much to go on in the report, Guv." Woodcroft declared, placing his half-empty mug of coffee on the desk. "I think Taylor is too much of a wimp to attack anyone. He's so scrawny I bet he couldn't knock the skin off a rice pudding."

Cunningham nose laughed, then cupped his chin, eyes focused somewhere in the distance. "Think what you like, Woody. Given the right circumstances, I'm certain that even the scrawniest of blokes would be more than capable of summoning up the strength to fight."

"Maybe."

"It's understood that Charlotte died as a direct result of being pushed backwards. Whoever did that also squeezed her throat. Maybe to prevent her from screaming."

"…and because she stopped moving, they ran off thinking she was dead and wouldn't be able to identify them." Woody interrupted. "You believe Norman is your man. Is it because he's weird or something?"

"That does come into the picture. He's been an oddball ever since he was a kid. No one really knows him. He gives people the creeps. Taylor always used to wear an old flat cap, paint-smeared jeans, grimy shirt, and jacket; he has done so for years. Did you notice his new cap and a change of clothes? I want to know why."

"I did notice, but he still stinks. What are you getting at?"

"In hindsight, I should've sent uniform to pick him up. Anyway. Forget that. Imagine you've just attacked someone and left them for dead. What would you do with the clothes you were wearing at the time of the attack?"

"I know what I would do. Get rid of 'em. Is he clever enough to think of that, assuming he attacked Charlotte?"

"He's not stupid. Clever and capable of deceit. Misguided intelligence is what drives him." Cunningham said, leaning back in the chair, fingers interlocked behind his head. "Think about it." He continued. "With such a miserable childhood, wouldn't he have learned to be deceitful and manipulative to avoid punishment when he supposedly did something wrong?"

"Yes. He would probably lie out of a situation to avoid punishment, if that's what you mean, Guv. I probably would if I were him. It's hard to understand why parents abuse their children. They don't deserve that."

Cunningham glanced at the family photo on his desk.

"There are countless reasons why parents abuse their children, and I don't believe they consciously make that decision. They fail to cope with the pressures of living, and by projecting their problems onto their kids and abusing them, they thereby relieve themselves of their frustrations. Anyway. Now's not the time. You hit the nail on the head when you mentioned lying out of a situation to avoid punishment. I'm sure Taylor has done that all his life, and he's doing it now."

Neither moved a muscle at that moment of silence. It was as if they were placing themselves in Norman's shoes to assess the mental scars and deceit forged by early childhood trauma.

"Mm," Cunningham mumbled, then returned to the now. "Let's see what Taylor has to say for himself." He said, picking up the manila folder from the desk and sliding a pack of cigarettes into his pocket. They continued their conversation in the corridor.

"Have you noticed how the innocent usually become angry when accused? They know they're innocent and shouldn't be in the position they're in. On the other hand, the guilty usually remain quiet and repeat their story word for word," Woody commented.

"Exactly. I want to push Taylor within an inch of the law to see how he reacts."

Norman had been waiting for almost an hour and was ready to explode at the first person who entered the room. Cunningham and Woodcroft were the first people to walk into the room, and fortunately for them, Norman curbed his pent-up anger. Cunningham sat opposite Norman, opened the manila folder, and spoke without acknowledging him.

"This interview is being video recorded for your protection?"

"I know what the cameras 'er for," Norman growled. Being so close to two authoritative figures suppressed his anger but not his contempt.

"You're here because we want to discuss the attack in your village resulting in the death of Charlotte Duval. To clarify, you're not under arrest, and you have the right to remain silent." Cunningham stated.

"Why do you wanna talk to me? I 'ad nuffin' to do with it."

"After being spoken to by the police the other day, there are certain facts I want to go over with you to hopefully eliminate you from our inquiries."

"Eliminate me? I've done nuffin' wrong."

"All part of the procedure. We can't rule anyone out who lives in the village until we are satisfied that they had no connection with Charlotte's death. Do you understand?"

"Yeh! Yeh! Alright. 'urry up. You've kept me waiting for over an hour already. I need a smoke."

"I apologise. We had an urgent matter to deal with," Cunningham said. Norman muttered under his breath.

"I'm DCI Tim Cunningham of Swynbourne CID, and this is DC Nathan Woodcroft, also of Swynbourne CID. Please state your name and address."

"You know where I live. You just picked me up from me 'ouse."

"For the record."

"Suit yer-self." He snided, cap shading his soulless eyes. "Norman Taylor. Eleven, Church Lane, Ashmarsh." He said, arms tightly folded across his chest.

"Mr Taylor. You told my officers that you were home on the weekend of November 24th and 25th, stating that you had a cold. Is that correct?"

"Not agen. You dragged me all this bloody way to ask me that. You could have done that at me 'ouse."

"As I said, we need to review the details again. Please answer the question."

Norman hmphed.

"Yeah! I 'ad a cold and stayed in all weekend."

Slightly puzzled, Norman glanced over his shoulder, then turned back and gave the two detectives the same puzzled look. His eyes widened when Cunningham placed an open pack of cigarettes on the desk. With lightning speed, Norman snatched two cigarettes, lit one and stashed the other in his pocket. His face lit up from the glowing cigarette end as Woodcroft slid the ashtray across the desk. Norman blew smoke towards the ceiling and grinned like the cat that got the cream. Neither detective smoked, but Cunningham knew that by offering interviewees a cigarette, they often dropped their guard. He hoped the cigarette would have that effect on Norman.

Norman's confidence grew with each draw on the cigarette. He gazed arrogantly at the ceiling and blew smoke rings, then leaned back and beamed a sickening grin as clouds of grey smoke swirled into the air. The smoke wasn't swirling as much as Norman's mind was while he fabricated his lies.

THIRTY-FIVE

I rested against the wall and listened to Norman spinning his web of lies that poured from his mouth like water from a jug. Cunningham didn't suffer fools gladly and had no time for Norman or his games. I'm sure if it wasn't for lawful constraint and the fact that cameras were recording the scene, he would have gladly wiped the smirk from Norman's face.

When the interview began, I saw how smoking a cigarette had bolstered Norman's confidence. Tired of Norman's egotism, Cunningham put the pack of cigarettes in his pocket.

"Look, Taylor. This is a murder inquiry. How about showing some respect?" Woodcroft barked. "If you stayed home all day, how do you explain the mud on your shoes matching mud samples from the cemetery?" Norman leaned back in the chair, inhaled the smoke, and examined the burning tip.

"That's easy. Me Mam and Dad are buried there, an' I sometimes go and 'ave a look. That's 'ow I got a cold, I reckon." He said, exhaling smoke from his nostrils like a raging bull. He hated his parents and wished they'd been cremated to be rid of them forever.

"When was the last time you visited their graves?"

"I reckon it was the Friday before I got sick." Woodcroft and Cunningham exchanged glances with a 'this interview is going nowhere' look on their faces. Both the cigarette and the negative attention were giving Norman a cock-sure confidence not known to him in years. Woodcroft pressed on.

"You don't sound too sure. That aside, why have you bought a new cap?"

Norman's dark, suspicious eyes scanned the blue carpet tiles, buying him time to think.

"Them bloody kids sneaked up be'ind me and ran off with me' old 'un, an' I couldn't be bothered to chase 'em. They're always calling me names and making fun o' me. One of 'em chucked me 'at in the stream."

Woodcroft hmmd.

"We can arrange for a team to search the area." He threatened, noticing the beads of dirt-laden sweat forming on Norman's brow. His self-assurance dwindled as fear and tension grew, and he adopted a victim role. A twitch in his eye was a tell. He was on his back foot with nowhere to go.

"It'll be in the sea b' now, I expect."

"Didn't burn it by any chance?" Woodcroft accused. Norman stiffened. It was a wild shot, but he may have hit the mark. I had remained silent from the moment I arrived but couldn't keep quiet any longer.

"Yes. Yes, he did." I yelled, unable to contain myself.

Norman whipped his head around, then returned his gaze to the two detectives, with suspicion inscribed on his forehead.

"Am I being accused o' murder? You said you wanted to eliminate me from your inquiries. You keep saying, murder, but the news said she was alive when she went to the 'ospital. So 'ow is that murder?"

"You can't rely on the news to give the full story. For your information, Charlotte was deeply unconscious and passed away the following day. That's why it's a murder enquiry." Woodcroft clarified.

Norman arched his eyebrows. Now, it was Cunningham's turn.

"I repeat. What were your movements on the day Charlotte Duval was attacked? The truth."

"I'm telling the truth. I never left the 'ouse all weekend."

"Can anyone vouch for you?"

"What do you mean, vouch?"

 "A witness that was with you that day."

Norman scowled.

"I already told yer no one was with me. Anyway, they've stopped calling round, now me Mam and Dad's gone."

"Who's stopped calling?"

"Them witnesses."

"Witnesses?" Cunningham repeated.

"Yeah. Them whatchamacallits. Jehovah's Witnesses that stand at the door and preach about Jesus and stuff." Cunningham looked at Woodcroft and nose laughed. I had to stifle a chuckle, too.

"Not that kind of witness."

"Well, I dunno what yer on about."

"It's very straightforward. Was anyone with you who's willing to swear an oath that you were at home on Saturday, November 25th, between three and four pm?"

Norman shrugged. Then, it was Woodcroft's turn to question the scheming weasel.

"The sooner you start telling the truth, the sooner we can finish this."

My frustration grew as Norman dodged and weaved his way around crucial questions. Perhaps I could write a message on the folder on the desk, but I can't hold a pen, so that won't happen. I tried scratching the folder with my fingernail, but I didn't leave an impression, so now I've run out of ideas. I tried talking to the detectives, but neither could hear me. So, what now?

Tired of Norman's flippancy, Cunningham peered deep into his dark and soulless eyes. Another hour had passed, and the interview had achieved very little.

Cunningham wouldn't let go of his hunch, but Norman's story was so well rehearsed it had become his truth. I knew the truth and hoped that using their detective skills would allow them to penetrate Norman's dark and secret mind. Cunningham slammed his hand down hard.

"Do I need to remind you that this is a murder inquiry? I want answers. Did you attack Charlotte Duval on November 25th last month?" He yelled. Norman flicked the ash from his cigarette, then stared at the ashtray.

"Should I 'ave a solicitor or summats? I never attacked 'er. I didn't like 'er and never went near 'er."

"If you didn't like her, wouldn't that be a motive for murder?" Cunningham stared him in the eye, looking for a tell, a clue, anything to probe the inner workings of Norman's sordid mind. Norman sniffed.

"I don't like anybody, but that doesn't make me a murderer. You've got the wrong guy. Leave me alone. Go and catch some real criminals?" He said, crushing the cigarette into the ashtray. "'aven't you got anything better to do?"

"Liar," I shouted. Norman glanced behind him again. Could it be possible for him to hear my voice? Woodcroft kept the pressure on.

"Look at me, Norman. If you admit you attacked Charlotte Duval, you can make things easy for yourself. Do that, and you'll receive a lighter sentence. What have you got to lose? Sign a confession; then, you can relax, knowing you've done the right thing. It will be much worse for you if you continue to lie. Mark my words. The truth will come out." He paused, then changed his approach. "What about her parents?" He said, playing good cop. "How must they feel knowing that their daughter's attacker is at large? Do the right thing and confess. At least give them peace of mind." Woodcroft sat back and waited for a reply. Norman picked at the paint on his fingers, rubbed his stubbly chin, and then stared at the paint fragments on the desk. Cunningham jumped in with a bad cop routine.

"What kind of weapon did you use?"

"I never used a weapon."

"So, how did you fracture her skull?"

"I didn't fracture 'er skull. She must ov fell and 'it her 'ead, or summat."

"You mean you pushed her backwards, and she hit her head?" Cunningham accused.

"No, look. I d'know. I — I. Oh God! Stop! Stop! I can't think straight. You're trying to trick me into admitting summats I didn't do."

"Go on. Tell them how I hit my head, Norman. Go on. Tell the truth." I shouted. Norman scanned the room, fire burning in his eyes. He turned around, then closed his eyes and hummed quietly to himself, his way of escaping reality. He opened his eyes a short while later.

"I — Look." He sighed, and then his demeanour changed like a switch had been thrown.

"'ow the 'eck should I know 'ow she fractured 'er blinking skull. I wasn't there. You're supposed to be the smart guys. Why don't *you* tell *me* 'ow it 'appened?"

"We don't have all the answers. But we intend to find out, and your vagueness isn't helping."

"I can't 'elp yer. You've got the wrong guy."

"Stop it, Norman. Admit it. It was you who caused my death."

"Shuddup, 'hoever you are." He said in a lowered voice.

"What was that?" Woodcroft asked.

"I can 'ear someone talking. It's driving me mad. Can't you 'ear it?"

Woodcroft ignored Norman and kept up the pressure.

"Charlotte told her parents that before the weekend of the attack, you were watching her from the cemetery gates, and you hid when she saw you. Is that correct?"

"I dunno. Can't remember."

"Was that you or not?" He yelled.

"Keep your bloody 'air on. Yeah. All right. It was me."

"Why were you watching Charlotte in the cemetery?"

Norman sighed. "If yer must know, I'd bin to me Mam and Dad's grave and saw 'er in the distance." He said, dropping his gaze. "I didn't want 'er to see me, so I 'id until she'd gone."

"Did you often spy on Charlotte?"

"No. Never."

"Liar. You watched me all the time. You watched me from behind the curtains when I walked past your house."

"I told you to shuddup." He said in a loud whisper.

"I'd prefer you to concentrate on the questions instead of listening to some non-existent voice?" Cunningham requested.

"It's not my fault someone keeps talking to me."

"Do you often hear voices in your head?"

"Nope. Besides, the voice isn't in me 'ead. It's be'ind me."

Cunningham looked at Woodcroft, and you could almost hear his eyes rolling. They had tried to push Norman, and although his alibi was weak, he remained firm.

"All right, Mr Taylor, that's all for now." Cunningham sighed. "You're free to go, but don't leave the village. I'm not done with you yet. Take my advice —" Cunningham said, opening the door, "— go home, take a shower — and for goodness' sake, clean your damn teeth. Now follow me." He ordered. Norman leapt from his seat, murmuring 'tosser' under his breath. Cunningham walked Norman to the front steps.

"Wait here, and one of my officers will drive you home. Can't have you catching another cold walking home, can we?" He added sarcastically. "You'll receive a video copy of the interview in due course."

Norman supported himself against the wall and lit the cigarette he'd stolen from Cunningham. He stared at the pavement while he waited. He may have won this round, but I now know he can hear my voice. Maybe this is what I've been waiting for.

THIRTY-SIX

With a hint of makeup and hair tucked behind one ear, Katrina casually flipped through the pages of a glossy magazine while rocking gently in her mother's old rocking chair. Sandy moaned from his basket like a sleepy octogenarian, then barked when he heard a car outside and the humming of the garage door. Katrina leapt from the chair, smoothed her skirt, checked her hair in the hall mirror, and then waited by the kitchen doorway. Resplendent in a knee-length grey skirt, a pale lilac Stella McCartney top, and shoes by Sanders, she could have been a model from the pages of the Vogue magazine she'd been reading. A combination of cooking and perfume met Philippe in the hallway. He stopped and stared at the enticing beauty in the doorway, briefcase in hand.

"Who are you, and what have you done with my wife?"

"Cheeky."

"Tu es belle, ma cheri." (You are beautiful, my darling.)

"Merci beaucoup." (Thank you very much.)

He set his briefcase down. "Come here." He said, then drew her closer and slipped his arms around her waist.

"Don't tell me. I've forgotten our wedding anniversary."

"No. You haven't forgotten our Wedding anniversary. It's in May, and well, you know it. I wanted tonight to be a surprise."

"It is." He said and sniffed the air. "Something smells good."

"Dinner will be ready shortly. Would you like a glass of red wine before dinner? I've already opened it."

"Later. C'mere. Let me look at you, you ravishing beauty."

He stepped back to admire her, then pulled her closer. Together, they swayed rhythmically to a familiar, silent melody.

🐘

When Katrina opened her eyes and blinked, it was dark. She gazed at the shadows dancing on the wall like puppet silhouettes caused by moonlight filtering through the curtains. Her eyes shone like diamonds as she tucked the duvet under her chin and turned to Philippe to see if he was awake. He was also lying on his back, staring at the ceiling.

"Can't you sleep?" She said, searching for his hand under the duvet.

"Huh? Sorry. I didn't know you were awake. I was thinking about last night. I love you so much. You looked so beautiful."

"I love you too." She said, averting her eyes. "I hadn't been looking my best lately, you know, since we lost Charlotte. She wouldn't want us to be sad, so I tried to cheer us both up." He brushed her hair from her face, then gazed deep into her eyes. She turned onto her side to face him.

"Losing Charlotte has left an enormous hole in our lives. We'll never get over losing her, but we'll eventually accept her loss. We must; otherwise, what is the point of living? The heartache will fade, but she'll always be in our thoughts. Our time with Charlotte was precious, and we must celebrate the good times rather than live in sorrow for the rest of our lives. Last night's dinner was my way of showing you how much I love you more than ever now. There's only you and me now." Her shoulders shuddered as a gentle tear fell. He reached across and held her in his arms.

"Shhh. It's okay. It's okay. Everything was perfect last night, and I know Charlotte would have agreed." Philippe said. Katrina kissed his cheek. His brow furrowed.

"It breaks my heart to look, and she's not there. Life seems unbearable without her. She was special, but let's not forget about us. I'm sure that's what Charlotte would have wanted."

"I'm fortunate enough to have you for my husband…" The shrill tone of the alarm clock interrupted her. She tutted. "What a shame you have to go to work."

"Speaking of work. Ron and Joyce send their love, and if there's anything they can do, just ask. He gave twenty pounds towards the memorial bench. Help yourself. It's in my wallet."

"That was generous of him." She said, and her eyes flicked to his jacket, which was laid on the chair. "Ron and Joyce adored Charlotte. I'm sure they miss her as much as we do."

"I doubt that." He said, throwing back the duvet and swinging his legs to the floor.

Katrina removed Philippe's wallet from his jacket while he was in the shower, and a small, creased photo fluttered to the carpet. The photo was of her with Charlotte on her knee. She was only a few weeks old, and what caught her attention was the gold locket around her neck. She removed the crisp twenty-pound note, slid the photo back inside the wallet and returned it to his jacket.

The heavy scent of pine shower gel drifted from the ensuite as Philippe stepped out of the shower, a towel wrapped around his waist.

"It's lovely that you keep that photo in your wallet."

"I've always kept it there."

"It's like it was only yesterday." She said, sitting on the edge of the bed. "Where has the time gone? I remember that day vividly. Charlotte cried all morning and wouldn't stop until I let her play with the locket I'm wearing in the photo."

"The one your mother gave you on your thirteenth birthday."

"Yes. It belonged to my grandmother. Do you remember the morning I climbed out of bed, and something triggered my memory, but I couldn't remember what it was?"

"Mmm. Vaguely."

"That was it. I gave the locket to Charlotte when she turned thirteen, and I'm sure she wouldn't have left the cottage without wearing it that morning. My point is. It wasn't with her belongings at the hospital. It could be in her room, but I haven't found the courage to go there since I went in there with Tim. I feel sad thinking about it."

"I can go into her bedroom and look for you unless you'd rather look for it when you feel stronger."

"It's all right. I will have to go into her room, eventually. Maybe later today. I don't know. If it's not there, then I'll phone Tim. It may be of importance."

Katrina plucked up the courage to enter Charlotte's room that afternoon after she'd had a heart-to-heart talk with Anne from next door. She stepped inside for the first time in days and stood in silence in the middle of the room. The bed was unmade, clothes were stacked neatly in a chair, and make-up was scattered on the top of the IKEA unit. Everything in her room was exactly how she'd left it that fateful morning. Time was frozen in Charlotte's boudoir, and each item of her belongings was Katrina's personal heartache. She gathered a T-shirt from the pile, raised it to her nose, inhaled its fragrance and was immediately reminded of when Charlotte was a baby, and the smell of talcum powder lingered on her tiny blanket. She held the T-shirt to her bosom and cradled it like a mother cradles her baby, then heard Charlotte's laughter echoing from the walls. Tears filled her eyes as memories of tucking her into bed came to the fore. She glanced at a snapshot of Charlotte on the dresser and mouthed 'elephant juice.' The private moment was interrupted when heavy paws thundered up the stairs and burst through the door. Sandy leapt onto Charlotte's bed and panted. Katrina stroked his ear and raised a smile through salty tears. Sandy loved Katrina fussing over him, but he couldn't hide his sadness about Charlotte not being in her room.

THIRTY-SEVEN

Philippe took a short break. While he gazed out the office window, observing the street below, a narrow shaft of sunlight between Swynbourne Cathedral towers caught his attention. The sunlight shone onto the pavement below like a golden carpet, momentarily sweeping him away from reality. His mobile phone interrupted his spiritual experience.

"Hello, Philippe. It's only me."

"Hello, Katrina. Did you go into Charlotte's room and look for her locket?"

"That's why I'm calling."

"You did! Well done?"

"I searched Charlotte's room after having a heart-to-heart talk with Anne from next door. It was quiet when I stepped into her room, and I felt guilty because of how intrusive it felt to search through her possessions without permission. I took my time but didn't find the locket. Even Sandy was confused."

"It must have been difficult for you to take that step."

"It was a huge leap forward for me. Real progress."

"Yes. A huge achievement, but you didn't find the locket."

"Unfortunately, not. I thought I would let you know. I'll ask St Anthony, the patron saint of finding lost and stolen articles. He'll help us find the locket."

"Forensics couldn't find it, so you may as well try."

"I will, as soon as I've let Sandy out into the garden. He looks desperate, so I'll have to go. Talk to you later. Bye." And she was gone. Philippe called Cunningham.

"Hi, Tim. How's your day going?"

"Could be better. What can I do for you?"

"The other day, when we spoke, you asked if any of Charlotte's possessions were missing?"

"That's right. Have you remembered something?"

"Yes, well, Katrina did. She remembered Charlotte's locket, which we hadn't seen since before she died. It's not in the cottage and wasn't returned with her personal belongings. She would never go anywhere without it, so we thought you should know it's missing."

"What kind of locket?"

"It's a Gold, oval-shaped, Victorian locket with an intricate pattern and the initials KT engraved inside. It has a delicate gold chain with close-set links. Katrina's grandmother's initials were KT."

"Thanks for that, Philippe. That may help with our inquiries."

"Glad to be of assistance."

Cunningham ended the call abruptly. Although a close friend of the family, he was a different person at work. Phone calls were often short, sharp, and to the point. He wasn't being rude; it was his way.

Would the investigation gain momentum if he saw the correlation between the missing locket and Charlotte's attacker?

THIRTY-EIGHT

With his blessings, the vicar permitted a memorial bench to be installed in the cemetery in Charlotte's honour. Enough money was raised, and Mrs Harper phoned Katrina with the news that the bench would be installed a week on Monday, and the unveiling would take place the following Saturday, at ten, weather permitting.

"Thank you, Mrs Harper. I'm looking forward to seeing the new bench. The brass plaque is on my kitchen table." She hung up and gazed dreamily out the kitchen window. No parent should bury their child. *How is it possible that there is a bench in memory of our sixteen-year-old daughter? She had her whole life in front of her.*

Katrina's life changed the moment Charlotte was born. At the time, she had no notion that it would be a brief encounter, a speck of dust floating by on the breeze of history, her butterfly child.

The oak bench was secured to a previously laid concrete base and then covered with a green tarpaulin to screen it from prying eyes.

On the morning of the unveiling, the weather was bitterly cold. Philippe and Katrina crunched along the gravel pathway to the chosen area. In all its splendour, the pristine bench was concealed beneath a crimson silk sheet borrowed from the vestry. The vicar waited for silence before addressing the assembled villagers.

"May I welcome you to the dedication of this wonderful gift to our community in honour of Charlotte Duval. May I also share a special welcome to Philippe and Katrina Duval, with whom I'm sure most of you are acquainted. Charlotte was the kindest, loving person one could ever meet. Loved by all, she left a lasting mark on the village. We don't often pay tribute to the young, but sadly, Charlotte was taken into the Lord's care far too soon."

Katrina was fully immersed in the vicar's kind words as he blessed the bench. Meanwhile, a dubious man was watching the unveiling. Unsure of himself, he remained out of sight behind a tall headstone.

"…and so, without further ado, I am honoured to unveil the Charlotte Duval memorial bench, donated by the residents of Ashmarsh."

The gathering gasped when the silk sheet slipped to the ground like a crimson waterfall. Katrina had repeatedly read the inscription on the brass plate as soon as it arrived. Even though she knew each word by heart, she reread it now that it was fixed firmly to the bench. Suddenly, it was real.

In Loving Memory

of

Charlotte Beatrice Duval

Donated by the citizens of Ashmarsh

God has you in His keeping;

We have you in our hearts

Dressed head to foot in denim, cap pulled over his eyes, a man in his mid-forties stepped timidly from behind a headstone. He balanced precariously on the top of an uneven grassy mound to get a better view of the unveiling. And with hands deep inside his pockets, he lost his balance. His hands shot from his pockets, and he waved his arms to regain his balance. He was oblivious that a shiny object had shot from his pocket and landed on the grass behind him. A sharp-eyed magpie swooped down from a tall tree, snatched the shiny object from the ground and flew to its nest.

The group slowly dispersed, and Katrina and Philippe were alone with the vicar. They thanked him for his kindness, and then he tucked the crimson sheet under his arm and walked to the vestry. Katrina ran her fingers along the bench, stopping at the brass plaque fastened to the backrest. Her finger followed the curves of the engraved letters, orderly and perfect — how her father would have liked them. *'If a job's worth doing, it's worth doing well,'* he always said.

Her reason for living was challenged, and life was far from orderly and perfect since the loss of her child. Those who rest upon the bench will become immersed in peace, tranquillity, and a spectacular view of the church. Only peaceful hearts and minds will hear the memories whispered imperceptibly from passed loved ones, and over time, spiritual essence will permeate every fibre of the oak bench and imbue it with memories indelibly etched into the grain like Akashic Records.

Warmed by central heating, the cottage was Katrina's sanctuary. She was feeling optimistic when it was time to take Sandy for his afternoon walk. Was her optimism about to be tested?

THIRTY-NINE

Sandy growled low in his throat as he approached Norman Taylor's house. The hair on the back of his neck stood. He barked fiercely, yanked on his lead, and almost dragged Katrina off her feet. His bark intensified with each step. In front of Norman's house, Sandy bared his teeth and growled fearlessly at the sallow face in the window.

"Sandy, stop!" She ordered. "What's wrong with you? Behave." Sandy wouldn't stop barking and growling, so Katrina wrapped the lead around her wrist and hauled him away. Reluctant to leave, Sandy's claws scratched along the pavement, but he eventually lost interest in Norman's house. They crossed the road as a rabbit hopped into view, sending Sandy into a frenzy, the opposite of his behaviour outside Norman Taylor's house.

The village green was a myriad of trails and scents for Sandy, where he could roam safely and freely. Katrina unleashed Sandy and watched him chase the rabbit while she sat on the base of the Celtic cross. He sniffed his way along the perimeter, zigzagged across the green, paused to sniff a shrub, picked up another rabbit scent and disappeared into a rhododendron bush. Katrina laughed at Sandy's antics as the sky slowly turned purple. The sun dipped below the horizon, and the sky turned thundery black. She called Sandy, and he ran to her, carrying a stick in his mouth. He dropped the stick at her feet and panted, but there was no time to play. It looked like there may be a storm, and she wanted to get home and tell Philippe about Sandy's reaction outside Norman's house.

FORTY

When I stepped into the village hall, the combination of lavender polish and fresh flowers greeted me. It reminded me of my youth club days, not that long ago when music pulsated from subwoofers like Jumanji drums. At the Youth Club, we gathered in a corner and giggled. We talked about the latest hot guy in school and admired selfies while the old wooden floorboards bounced to the rhythm of those who preferred to dance.

The hall was quiet tonight, but polite smiles gave way to conversation, and voices grew louder when more people joined in. Laughter erupted as people familiarised themselves with the person sitting next to them. Considering the damp and drizzly night, it was a decent turnout. Cunningham stepped onto the stage and sat beneath a lone spotlight. He checked his watch and raised his voice above the chatter at the stroke of seven.

"Thank you. Thank you. Can I have your attention, please?" He shouted, waiting for the chatter to die down. "It's not the best night to be out, so I would like to thank you all for being here tonight." He waited for the mumble of chatter to die down again.

"My name is Detective Chief Inspector Tim Cunningham of Swynbourne CID…"

He'd barely finished introducing himself when the lights went out, and the emergency lighting immediately came on.

"Please stay in your seats. I'm sure the lights will come on again shortly."

Two minutes later, the main lights came on again, causing a cheer in the hall. Old Jake apologised from the back of the hall and said it was a nuisance breaker trip.

"And hopefully, the annual village fête raised enough money for the hall to be rewired." Cunningham quipped. "I'm sure that won't happen again." He said, giving Old Jake a long, cold stare. "I'm sure you're all aware of the recent tragedy in the village. That's why we're here. My purpose tonight is to reassure you and your families that Ashmarsh is a safe village and not to provide you with information about our ongoing inquiries. The meeting will benefit everyone. That said, I will answer questions about village safety." Cunningham said, then softened his tone. "There's no reason for anyone to live in fear. The recent attack in the cemetery was the first incident of its kind in over thirty years. Be vigilant, but don't let fear prevent you from living your life. Times have changed, but let me reassure you that Ashmarsh has one of the lowest crime rates in the county."

Do you know what I find frustrating? Cunningham hasn't told us anything we didn't already know. I'm guessing that the meeting is a PR exercise. Over half of the village is here, and I thought it would be the ideal place for him to ask for the public's help in solving the case. Well, if he's not going to, then I will. What an excellent opportunity to see if anyone in the audience can hear me. With great apprehension, I climbed onto the stage next to Cunningham and waited for a suitable gap in the conversation.

"Can anyone see or hear me? Anyone?" I said, projecting my voice as far as it would go. There was no noticeable response, so I yelled again and scanned the sea of faces for clues.

"Please. Can anyone hear me? I'm Charlotte Duval, and it was Norman Taylor who attacked me," I yelled, then desperately waited for a response. Not one person flinched or even looked at me. Even Cunningham talked over me, and I was left feeling awkward. I was about to step down from the stage when a loud noise erupted from the back of the hall. The entire audience spun around to see the commotion. I watched the outline of a crouched figure dash towards the exit, lit by the oblong exit sign. Cunningham joked about someone wanting to leave quickly, but I knew the truth about who had run out the door. With my superior knowledge, I sat on the stage, dangling my legs. At the same time, Cunningham talked about how reliant the police were on CCTV footage and the fact that there were very few public surveillance cameras in the village apart from the ones at the train station. He said the station cameras had revealed nothing of importance.

"If anyone saw anything that night — anything — no matter how insignificant you may think it may be, call me, or call the police hotline. You can remain anonymous. My cards are near the door if anyone wants to contact me personally."

Hmm! I underestimated Cunningham. I could listen to him all night. He was an excellent speaker and kept everyone's attention for almost two hours. He'd kept the meeting light, informative, and on track.

"We're rapidly running out of time. To recap. I cannot emphasise enough that you and your children can walk safely around the village without fear. I believe the attack was opportunistic and not the work of a serial predator."

It was five past nine when Cunningham checked his watch. He drew the meeting to a close, and as the crowd were about to leave, the lights went out again.

Why was Norman Taylor in a hurry to leave? If Cunningham saw who it was, I bet his odd behaviour only added to Cunningham's suspicions. Did Norman Taylor leave because he heard what I said about him? I wanted to test this theory again, so I left the hall and walked to Norman's house in the rain. When I stepped indoors, Norman was smoking a cigarette at the table. *No change there.*

"Hello, Norman."

Norman swung around and knocked the glass ashtray off the table. It landed on his foot, and he yelled in pain. He cursed the ashtray, but the pain of the heavy ashtray landing on his foot was the least of his worries. I had verified that he could hear me, and maybe that's why he hurriedly left the hall. He may have thought that if he could hear me, everyone could. He clenched his teeth and tossed the ashtray onto the table. If only Cunningham could hear me.

FORTY-ONE

Cunningham oversaw the PowerPoint presentation. The large screen showed graphic scenes from Ashmarsh Cemetery while his team stood in front of the whiteboard. Charlotte Duval's name was highlighted at the top of the board and written in blue. He wrote two names underneath: Alan Rodrigues and Norman Taylor, and he underlined Norman Taylor in red.

"For those seconded to my team, my name is DCI Tim Cunningham, your SIO." (Senior Intelligence Officer). "As you may know, a lack of evidence is slowing our investigation. I'm proud of everyone for doing a great job under the circumstances, and I thank you for that. I've spoken with this Norman Taylor character, but I haven't finished with him yet. I want to dig further into his background to generate a criminal profile. We also want to speak to Mr Rodrigues." … he said, tapping the board with the marker.

"The scene was remarkably clean. Initially, no hair samples, DNA, or textile material were found."

"Initially, sir?" A female detective queried.

"Initially, yes. That was my next point. We have an update. Forensics found the tiniest fragment of, yet-to-be-identified fibres from the victim's clothing. The assailant may have worn a woollen jumper or gloves, but we don't know at this stage. We need some good old-fashioned detective work in conjunction with modern technology. That said, instead of sitting at your desk all day, I want you out on the streets asking questions and making nuisances of yourselves. Not you, Rob. I need you in the office. And Woody, you'll be teamed with me."

A low humdrum of chatter erupted. "Quiet. Quiet." Cunningham ordered. "Getting back to Norman Taylor…"

"…you mean creepy Norman?" Someone remarked.

"Yes. If that's what you want to call him. Soil samples detected on Taylor's trainers matched soil samples from the scene. His parents are buried at the cemetery, so it's feasible he may have visited their graves at some stage, and that is how his trainers were contaminated. Well, that's what Taylor is saying. Alan Rodrigues hasn't been seen since the day of the attack, and I want to know where he is. Until we determine his movements that day, he's in the frame. Jayne? You were dealing with that. Any progress?"

"I received an email a few minutes ago from immigration saying he flew to Hong Kong late that afternoon, and I'm working with Interpol to get more info."

"Excellent. If we can eliminate him from our inquiries, then we can concentrate on this slippery character," he said, stabbing Taylor's name on the board.

Cunningham usually held his cards close to his chest. He was a team player, not necessarily keeping information to himself, but his mind was often too busy, and there wasn't time for him to share his knowledge. He acted on impulse before sharing information with the team. The purpose of the meeting was to exchange information and share any valuable snippets gleaned from his own investigations.

Cunningham changed the PowerPoint slide, and the team studied the disturbing image.

"To bring latecomers up to speed, Charlotte suffered blunt trauma to the back of the head. Initially, she was thought to have been struck with a blunt weapon. We now know that Charlotte fell backwards and hit her head on a grave surround, and as a result, she suffered severe, irreversible brain damage. Samples of blood and tissue lifted from the grave surround confirmed this. For her to have struck her head so hard, we believe she was pushed violently."

A comment came from the back. "One more reason to catch the perpetrator."

"If we need any more reasons," Cunningham quickly replied.

"Taylor's flimsy alibi doesn't sit well with me, and he fits the profile." A female remarked. Cunningham sighed.

"I also have my suspicions about Taylor." He studied the sea of faces. "He has no previous convictions, but he can't be arrested on a gut feeling no more than he can for being a bit of a weirdo. I can smell it, but evidence based on olfactory prowess is inadmissible in a courtroom" The team chuckled. "We need hard-based evidence and facts to take to Crown Prosecution Services" (CPS), he said, staring hard at the name Norman on the whiteboard. "I understand how you all must feel. I, too, have a hunch, but our hands are tied. First, I'd like to rule out Alan Rodrigues; then, we can concentrate our resources on Taylor."

"Did Charlotte have any enemies, either male or female?"

"Our focus is on males, primarily, but females haven't been ruled out. Charlotte was well-liked and, as far as we know, hadn't ruffled anyone's feathers. One other thing I want to mention. In the notes, the coroner stated bruising to Charlotte's throat indicated her assailant was left-handed."

"Thanks, Guv."

"Now. Are there any further questions?"

"I have a question," Woodcroft stated. "Has any more thought been given to the tragic drowning of a young boy in Ashmarsh stream over a decade ago?"

"You already know, Woody, that I retrieved the archive file yesterday and skimmed through it. The coroner recorded the child's death as misadventure, so I want you to go over the file in detail, Woody." Cunningham cast his eyes to the floor as clear pictures of the incident flashed through his mind. Everyone in the room remained silent as Cunningham put down the marker pen and lifted his gaze.

"That concludes this morning's meeting unless you have any more questions." He paused to look around the room. "No? Okay." He said, straightening his back and clapping his hands. "I want results. We're investigating the death of a young girl, so let's give it all we've got."

Cunningham went back to his office, and Woody joined him shortly afterwards.

"That was a good meeting, Guv. Nice bit of team building."

"Thanks, Woody."

"We should question Taylor again. His alibi is too vague."

"And we will, Woody. My gut feeling says he's our man. I've spent many an hour in the company of the guilty, proclaiming their innocence. Taylor is mentally scarred and has needs. It's all in the eyes, and I know the look. They say the eyes are the windows to the soul, and I can see right into Taylor's."

"But CPS wouldn't agree to a trial on that alone? What other evidence do we have?"

"We haven't much to go on at this stage. But we wait. Slowly, slowly, catchy monkey.

FORTY-TWO

I so miss things that I used to take for granted. Most of all, I miss being unable to converse with Mum and Dad. After a demanding day, I miss a tingling hot shower or a relaxing hot bubble bath: Mum's delicious dinners, especially her Spag Bol. Then there's the milky smoothness of chocolate, the creamy taste of ice cream, the sensation of a boy's hand in mine, and a shared kiss. Next, after my parents and friends, comes Sandy, then Abigail, and Isabella. Although I haven't been in spirit long, I cannot interact with them, and I've already become a distant memory. Am I being paranoid? *Damn you, Norman Taylor.*

I have much to learn about love, compassion, and forgiveness, but I'm determined to bring Norman Taylor to justice before I can show him my compassion. Gran said to send him love and light and let go, and I will — but in my own time. Mum always said I was stubborn, and I suppose I still am, but I can laugh about it now.

Ness took the opportunity to clean the ground floor While Mum pottered in the back garden. I glided into the garden and caught her pruning shrubs, wearing her green wellies, denim jeans, Berber jacket, gardening gloves, and a woolly hat. Sandy was panting while stretched out on the lawn after playing with his favourite soft toy. His ears twitched as I approached, and he barked softly. I'm sure he's aware of my presence. Perhaps he no longer wanders from room to room, looking for me.

"I miss our walks across the rabbit-plagued meadow," I said to him, then knelt alongside. "It's not the same walking with you and Mum. If I could tell you who contributed to my death, you might be able to tell someone or at least give them a hint, and then I will be ready to go to the light." I bit my cheek. "Norman is only human, and even monkeys fall from trees," I said, but I knew Sandy wouldn't know anything about monkeys. He scrambled to his feet and tilted his head to one side.

"You know I'm here, don't you, Sandy?"

I overheard Mum talking on the phone about Isabella and how she would return to school at the beginning of the new term. While she was on the phone, I walked to Isabella's house.

Isabella's mama was talking on the phone, and Isabella was on the sofa, watching TV with her knees tucked under her chin, and for the first time, in like, for-ev-errr, her cheeks glowed. The large Tupperware box on the table next to her was brimming with blister packs and plastic bottles. The numerous daily medications she had to take were a small price to pay for a new life — for a life. I'm so grateful she has received a new heart, and not before time. We take our breathing for granted, but for most of her life, Isabella had fought for every breath. I can't imagine anything worse, apart from being in spirit. Death takes some getting used to, but being in spirit has advantages.

"I'm over the moon now you can live life to the full, Isabella. My only regret is that I can't share in the celebrations."

Something on TV amused her, and she laughed. This was the first time I'd heard her laughter in, like, ages.

"Don't forget to walk Sandy when you can. I'll be alongside you, I promise. He misses you. Me too."

It was good to see Isabella looking a picture of health. I sent her love and light, although she doesn't need it. I can't believe how well she looks, and it's great to see her leading a near-normal life. Maybe I can stay a while longer if Gran agrees.

FORTY-THREE

The grey outline of a farm tractor slipped behind a veil of murky mist at the far end of Bottom Field. The tractor would have gone unnoticed without the aroma of freshly tilled soil and faint seagull cries. Unaware of the tractor as she laboured in the garden, Katrina was grateful for the cottage in the country. They lived far enough away from the city to escape the hustle and bustle yet within easy access to major chain stores. Besides the elderly and retired, villagers were often too busy to stop and talk. The garden was her spiritual space, her sanctuary. It was a place to relax, to be herself, and to sort out life's worries, free from interruptions. Ness had left by the time Katrina put the garden tools away. She showered and changed, then collected Sandy's lead from the hook on the back of the kitchen door.

Sandy walked obediently by her side, and while they were out, she left a bunch of freshly cut flowers at the church, then crossed the road to the meadow to let Sandy off his lead. After chasing anything that moved and exhausting himself, Sandy trotted back to Katrina, and she decided to take the long route home. Midway along Cooper's Passage, Sandy's hair bristled as a scruffy man in his thirties walked towards them. Sandy bared his teeth and growled. He snarled at the man like a rabid dog and behaved as he had outside Norman Taylor's house recently. Katrina held him back by tugging on his lead.

"I'm so sorry. He doesn't usually behave like this."

"Keep that bloody mongrel away from me, or I'll kick it." The man growled. Trapped between a hawthorn hedge and a wall, the man held his hands in the air, well out of reach of Sandy's sharp teeth.

"Idiot. Can't you control that damn thing? Silly cow, you should 'ave it put down."

"How dare you speak to me in that tone. He's protecting me and means you no harm."

"Yeah! Such a friendly mutt." He said sarcastically. "I ain't gonna 'arm yer."

"That's a relief." Katrina gulped. Sandy lurched forward and barked fiercely.

"Is that you, Norman? It is you. I barely recognise you now you've shaved and had a haircut."

"State the blinking obvious, why don't you? It's none of yer damn business. Keep that ruddy dog away from me."

"Don't be rude. I told you he means you no harm." She assured him. Sandy snarled at him again.

"Sandy! Stop!" She ordered. "Norman. If you can't speak to me in a civilised manner, then don't speak to me at all. Goodbye." She huffed and jerked Sandy away. Norman cursed under his breath as he inched his way past.

The incident in Cooper's Passage had triggered Katrina, and she needed a moment to sit, so she made her way to the nearby bus shelter. Emotionally scarred from losing Charlotte, she sat with her eyes closed and breathed deep and slow.

When she opened her eyes, she first noticed the swing hanging from a tree on the other side of the road. Philippe made that swing for Charlotte some years ago. She imagined Charlotte gripping the ropes, kicking her legs into the air, and squealing when her toes scraped the ground on the backward swoop. Katrina's moods were like that swing, and today, her mood was arguably a fairground carousel with galloping horses surging forward after meeting Norman in Coopers Passage. Why should she let his behaviour spoil a beautiful day when there were more important things in life?

The sweet warbles of a songbird raised her spirits, and the church clock chiming the hour startled pigeons into flight.

🐘

Sandy was the first to enter the boot room, followed by Katrina. Philippe spun in the office chair to face the open door.

"I'm in the study, Katrina," Philippe shouted down the hall.

How was your walk?" He called. Katrina stepped inside the study and kissed him on the cheek.

"Hmm! Not without incident. Anyway. Sandy must have known you were here as he rushed home. He practically dragged me here." She said and laughed. "I enjoyed our walk, apart from the cold wind and..."

"You've been busy in the garden, I see." He said, cutting her off. "It always looks lovely after you've worked your magic."

"Thank you. I'm glad you noticed. When working in the garden, I can put the world right."

She told Philippe about Sandy and how he behaved toward Norman, her eyes widening with each syllable. She told him how rude he was and how upset she'd become.

"I'll speak to Tim. He'll know how to handle him."

"No, don't. It'll only make matters worse; besides, there's no permanent harm. I imagine Sandy didn't recognise him now he's altered his appearance. Norman has issues and overreacted. Sandy behaved like he did when we passed Norman's house the other day."

"I would say that Sandy was protecting you."

"That's as may be. I could barely hold him back; he's that strong." Philippe stood, then held her in his arms.

"Like I said. Sandy didn't recognise him. Don't worry. He will next time he sees him, you'll see." He said reassuringly. She lay her head on his chest.

"It was more than Sandy protecting me. I'm sure he was trying to tell me something. He's smart." She said and laughed at how ridiculous her suggestion sounded.

.

FORTY-FOUR

Mum and Dad woke to a dark, damp, and misty morning. Dad went to the kitchen, helping himself to a bowl of cereal, when he heard a van trundling down the lane.

"The florist van is here."

"Thank goodness. I've been waiting for him." She said, dashing to the window to catch a glimpse. "We'll pop into the Post Office to buy fresh flowers on our way to the cemetery," Mum said, picking up her phone from the kitchen table.

"Hi, Isabella. How are you today? — Oh. That's good. I'm so pleased to hear it. Would you mind looking after Sandy this morning while we visit the cemetery?"

"What time? Well — whenever you're ready. Sandy's been fed, so no doggy treats, please." She teased. Isabella giggled.

Within fifteen minutes, Isabella crunched across the drive. Her cheeks were glowing, and her smile oozed a self-fuelled charm.

"Hello, Mrs Duval." She said, waiting outside the boot room door.

"Hello, Isabella! You look wonderful now you've gained a little weight!"

"Yes, and I feel better for it. I have decent curves now." She said, showing off her hips. "Mind you, I don't want to end up looking like Mama. Oh! Don't tell her I said that." She said, grinning mischievously.

"You look well," Mum said, straightening Isabella's woolly hat.

Isabella wore a permanent apprehensive expression before her operation. But today, she was glowing radiantly. Mum was fussing over Isabella like she used to fuss over me until I told her I was no longer five, and she eventually took the hint. We're alike.

"Sandy has been waiting at the door ever since I phoned you. He knows when you're coming to collect him."

"I told him I would be walking him again soon. He's very smart. He has a sixth sense or something."

"I agree. I shouldn't be telling you this, but we met Norman Taylor in the lane the other day, and Sandy snarled and growled at him. Norman was afraid, which was quite natural, I suppose. I was surprised because Sandy is everyone's friend, as you know. He knows something isn't quite right with that man. Anyway. I won't bore you with the details. Be careful, won't you? It wouldn't do for Sandy to drag you down the lane if he sees Norman, would it?"

She laughed, brushing off Mum's half-hearted joke.

"He is a bit weird, isn't he?" Isabella then regretted her judgment after realising she was in no position to judge, not after being given a second chance. Dad leaned into the boot room.

"Hi, Isabella. Did someone mention Norman?"

"Hello, Mr Duval Yes. I did." Isabella said, blushing with embarrassment. "Forget I mentioned his name. Well. I'll get going. Give Charlotte my love, won't you? I plucked up the courage to go to her grave last week and had like a tickling sensation in my hair. It was weird, as though I had, like, fleas or something." She clucked her tongue. "I'm not a hundred per cent yet, so I'll walk Sandy round the block, then take him back to mine. Papa said I can bring him to the house if I wish. He's been so nice lately."

"How sweet. Don't wear yourself out, will you, sweetheart? You're still recovering from your operation."

"Mama says the same thing. I'll take my time, Mrs Duval. I know when I need to rest. When I last saw the specialist, he was like… 'The more exercise you do, the stronger you'll become.' And I was like… 'Not quite ready for the Olympics.' Anyway, I'd better get going before Sandy runs off without me. Byeee. See you later." She said, holding Sandy at heel. Mum and Dad rushed to the kitchen window and watched her walk up the drive.

"Isn't she sweet, Philippe? She looks a lot like Charlotte from this angle."

"There is an uncanny resemblance, especially wearing Charlotte's woolly hat. She walks like her, too." Dad commented.

Mum gave Isabella my woolly hat when I grew tired of it. I also gave her many of my old clothes when they no longer fit me or when I stopped wearing them. They suit her now she's gained weight. We often borrowed each other's clothes, but Isabella wasn't just wearing my clothes: she was slipping into my old life, and I was a teeny bit jealous.

Dressed suitably for the cold, they called into the Post Office on their way to the cemetery. Earnest was in the stockroom watching TV, and Mrs Barnes was leant on the counter, reading a glossy magazine wedged underneath her ample bosom. She glanced up when the bell jingled.

"Good morning, Mrs Barnes," Katrina said merrily. "I noticed the curtains are drawn at the Old Bakery."

"Yes. Mr Rodrigues closes them — for security reasons when he's away. — He's often gone for long periods." Mrs Barnes said boastfully.

"I've never met him."

"I spoke to him in the lane once. He's very reserved." Philippe said.

Even Mrs Barnes didn't know much about him, which says a lot.

"I'm looking for flowers for my mother's grave. The ones in buckets outside are wilting. I saw the delivery van earlier. Can we buy a bunch from those instead of the ones outside?"

"I'd rather..." Mrs Barnes stopped herself. "The flowers outside — are past their best," she agreed. "If they're not sold — I leave them at the church." She added. "The new delivery has only just arrived — and I haven't had time — to sort them."

Mrs Barnes was eager to sell old stock first, but today's customers are more discerning. They demand freshness and quickly complain if goods have exceeded their 'best before' date.

When we were kids, Isabella and I were curious about the bins at the rear of the Post Office. We used to check them to see if Mrs. Barnes had thrown anything useful away. Isabella was breathless and couldn't climb the high wall into the yard, so she kept watch while I clambered over, skinning my knees every time.

We soon learned that Mrs. Barnes rarely threw anything of any value away. Neither of our families was poor, but it was our way of entertaining ourselves during school holidays.

'What if we get caught?' Isabella fretted. 'We'll only get a telling-off,' I said, trying to ease her worry. But if Mum ever found out, I would have been grounded, like, for-ev-errr. Mrs Barnes always gave me sweets or crisps, and I felt guilty after we'd been rummaging through her bins earlier. I never refused a treat.

Mrs Barnes swept the curtain aside and disappeared into the back room. Dad browsed the merchandise, and with barely enough room to swing a cat, finding a particular item was, how should I put it, 'challenging?' Gasps and wheezes grew louder when Mrs Barnes returned with two bunches of freesias, glistening with condensation.

Mrs Barnes' shortness of breath was due to her being overweight. She had been that way for as long as I could remember. Her health was declining, but she would always manage a smile.

The bell jingled, and another customer walked in. Mum and Dad said goodbye to Mrs Barnes before she began chatting with the new customer. *It was more like an interrogation.*

When I ran to the cemetery, I found Gran sitting beneath a tree, so I sat beside her on the soft grass.

"I thought you'd deserted me." I teased.

"You're doing so well; I trust you."

"Don't I get a hug?"

Mum and Dad walked through the cemetery and trod the familiar path to our graves.

"Have you been able to communicate with anyone yet?" Gran enquired after we gave each other a warm hug.

"I'm so excited because I worked out that Norman Taylor can hear me, and I may have half scared him to death at the meeting the other night."

"Then, are you ready to leave?"

"Goodness no. Not yet. My business with him isn't over."

Cunningham is smart and will work out that Norman Taylor was my attacker. I'm limited in spirit and haven't yet discovered a way to help Cunningham. But me being stubborn…

She knelt at my graveside and placed flowers in the vase, matching the one on her mother's grave. Dad put a hand on her shoulder while she whispered a private prayer. She shuddered as grief rose to the surface. Grief is the price of a lost loved one. He helped her to her feet when she indicated she was ready to stand.

I had no understanding of how losing a daughter must feel. Isabella brought them joy, but that was on hold for now. Mum kissed her fingertips, touched my headstone, and whispered, 'elephant juice,' as a shaft of sunlight shone on my headstone. *Perfect timing.* She saw it as a positive sign, and it helped calm her emotions. The granite Angel on my headstone was gazing heavenwards with her hands in the prayer position. My full name and date of birth were engraved below the Angel, then a black line, followed by the date of my earth death: a beginning, a middle, and an end. The thin black line represents my life, which, over time, will fade. By then, not a single person alive would remember me or anything about my life. Sixteen years: a meagre moment in time. It's easy to forget that the person beneath a grave once lived purposefully. We are born. We live. We die. During that time, we are presented with growth opportunities and a chance to improve the world.

It took Mum a moment to read my name out loud. She wasn't ashamed to read her daughter's name on a gravestone, but it was a step too far. I had left her before my time, and she will have to live with her guilt because she thought she'd failed me. She taught me to be aware of my surroundings and thought she'd failed there, too. She taught me that nourishing my soul and caring for myself wasn't selfish but self-preservation. She felt she had failed there, too and chastised herself for being weak in God's eyes. Dad said that God wasn't judgmental, but that didn't help. She had turned a corner, but seeing my name on a new headstone had ruthlessly thrust a sword through her grieving heart. Her world had changed, and she needed more time to adapt. We had spent sixteen wonderful years together, but she'd been robbed of a daughter, a friend. And as she had come to terms with the loss of her mother, she would also accept my loss. Life must go on. I sent love and light, and tears turned to joy as Mum found her inner peace.

Isabella had become a large part of her life, and Mum realised that the dividing line between Isabella and me was blurring.

"I'm sure Charlotte is guiding Isabella to help ease our pain," she said, wiping her eyes. "She is with her Gran now."

They stepped to one side, and Mum arranged the remaining flowers in the identical vase on her mother's grave. She said another private prayer, then turned to Dad.

"I'm okay, Philippe. I'm ready to go home."

They strolled through the gates, arm in arm, and Mum relaxed once they reached the car park. Mum's behaviour wasn't the end but the beginning of a new chapter. One thing of concern is whether her sadness will return when she learns who attacked me.

FORTY-FIVE

Philippe's mobile rang as he stood at the network printer, waiting for documents to print.

"Hello, Philippe." The leathery voice said.

"Hi, Tim. How are you?"

"I'm good, thanks. If you're not too busy, I have some questions."

"Hah! I'm always busy, but ask away?"

"Does the name Alan Rodrigues mean anything to you?"

"There is an Alan Rodrigues in the village. He lives at the Old Bakery, if that's who you mean?"

"That's the guy. Are you two acquainted?"

"No. Not really. Only to say hello to. He keeps himself to himself. Talk to Mrs Barnes; she knows everyone's business."

Cunningham knew Mrs Barnes and her unique way of levering information from unsuspecting customers.

"I will talk to her since she's the local Oracle." He said, and nose laughed. "Has he ever spoken to Charlotte?"

"Absolutely no idea. She never mentioned him."

"Mm," Cunningham mumbled. "The cottage is deserted. Is it an Airbnb, or is it his permanent place of residence?"

"I've never seen strangers there, so I don't believe it's an Airbnb. Mrs Barnes told me he travels to Hong Kong regularly."

"Interesting. Do me a favour, Philippe. Keep an eye on the place and let me know if you see any activity there."

"Absolutely. No problem at all."

"Okay, Philippe. Thanks for that. I'll be in touch. I've got to dash. Bye."

Philippe pondered Cunningham's words. He didn't give a reason for wanting him to keep an eye on Mr. Rodrigues.

Philippe was blaming Ness for hiding his slippers, and he was in the middle of a frantic search of the bedroom when he noticed a change at the Old Bakery. He recalled the conversation with Tim about keeping an eye out for Mr Rodrigues earlier in the week. So, when he saw the curtains were drawn and a light was on, he phoned Tim straight away, and within half an hour, Cunningham's Chrysler 300 stopped outside the Old Bakery. Cunningham waited in the doorway, hands in pockets, while focusing on the cemetery gates.

The Old Bakery was left empty for many years and, over time, fell into disrepair. Villagers complained to the Council about the eyesore until Alan Rodrigues bought and renovated the building two years ago. He had it converted into a magnificent, well-appointed home.

Mr Rodrigues invited Cunningham inside, then explained why he was there to Alan. Alan was visibly shaken to learn of

Charlotte's death and stared vacantly at the pile of unopened mail on the coffee table.

"My God. That's awful. Poor Mr and Mrs Duval. I didn't know them, but I'd heard many good things about Charlotte, mainly from the old gossip in the Post Office. Can't stand her. She wants to know everyone's business." Alan said, then apologised for his outburst. Cunningham kept his thoughts to himself.

"The reason I'm here is because you flew from Heathrow Airport on November 25th, the day of Charlotte Duval's attack."

"That's correct, Inspector. My taxi arrived at 3:30 to run me to the airport, and I flew to Hong Kong later that evening."

"Business trip?"

"Yes. I'm the CEO of a company in Hong Kong. I've been home for less than an hour." Alan said, smiling humorously. "The jungle drums must be working well for you to be on my doorstep within half an hour of me setting foot in the door." Cunningham mirrored his smile again without comment.

"Can I offer you a coffee?"

"Yes. Thanks. Milk, no sugar."

While unique coffee machine noises emanated from the kitchen, Cunningham scanned the room and its incredible array of extravagant antiques, watched by a sizeable ceramic leopard by the fireplace. The glass coffee table reflected the soft light from the Art Deco lamp, and a Chesterfield sofa and matching chairs complimented the luxurious burgundy carpet. Framed prints caught his attention, as did the Chinese Jian sword above the fireplace.

Alan brought in a wooden tray and placed it on the coffee table.

"You did say sugar, didn't you?"

"No sugar, thanks." He replied, taking a cup and saucer from the tray.

"I see you live close to the cemetery."

"Hah! That doesn't bother me if that's what you mean."

"That's not my point. Do you recall seeing anyone near the gates when you left for the airport?"

Alan rubbed his eyes.

"I vaguely remember seeing someone." He said, clawing back a hazy image from that afternoon. Cunningham wrote in his notebook.

"I recall it was a misty afternoon. You know, a typical November day. There was only one street light, so visibility was poor. Whoever it was wore dark clothes, a hat, long hair, and a stoop. They may have been wearing a scarf over their mouth, but I couldn't be sure."

Cunningham wrote it down.

"Would you say that person was round-shouldered?"

"A fair assumption."

"Was their behaviour unusual?"

"Yes. It could be described that way. They were hesitant and edgy as if they were trying to hide and doing a poor job. Look, inspector, I'm tired, and my mind isn't clear." He said, glancing at the clock and stifling a yawn.

"Your recall is admirable, considering you're tired. I won't keep you any longer. I know jet lag dulls the mind."

"Somewhat understated. It was only a brief glimpse, and I couldn't tell whether it was male or female. I had so much on my mind that I'd forgotten until you mentioned it. The fog was closing in, and I lost sight of them when the taxi turned in the lane."

Cunningham slid his notepad into his pocket.

"I can't see any problems after confirming your alibi. Of course, we'll need to verify your travel itinerary; then I'll get back to you." Cunningham finished his coffee and left a business card on the table. "If you remember any details in the morning, call me on that number. Do you plan on returning to Hong Kong any time soon?"

"Not for a couple of weeks unless there's a problem." He said, handing Cunningham his business card. "You can contact me on that number."

"Thanks. One final question before I leave. Would you recognise the person if you saw them again?"

"I doubt it, although whoever it was had round shoulders, as I said. It could have been either male or female. Doesn't that scruffy bloke up the road walk with a hunch?"

"Norman Taylor?"

"If that's his name."

"Could it have been him you saw that afternoon?"

"I couldn't say for sure, although he does mooch around the village rather creepily. Sorry. I shouldn't judge. The fog was getting worse, and I was worried in case it was a slow drive to the airport."

"Okay," Cunningham said. "I'll leave you to get some rest."

Alan smiled thinly.

"The joys of long-haul flight. There was one other thing. I saw the bloke who locks the cemetery gates staggering down the lane at about the same time. I see him every night when I'm home, so it wasn't unusual. He may be able to help."

"We have already spoken to him. But thanks, anyway."

The leather chair creaked when Cunningham stood to leave.

"We'll need to sample your DNA as part of our enquiry. A member of staff will phone to arrange an appointment."

"Understood," Allan said as they shook hands. Cunningham automatically glanced at the proximity of the cemetery gates as he walked to his car.

One of his team members was on maternity leave, so DS Woodcroft took over her role and spent the morning checking Alan Rodrigues's travel schedule. By lunchtime, he confirmed Alan's schedule and, in a moment of self-gratification, put down the phone and smiled.

"Yes!" He boasted and rubbed his hands together in an unbridled display of pride.

"Alan Rodrigues' story checks out, Guv." He said to Cunningham, at his desk in the corner, face buried in a folder. Woodcroft read his notes out loud.

"The taxi company confirmed the arrival time of Rodrigues's taxi, and the driver said he waited for about two minutes before his client came out of the house."

Cunningham stopped reading and looked up.

"Great work, Woody. Interpol can be hopeless at times. I spoke to Mr Rodrigues last night. He said he saw a person near the cemetery gates on the afternoon of the attack, although he didn't get a good look at them. He also saw someone staggering down the lane, which I presume was Old Jake. Damn. I'd love to know who was at the boneyard gates that afternoon. Where are the security cameras when you need them? We'll have to wait for Alan's DNA sample to be processed before he can be eliminated from our enquiries. I'm confident he will be." Cunningham said, handing Woody a description of the person seen at the gates that afternoon.

"Mm! That reads like a description of Norman Taylor to me, Guv. His hair was long, and he wore a cap and scarf. He's round-shouldered, and his alibi is so flimsy a puff of wind would demolish it."

"He's very guarded," Cunningham remarked. A vivid image flashed through his mind of how Norman usually dressed in winter.

"I think it's time we paid Taylor another visit."

FORTY-SIX

Cunningham realised that the theory, the wheels of justice grind slowly, was true since it took the judge two days to grant a warrant to search Norman Taylor's house, despite the connection to a murder enquiry. Warrant in hand, he and Woodcroft joined the motorway to take them to Ashmarsh.

The sign above the door read, 'G & R Taylor.' Woodcroft knocked while Cunningham eyed the cemetery gates and tried to picture Taylor behind the stone gate support that afternoon. His stomach stirred as his thoughts turned to Charlotte, not only because she was a family friend but also because of the events leading to her death. His boss had warned him to remain impartial, and he'd assured her of his utmost professionalism.

Cunningham braced himself for the stench that would greet him when the door opened. A clean-shaven man eyed them in the doorway. The man wore faded, dirty jeans and a black T-shirt. He also had a cigarette dangling from his lips.

"Oh! It's you two muppets." The man growled, cigarette dancing between his lips. "Waderyawant?"

Cunningham thrust an A4-sized sheet of paper at Norman Taylor.

"We have a warrant to search your premises?" He said and barged past Norman. Woodcroft followed him.

"Come in, why don't yer?" H said, flicking the cigarette end into the garden. They squeezed down a path in the hall, barely wide enough to walk safely, and Norman barged past them on his way to the bay window in the lounge. He sat at the table in the window and lit a cigarette. Woodcroft looked around the kitchen while Cunningham talked to Norman.

"If it's a complaint about the bonfire I 'ad, then I don't care. Everyone 'as a fire on Bonfire Night. Why single me out?"

"We don't need a warrant to search your bonfire. That's not why we're here."

"Then why 'ave yer got a search warrant?"

"Because, Mr Taylor, new evidence has been uncovered in the Charlotte Duval case. We're here to search your premises, and you'll be helping with our inquiries."

Norman shrugged. "Suit yer sen. It's got nowt to do wi' me." He said, voice gravelly and low.

"A person matching your description was seen near the cemetery gates on the afternoon Charlotte Duval was attacked. That person was thought to be wearing a flat cap, a scarf around their mouth, a shabby jacket and jeans, and their hair was long and straggly!"

Norman leaned back in the chair, exhaled a billowing cloud of smoke, and gazed out the window down the deserted lane.

"Look. I don't own clothes like that. Anyway. Everyone wears clothes like that in winter."

"Don't lie, Taylor. Until recently, you wore clothes like that every winter. If those clothes are here, we will find them."

Norman smirked. He knew that they wouldn't find clothes matching the description. Cunningham searched drawers and cupboards, opening them with his pen. After finding nothing significant, he went upstairs, stumbling on papers piled on every step. Norman followed him upstairs.

Norman's bedroom was unremarkable. The few sticks of furniture dated back to the 1940s, and the wallpaper was from the mid-60s. Cunningham ran a finger along a line of clothing in the wardrobe, then examined a cluster of ornaments on the dressing table.

"Fascinated with death, are we?" Cunningham remarked.

"The glass skull's an ashtray…" he said, and crushed a cigarette into it, "…an' the coffin's a wind-up money box. Put a coin on the top, an' a skeleton's 'and shoots out and snatches it away."

Luckily, Norman didn't go anywhere near Charlotte's casket at her funeral. Otherwise, she may have slid her hand out and dragged him inside like a coin.

The remainder of Norman's gadgets were of little interest to Cunningham. He drew back the dusty grey net curtain with his pen and peered up and down the lane. He released the curtain, sending a cloud of dust into the air. Cunningham shot out of the bedroom to avoid inhaling years of dust.

Woodcroft raked through the remains of a bonfire using a bamboo cane. Cunningham joined him in the back garden, and Norman smoked a cigarette while leaning against the door frame.

"Had a fire?" Woodcroft asked, more of an accusation than a question.

"State the blinking obvious, why don't yer? I already said I 'ad a fire on Bonfire Night."

"Didn't burn clothes by any chance?" Cunningham asked. Part guesswork, part intuition. His guesses were usually accurate.

"I burned branches an' stuff. It's the only time I can 'av a fire without me nosey neighbours 'avin' a go at me or grassing me up to the council. 'Do you 'ave to light a fire so close to the 'ouse, the smoke is coming in my window?' ALWAYS BLOODY COMPLAINING." He said in a voice loud enough for the neighbour to hear.

"Want to know what I think?" Cunningham asked.

"No. But I s'pose you're gonna tell me."

"I believe it was you outside the cemetery that afternoon."

"Not me. I told yer, I stayed 'ome all day. I can't 'elp it if yer don't believe me." Norman said, scraping his heel on the step. "I keep telling you; I never left the 'ouse all weekend. End of."

"I'll get the truth from you if it takes me until next Christmas. No one can verify you were at home that weekend, and the person seen at the cemetery gates matched your description."

"And…? You've done enough of your searching; now piss off and leave me alone." Norman growled. He lit another cigarette and flicked the old stub into the garden.

Cunningham thrust his hands deep inside his coat pockets.

"We're not done yet. Forensics are coming, but before they arrive, tell me, why have you tidied yourself up?"

Norman lowered his gaze, and the cigarette quivered between his lips.

"I 'ave feelings yer know, even if you think I don't. People think I can't 'ear 'em when they talk about me be'ind me back. I can 'ear their snide remarks, and they 'urt. I thought they'd leave me alone if I smartened me'self up."

"Mmm" was all Cunningham said. He walked to the hall and turned on the spot.

"Are you sure you were at home all day the day Charlotte Duval was attacked?"

"Oh, fer God's sake. 'ave you not been listening to a word I said? 'ow many times do I 'ave to spell it out to you? I NEVER LEFT ME 'OUSE ALL WEEKEND."

Every word was drenched in frustration. Cunningham noticed Norman's quick temper, which would be helpful if used against him. The fact that Norman was sensitive to criticism was a surprise. And there he was, thinking that Norman was cold and emotionless.

Cunningham wouldn't allow Norman's feelings to get in his way. He needed proof, solid evidence, something to put Norman at the scene to prove his guilt. Frustration grew, and each line of investigation had drifted away like the smoke from Norman's cigarettes.

"How do you explain the metal buttons and zip in those ashes?" Woodcroft queried. It was a fair question since Norman said he had only burned wood and paper. Norman shrugged, and the question was left unanswered.

Norman stood in the doorway and watched Cunningham and Woodcroft step into the front garden.

"Goodbye, and good riddance."

"I told you! We're not done with you yet. Forensics will be here soon." Cunningham informed Norman. Norman tensed. Filled with dread at the thought of forensics scouring the house, guilt and horror washed over him in the minute it took him to process the information. His thoughts were interrupted when three vehicles stopped outside his gate. A team of six walked down the path, and both detectives stepped aside as they filed through the door. Norman followed them inside, lit a cigarette, and gazed at the vans from the bay window, feeling less smug than five minutes ago. The two detectives sat in Cunningham's car.

"You think you've got away with murder, don't you, Norman Taylor?"

"What the…?" He scanned the room, then stared accusingly at the two forensic officers rifling through his cupboards.

"'oo are you? Show yerself." He said, in a state of fear.

"They will find evidence." The voice said. "You caused my death. Confess, or things might become difficult?"

The cigarette fell to the floor when Norman's jaw dropped. He glanced over at the two officers.

"Which one of you is doing that? Stop mucking me about, ye'r doing me 'ed in."

The officers exchanged puzzled glances.

"It's me. I'm over here."

"Come out where I can see yer." He said, stamping on the cigarette, burning a hole in the carpet.

"I know you can't see me, Norman, but you can hear me. It's Charlotte. You attacked me in the cemetery, remember?"

"Impossible. She's dead."

"Then who do you think is talking to you?"

"I dunno. Cunningham left a loudspeaker or summats, or them two goons are doing it to scare me."

"I don't think so, Norman. There is no speaker. It really is me."

"Impossible. Dead people can't talk..." Both officers looked at each other in dismay. Norman lit another cigarette mid-sentence.

"...so why don't yer leave me alone? I can't stand it anymore."

"You should have thought about that before you attacked me."

"Stop! Stop! You're scaring me. STOP!"

"I'll leave you alone if you promise to make a full confession to the police."

"I - I - can't. I'm scared of what might 'appen to me."

This could be the breakthrough I've been waiting for. Norman can hear me, and he's scared of me.

FORTY-SEVEN

If or when Cunningham required personal space, he looked for a quiet place to be alone. While forensics searched Norman's house, he walked from his car to the cemetery, an ideal place for him to toy with his thoughts.

Hands deep inside his pockets, he walked the gravel path until he arrived at the recent burial part of the cemetery. He stopped, rubbing his chin thoughtfully.

Is there a similar case to Charlotte's? Does Taylor have murderous traits? How does he function? What is he capable of? Do the limitations of fear and paranoia bind his life?

There was something about Norman Taylor that troubled him. The handful of details he had weren't adding up. For once, he wished that answers would fall into his lap.

Woodcroft knew to leave Cunningham alone when he was 'in the zone.' Still, rather than wait in the car, he walked to the cemetery, wandered to the opposite end of the cemetery from where Cunningham was, and searched the area for whatever might turn up.

As a schoolboy, Cunningham rarely asked for help and usually found the solution alone. His method had taught him the basics of understanding fundamental concepts and aided him in assembling essential building blocks of his life. He took his quirky characteristics with him through his university years, which paid off. Now in charge of a Murder Investigation Team, he led by example and, using his ingrained characteristics, jumped head-first into solving problems. He loitered amongst the graves, then happened upon Katrina's mother's grave alongside Charlotte's. He cringed when images of Charlotte lying helpless on the grass invaded his thoughts.

Forensics occasionally make mistakes. If Charlotte's locket wasn't found during the search, someone must have it…' A magpie cackled in a nearby tree. '*…or, a magpie may have flown it to its nest.*' He thought, recalling Katrina's story about a magpie stealing her earring from the garden table last summer. The icy wind took his breath away, and he held onto his hat to glance up at the lofty branches of nearby trees. Then, a magpie cackled again, almost as a reminder. '*Magpies have nested in that tree.*' Then, resisting the urge to climb it and risk falling and breaking his neck, he ran a scenario in his head. He then moved on, hopefully heading physically and mentally in the right direction. A jumble of gravestones, obelisks, and long grass hindered his progress. He probed a pile of leaves gathered against a gravestone with a discarded stick, then weaved between gravestones and combed through more leaves and debris in the hope of finding the lost locket or anything that might be of interest. His search ended at a row of shrubs hugging the cemetery wall.

Twenty minutes later, cold, tired, and hungry after searching through copious amounts of plastic bags and sweet wrappers, Woodcroft was sitting in the car when Cunningham returned.

"Start the engine, Guv, I'm freezing." Cunningham started the engine without comment.

"Any luck?"

"I didn't find anything useful, if that's what you mean?" Cunningham said quietly. He breathed in three deep breaths, U-turned the car and shot up the lane, snapping twigs like tiny bones beneath the fat Dunlop tyres.

"Damn." Cunningham spat and hit the steering wheel with his palm.

"I didn't find anything either if it makes you feel better."

"It was you I saw in the cemetery."

"Yes. I thought I'd make myself useful."

Woodcroft gazed at the white vans outside Norman's house as the Chrysler shot past them.

"Steady, Guv. I do have a family to go home to." Woodcroft fretted. Cunningham realised what he was doing and eased off the accelerator.

Each line of inquiry resulted in a blank, and like Cunningham's search in the cemetery ending at a brick wall, so too had the investigation. It was a process based on facts, and he had nothing — zilch — a big fat zero.

Cunningham had dealt with his anger and was relaxed on the journey back to Swynbourne Police Station. Something was niggling him, but he wouldn't discuss it until he had given it more thought. The clues so far were 'Norman Taylor's flimsy alibi, a mystery person resembling Taylor seen at the church gates, and a missing locket.' Those thoughts ticked over in his mind much faster than the indicator for the right turn into the station car park.

"You coming, Guv?"

"You go ahead. I'll be there shortly."

"Okay."

Woodcroft closed the car door and ran up the concrete steps to the main entrance.

It would take enormous brain power for Cunningham to process the information before he could even consider returning to the office. His intuition usually told him when things weren't right. More than crumbs of evidence were required to solve a case close to his heart, and today, his intuition was screaming from the rooftops.

🐘

Freshly motivated, Cunningham climbed the station steps, not ready to return to his office. The overly large atrium was a jumble of direction signs, so he read the sign directing him to where he needed to be and followed the arrows to a flight of stairs leading to the lower floors. A middle-aged woman was behind a desk, halfway along a bright corridor, and she directed him to the office he was looking for.

When he reached the office, a man in a white coat had his back to the door with arms searching the insides of a filing cabinet. The man turned and peered over his gold-rimmed glasses when he heard a knock on the door. He recognised the caller immediately.

"Hi, Tim! Come on in." Professor Craig Marsden said. "It's so good to see you." He shook Cunningham's hand with a firm grip.

"Good to see you too, Craig."

"Now. My guess is you haven't come to the bowels of the building to say hello."

"You're right. I know I haven't been in contact lately, but I'm investigating the recent murder of Charlotte Duval, and I believe you were involved in the case."

"That's right. Happened in Ashmarsh cemetery."

"Yes. Near to where I live."

"So sad and a bit too close to home. How can I help?"

"I have an idea. I know your guys combed the cemetery but did their search include the perimeter wall area?"

Craig wiped the lenses of his glasses on his jacket.

"Both sides of the perimeter wall were thoroughly searched. Every inch, finger searched on hands and knees. The dog squad was involved, too. I'll check the database." He said, settling his glasses and standing behind his computer.

"If, for example, a gold locket was found, you'd know about it, right?"

"Of course. Everything from the scene was bagged, tagged, and recorded on the database. Are you missing a gold locket? I don't recall there being one found, though. Give me a moment." Craig tapped the keyboard. "Mmm. There's no mention of a locket. If there had been a locket, it would have been labelled on the diagram." He turned the monitor to face Tim. "See for yourself. We have drone footage of the area if you'd like to see it."

"That won't be necessary, Craig." He said, studying the monitor. "I was hoping your guys had found a locket at the scene, as it would make my life a whole lot easier."

"We could all do with a lucky break at times, Tim. Sorry, I can't help you. What's this about?"

"Charlotte wouldn't leave the house without her gold locket. You've confirmed it wasn't at the scene, it wasn't with the clothes she was wearing on the day, and it wasn't in her school locker or at her home. It suggests to me that she either lost it before the attack or her assailant had it. That's not much to go on, I know. My other thought was that maybe a magpie found it and flew it to its nest."

"There's more to this than you're saying, Tim."

Cunningham sighed.

"You're right, Craig. Charlotte was the daughter of close friends of mine, and it breaks my heart knowing her killer is on the loose. I want this crime solved, not for me, but for her parents."

"Are you okay, Tim?"

"I'm upset, naturally. But I can't let my feelings get in the way. That's what's driving me."

"Keep a clear head, Tim, and I'm sure the locket will turn up. It's odd because the crime scene was unusually clean."

"Never has a crime scene been so clean, Craig."

"It is unusual. You are a remarkably talented detective, Tim, and with your intuitive abilities, I know you'll find something. There's still time for more evidence to surface." He said, trying to identify the bee in Cunningham's bonnet.

"We obtained a warrant to search the house of a local chap, and I'm waiting for the report."

"Yes, I know. My guys are involved, and I'll contact you when I receive that report." Cunningham glanced at the time.

"I'll leave you to it. Thanks for your help, Craig. It was good to see you again."

"Hang on, Tim. I've just received an email." He read it quietly, then peered over his glasses. "Interesting. This could be the lead you're looking for, Tim."

Cunningham read the email without comment. "Thanks, Craig. I'll get back to my office. Keep me in the loop." He said, preparing to leave. "Will you forward the email to me?"

"Can do, Tim. Good luck, and I'm sorry about losing your friend's daughter."

"Yeah. Me too."

Cunningham went to his office, and although he was pleased with the news, he wondered whether the missing locket was sitting in a magpie's nest close to the cemetery. Would it be worthwhile for him to organise a team with a cherry-picker to search the trees around the cemetery?

FORTY-EIGHT

"Are we able to move objects with our thoughts, Gran?" I asked, hoping her answer would be yes. I'd been trying to move objects without success and was curious whether it took practice.

"We can, but it's not that easy," Gran said, preparing herself to explain the intricacies of spiritual telekinesis. "Moving objects requires a great deal of energy and is usually restricted to Angels and higher spirits. Poltergeists have an abundance of energy, but they are misguided. Spirits may become trapped between two worlds and often attract attention by moving an object gently or violently. Why do you ask?"

"I would like to be able to do that as I think it would be fun."

"You still have your playful streak," Gran said, recalling her first days in spirit when she tried to move an object. We sat on the bench closest to the church, and Gran turned to me.

"We can have fun in spirit without the ability to move objects. I understand you have already communicated with one individual, although I can't imagine it was fun for him."

"I think I mentioned it to you before. I was going to talk to you about that in detail."

"You must have terrified him."

"I did scare him, and later, I felt sorry for him. I can't move objects, but I'm excited now I've established that he can hear me. I will talk to him again and try to persuade him to confess."

"In God's name, be careful. We must adhere to the code." She cautioned.

"More rules. Huh! I obeyed the rules on earth, and where did that get me? And now I must obey rules in spirit." Is there no end to this control?

"Not so much rules; more like guidelines."

I wish DCI Cunningham could hear me. Norman can hear me, I know that now, but if I talk to him, will he own up to his crime? Can you imagine what he would be like at the police station? 'I'm here to confess to the murder of Charlotte Duval because she told me to.' Like, that's going to happen.

When we began to walk, Gran sensed something was wrong with her daughter. She turned quickly and walked towards the cottage.

FORTY-NINE

Sandy paid little attention to his surroundings when he was devouring his food. He didn't notice Katrina watering the cactus on the kitchen windowsill or Philippe walking into the kitchen.

"It's time I fixed the shelf in the hall." He announced. "It's been loose for months, and I need screws and filler. Would you like to ride with me to the DIY store?"

"I was wondering when you would get around to fixing it. I will come with you on one condition…"

"I thought there'd be a catch." He said with a smirk.

"I want to call into Harvey Nichols to collect the Dolce & Gabbana top I ordered."

Philippe was taken by surprise.

"Is it for a special occasion?"

"Kind of. I thought I'd mentioned it to you. Graham from Paige & Neilson phoned to ask if I would like to work for him again. He doesn't know about Charlotte yet."

"Don't rush into anything. It's early days, yet."

Katrina placed the miniature watering can in the sink.

"I know, but I have been thinking about doing something fulfilling for a while now, something to challenge me. Lately, all I ever seem to do is play bridge or stare at these four walls, although

I enjoy gardening. Besides helping at the church, I haven't done anything constructive since Charlotte was born. I want to challenge my intellect…"

"… and helping at the church isn't enough?"

"I enjoy giving my time to the church, but I'm sure I'll go crazy if I don't do something more gratifying. Graham suggested I work part-time to begin with…"

"…to begin with?" He interrupted. "Do you plan to go full-time?"

"Yes, if I enjoy the work." She said flippantly. "Look. It's not cast in stone, especially so soon after — well, you know, losing Charlotte. Technology has changed in the last decade, so I need to upskill. There's no harm in going for an informal chat with Graham. I may leave it until spring."

"Have you given any more thought to starting a business? You've always talked about it ever since we met."

"True. If things don't work out with Graham, I wouldn't mind working for the Grieving Parents Support Network. (GPSN). They've been so supportive, and I'd like to give something back. It is paid work."

"GPSN has been amazing, but don't be in a rush," Philippe said, glancing at the clock. "We can talk about it over lunch in Swynbourne."

"Let's go to the new Bistro in the High Street."

"Sounds like a plan. I'll get my jacket."

Katrina finished watering the cactus and remembered that Spaghetti Bolognese was Charlotte's favourite dish. The mere mention of pasta had opened a wound, and then an emergency wailer in the distance disturbed her thoughts.

Philippe heard the wailer grow louder while deciding which jacket to wear. He peered out of the bedroom window in time to see an ambulance responding car hurtling down the lane. Katrina watched from the kitchen window and saw the vehicle stop outside the Post Office. Philippe shot downstairs.

"Are you all right? I heard the wailer from the bedroom. Mrs Barnes has probably cut her finger on the bacon slicer or something," Philippe rationalised.

"Something may have happened to Mrs Barnes. I hope it's not serious. I'll pop over to see if there's anything I can do. Are you coming?"

"No. I'll stay here. There's not much room in the shop, and besides, what can I do?"

Sandy made an opportunistic dash for the open door while Katrina slipped her shoes on.

"Sandy. No!" Ordered Philippe. Sandy sloped off back to the kitchen.

When Katrina left, Philippe had an excellent opportunity to move the hall furniture. He was about to move the phone table away from the wall when a breathless Katrina burst through the door and threw herself into his arms.

"Mrs Barnes had a massive heart attack." She sobbed. "The paramedic worked hard to save her, but she didn't respond."

"My goodness. I'm so sorry." Philippe said as he comforted her in his arms and felt her body shudder.

"I left when the vicar arrived as there was nothing I could do. There was nothing anyone could do." She said and breathed a slow, juddering sob. He walked her into the kitchen.

"Take a seat, and I'll make you a coffee."

They moved into the cottage twenty years ago and became close to the joint owner of the Post Office. Out of respect, she was always called Mrs. Barnes. When her driving license was cancelled due to ill health, Katrina drove Mrs. Barnes to the wholesalers until deliveries could be arranged.

The old Post Office was a hobby and a convenience to the community, but with Mrs. Barnes gone, will the shop close forever?

The Reverend Nigel Goodfellow offered Earnest Barnes his blessing, and then a team of muscly men carried Mrs Barnes outside to the deliberately anonymous hearse. Its soul left when Mrs Barnes' body was removed; then there was calm, a rift in time and space that wandered through the shop like a stranger in a silent forest. The Post Office seemed empty. The last time Earnest took charge was when Mrs Barnes asked him to look after the shop while she played the organ at Charlotte's funeral service.

Philippe continued to repair the hall shelf, which helped take his mind off Mrs Barnes. Katrina sipped her coffee while nervously pulling at a damp tissue, and Sandy stared at the AGA from his basket. He clambered to his feet and nudged Katrina's leg with his muzzle. She ignored him and tore the tissue into a thousand pieces.

After securing the hall shelf using old screws he had in the garage, Philippe leaned into the kitchen.

"Are you feeling any better?"

"Yes. Thank you. I haven't taken it all in yet. The village won't be the same without her. Thanks for being so patient. I needed to gather my thoughts."

Philippe sat at the table while Sandy concentrated on a space near the AGA.

The invisible cord that binds a mother and daughter is stronger than spider silk, and Gran was inexplicably drawn to her daughter, and Charlotte went with her.

"I doubt if Earnest would manage on his own. It will be a huge loss to the village if the Post Office closes." Katrina remarked.

"I doubt he's had much time to even think about it. We'll know soon enough." Philippe said, examining his dusty hands. "I'll clean up in the hall, and then I'll make us a coffee."

"It's okay. I'll do it. It'll help occupy my mind."

Would Katrina consider helping Earnest in the shop? If so, she would undoubtedly recommend changes.

Katrina lost a daughter and a close friend, all within a short period. Mrs Barnes was the last person to speak to Charlotte before the attack, which bothered Katrina. Gran watched her daughter while standing beside the warm AGA. How could one person endure so much grief in such a short period?

FIFTY

The morning of Mrs Barnes's funeral, although unspeakably sad, began with a Christening in which the baby cried throughout the service. It stayed dry, but high winds were whipping through the village, causing minor structural damage. The church porch behaved like a wind tunnel, and heads turned as the ancient oak door slammed shut with an almighty crash. It took two strong men to heave the door open against the wind, allowing the vicar to simultaneously greet guests and hold down his cassock. Previously recorded organ music played softly before the funeral service began.

Now that everyone was safely inside and the door was closed to keep out the wind, the vicar conducted a heart-warming service to celebrate Mrs Barnes's life. He read the 23rd Psalm while her coffin was wheeled to the door. The Votive candles extinguished as soon as the door opened, and brave pallbearers battled against the wind to carry Mrs Barnes to her final resting place.

With the burial over, Katrina and Philippe waited for everyone to leave before fighting their way to her mother and daughter's graveside. Philippe stared fearfully at the huge branches thrashing perilously in the relentless wind.

"I hope those branches hold. We shouldn't stay too long…" He shouted above the booming wind. "…it's too dangerous."

"I'll only stay for a few minutes," she said distractedly. Something out of place on the ground caught her attention, so she stooped to look at it. Realising what the object was, she brushed leaves and twigs aside and rescued it from its lonely resting place.

"Look, Philippe." She said, holding her open palm to show him her find.

"What is it?"

"What are *they*?" She said, closing her eyes and clasping two shiny objects in her palm.

"It looks like my lost earring entangled with Charlotte's locket and chain." She said, examining the objects in her palm. "It is Charlotte's locket and my lost earring. I would know them anywhere, even if they are covered in bird poop. They must have fallen from a nest." She proclaimed, pointing at the furthermost branches of a towering tree, limbs waving wildly as if trying to attract her attention. Katrina untangled the earring and handed it to Philippe but held on to the locket like a child clutching their favourite toy. Her emotions skipped and danced between adult and child, and like a mother doting on her sleeping infant, she gazed tenderly at the locket. She unpicked the knotted chain, and memories of the day she gave it to Charlotte rushed in like a tidal bore. The family heirloom was handed to Charlotte when she turned thirteen, and she was expected to hand it to her firstborn girl when she turned thirteen. With her hopes and dreams now in tatters, Katrina knelt at her daughter's grave, fully aware that she would never be a doting grandmother.

Philippe tapped the ground with a stick while Katrina faced reality. She clambered to her feet, wiped her eyes, and turned to Philippe.

"I'm Sorry." She yelled above the deafening wind. "I needed to deal with the shock of finding Charlotte's locket." She said, examining it in her palm. "Everything came flooding back. Charlotte had so much to live for. Why did she have to die so young? It's so unfair."

Philippe let the stick fall to the ground and hugged Katrina.

"It is unfair." He agreed, staring up at the thrashing and waving branches. "Come on. It's too dangerous here. Let's join the others in the hall. It'll be safer in there."

"Sorry. I was overcome. Memories of Charlotte catch me off guard now and again."

"Me too."

Philippe understood Katrina's reaction to the locket. Emotions welled, but he kept his in check. It was evident to him the wind had dislodged the locket and earring. At this moment, he wished the pain of losing his daughter could also be dislodged.

"What are the odds of the locket and earring falling from a tree and me finding them? I would never have found them if they had fallen and stuck on a branch. They would have been lost forever. For them to land on this spot was nothing short of a miracle. They mean so much to me."

"I'm pleased too. I know the locket has sentimental value."

"You gave me those earrings, and they are special, but the locket belonged to my great-grandmother and has enormous sentimental value — even more now Charlotte is no longer with us." Katrina paused. After a moment, a smile grew across her face.

"I'm glad I kept the other earring. I'll have a matching pair again if this is my lost earring." She said, rolling up her collar to stop the wind blowing down her neck. "I was upset when a cheeky magpie stole it." She laughed and glanced up at the branches thrashing franticly in the wind. "That's what happens when you ask the patron saint of finding lost and stolen articles. Thank you, St Anthony, for returning the locket and my earring. I'm forever grateful."

"It is remarkable that you found the locket after asking St Anthony to help us. It's great that two articles were found together, but it is feasible that the locket was lost before the attack, and Charlotte losing it was unfortunate. We should let Tim know that we've found the locket. He phoned and asked me to let him know if we do find it."

"Yes. It's up to Tim to decide whether it's relevant or not." Philippe recovered his phone from his pocket.

"No! Wait! If we hand it to Tim immediately, we may never see it again."

Philippe raised his eyebrows. It was something only a mother would understand. With no notion of how a woman's mind works, he agreed.

"If you're right, and the locket is admissible evidence, it may be a huge step forward with the inquiry. Tim will be amazed when I tell him where you found it."

Katrina pulled a doggie-do bag from her handbag and dropped the locket and earring inside.

"The locket has been missing for days, so another hour or two won't make any difference." She said, linking arms. "Come on. We should join the others in the hall. I need a hot drink to warm me up."

Katrina's thoughts were elsewhere as she battled the wind along the well-worn track to the hall. Will Cunningham investigate the missing locket?

FIFTY-ONE

The wind whistled through tiny gaps in the old wooden window frames, but even that couldn't blow away the optimism of Mrs Barnes' post-funeral gathering.

Philippe and Katrina left shortly after offering Earnest Barnes their deepest condolences. Although the wind had dropped, the footpath to the cottage was strewn with twigs, branches, and leaves.

Cocooned in the warmth of the cottage, Katrina couldn't keep her eyes off the locket she had placed on the coffee table, in two minds about whether to phone Tim to tell him or leave it for the time being.

An hour later, Katrina decided to call Tim, and he answered her call swiftly.

Katrina relayed the story of how the locket had come into her possession.

"Amazing. That was in Ashmarsh cemetery I take it?"

"Yes, and judging by the state it's in, it's probably been in a nest for a few days, at least."

"Are you home now?"

"Yes. We've been home for about an hour."

"We will need to test it for DNA. I want to collect it ASAP. Don't touch it any more than you already have."

"I only touched it once and then put it in a plastic bag for safekeeping."

"Good! I'll be there in ten. Bye, Katrina."

Sandy was alerted when a car drove into the drive. Tim knocked and walked in.

"I'm in here, Tim," Katrina yelled from the lounge.

"Hi, Katrina. Is Philippe here?"

"Yes. He's taking a nap."

"It's alright for some!" He quipped.

"I could do with a nap myself. The wind saps my energy. Anyway. As I said on the phone, the locket is caked in bird droppings, so we assumed it was dislodged from a nest." Katrina said, her words sounding like she was apologising.

"That's okay. DNA testing is extremely accurate these days."

"The wonders of modern science. It can work for or against you, depending on which side of the law you're on."

"Mmm," Cunningham uttered, deep in thought. "I can't begin to imagine how you both feel. The loss of Charlotte has affected my family deeply; in fact, the entire village is in mourning. The news of Charlotte's death was a huge shock to Mrs Barnes, which may have contributed to her death."

"Mrs Barnes had a bad heart for years, and it may have been the shock that killed her. We'll never know for sure." Katrina said regrettably. "Indirectly, whoever attacked Charlotte may have contributed to Mrs Barnes' death. The village has been thrown into turmoil over a gold locket. I realise your family have been affected too, Tim. I know you are doing your utmost to find the culprit, which means a lot to us."

"Even though I'm emotionally attached, I can stay on the case. I owe it to both of you and Charlotte. Celine and I have known Charlotte since she was born and were deeply saddened following her loss. You raised her well and should be proud of yourselves."

"Thanks, Tim. We did our best."

"Would you like a drink?"

"Err! No thanks. I'd better get some work done. I want to get this locket to forensics right away. I'll phone you later." Tim said and disappeared out the door.

The other day, when Cunningham was searching the cemetery, he had no idea that the locket was sitting in a magpie's nest only metres above his head, although it had crossed his mind. If Norman's DNA, fingerprints, or both are detected on the locket, then that evidence alone would be enough to arrest him. He clutched straws, but that straw may turn into a golden thread.

FIFTY-TWO

Rain was forecast for the afternoon, so Gran and I walked around the village while it was dry. Our peaceful stroll was interrupted by the growling of a chainsaw as an arborist cut branches brought down by the recent gale-force winds. As we approached the Post Office, Earnest Barnes attempted to attach a large poster inside the window, and every time he fixed one end, the other end fell. He finally got the sign in place, which read, 'CLOSING DOWN. UP TO 50% OFF. EVERYTHING MUST GO.' A 'For Sale' sign was also attached to the wall.

Earnest Barnes must have locked the Post Office door a million times. It was six o'clock when Earnest peered up and down the lane, locked the door and turned the closed sign for the last time. He glanced up at the brass bell, its spring curled like a chameleon's tongue, bouncing silently. The building appeared larger now that most of the stock had been cleared. The Post Office had been his passion after spending a lifetime behind the glass partition. It got him out of bed in the morning until central cutbacks forced the Post Office to close. That was when he lost interest in the shop, and it was up to Mrs Barnes to keep the business afloat.

Within weeks, a SOLD sign appeared on the Post Office wall, leaving locals wondering who the new owner was. Had a large multinational company bought the building?

Before he left the village for good, Earnest was presented with a nineteenth-century oil painting painted by a local artist. The principal subject was the building before it was a Post Office. In years gone by, the cottage nestled among trees and was edged by open fields, with cows grazing beneath ash trees lining the cart track called Church Lane. How have times changed?

Mum and Dad bought our cottage to escape city noise and pollution. However, due to its proximity to London, a new housing development had turned Ashmarsh into a commuter's paradise. Village culture changed, and the community spirit had all but vanished. The entire village speculated about who had bought the building and their intentions.

Cunningham climbed into his car after placing the bagged locket into his pocket. He drove out of the cottage drive and mistakenly turned left instead of right. He was about to make a U-turn when he noticed wire fencing surrounding the Post Office. For no other reason than curiosity, he stopped the car and eased through a narrow gap in the fence. He stepped into the dark interior and stared at the large, empty space lit by daylight from where the staircase used to be. A commanding male voice caught him off guard.

"What are you doing in 'ere?" The voice echoed, seemingly coming from nowhere. A stocky man stepped from a darkened room. He wore a white helmet, a blue and white checked lumberjack shirt and heavy-duty trousers. Cunningham spun sharply on the terracotta tiles.

"I thought the building was empty."

"And you decided to 'ave a look round while no one was 'ere." The man huffed. "What do you want?"

"I'm DCI Tim Cunningham of Swynbourne CID." He replied, flashing his warrant card.

"Oh. I thought you were one of them travellers. I get all sorts poking around in 'ere. I've gotta be one step ahead of those thieving so n' so's. I can see now the way yer dressed you 'ain't no traveller." They shook hands. "Stan's the name. Site foreman."

"Thank goodness I'm not dressed like a traveller."

Arms by his side, Stan stared at Cunningham with a measured expression.

"I'm a senior intelligence officer in charge of a murder inquiry."

"Is that why you're here? I'm not from around these parts, so I know nothing about a murder. There's not much left of the place, as you can see. You're welcome to look around, but you'll need that." He said, pointing to a grubby safety hat hanging on a nail.

"This was the last place the victim was seen alive."

"In this building? Sorry about that." Stan said. Cunningham swapped hats.

"Have you any objections to me looking in the backyard?"

"Help Yourself."

"Cheers."

Cunningham stepped outside and was confronted by a twenty-foot shipping container dwarfing the walled backyard. Building rubble and knee-high grass and weeds barred his way to the container. Cunningham flattened weeds and fought his way to the giant steel doors, then peered inside at the jumble of shop fittings, rolled carpets, wooden shelves, and cardboard boxes. With hardly any room to move inside the container, he inched along a narrow gap and was momentarily alarmed by his reflection in a large convex mirror. Arms held above his head, he nudged a cardboard box with his elbow and sent it toppling to the floor. The box burst open and spilt its contents, exposing a video recorder, CCTV camera, VHS cassettes, and a bundle of knotted wires. The sight of the equipment triggered a conversation he'd had with Mr and Mrs Barnes about security. At the time, they said they relied heavily on the convex mirror (the one that startled him a moment ago) and Mrs Barnes' sharp eyes for security. A green bracket on the camera suggested it had been fastened to a wall or similar at some point. He bundled them back into the box and was about to leave when he spotted a brass bell on the end of a coiled spring, the same bell that had, over many years, dutifully announced customers entering and leaving the Post Office. Its jingle was probably the last pleasant sound Charlotte heard before the attack. That bell could tell many stories if it could speak, and Cunningham thought the CCTV camera from the shop might tell its own stories.

As he was about to leave the container, rain crashed onto the roof with a deafening roar. The sharp shower quickly to drizzle, allowing him to rush back to the building without getting drenched.

Stan was in the same room he'd materialised from earlier when Cunningham stepped inside, put the box down, and shook his coat to remove raindrops.

"That box of video equipment was in the container. Have you any idea where its contents came from?"

"All the stuff left in the shop was shoved in the container. One of the lads must have stashed it in there."

"So, you're quite sure it came from the shop?"

"Pretty much. What interest are they to you?"

"The recorder may have vital footage."

Stan shrugged.

"You know what you're doing."

Cunningham placed the box on a trestle to focus on the green wooden beam above him. His leather soles scratched on the dusty tiles like fingernails on a blackboard, and his Cashmere coat swirled as he rotated on the spot. *Few customers look above the top shelves*, he thought, peering at the weight-bearing beam running front to back. *The bracket on the video camera is painted the same green.* He examined the beam, end to end, and discovered a small unpainted square with four screw holes. His heart skipped as he looked, first at the shop door and then at the unpainted area. Answers came fast. *If the camera was attached to the unpainted area, the bracket angle suggests it was pointing at the door rather than the cash register.*

"Stan. I'm taking this box with me."

"Keep 'em. They have no market value. Who wants VHS tapes these days, anyway?"

"You're right, Stan. Thanks. I'll give you a receipt."

"Don't worry about it. I hope you find what you're looking for."

The sky had cleared when he swapped hats, ready to leave the building site. The box was too large to fit through the gap in the fence, so he left via the side gate. Cunningham had his hopes set on the tapes, giving up their secrets, and hoped that his clouds of doubt would vanish as quickly as the rain did.

FIFTY-THREE

Time was of the essence. He parked the Chrysler in the Swynbourne police station car park and headed to the Forensics Department. He gave them the locket and told them he needed the results yesterday. He then collected the cardboard box containing the tapes from his car's boot and walked swiftly to the Media Room.

The room was damp and stale after being denied daylight and fresh air since it was commissioned. He disconnected the in-house recorder and connected the video player/recorder from the Post Office using the mishmash of cables. This action automatically initialised the monitor screen. The words, 'No Signal, check connections' were displayed on the monitor. Unperturbed, he checked the wiring. Everything was in order, so he inserted a second cassette and received the same 'No signal, check connections' message. To solve the problem, he disconnected the Post Office recorder and reconnected the in-house video player. A picture appeared on the screen when he inserted the Post Office cassette. *Progress at last.* He fast-forwarded the tape to the date and time of interest, then watched a grainy, low-definition image of Charlotte as she entered the Post Office, then left a few minutes later. What struck him as odd was the dark shadowy figure also caught on tape. Cunningham inched the tape forward and focused on the dark figure passing the shop door from right to left. He printed a screenshot. *'Image enhancement' can clean that up,'* he told himself. Some twenty minutes later, a similar dark figure ran past the shop, travelling from left to right. He printed that image and then flopped into a chair to examine them under a bright light.

FIFTY-FOUR

I'm bored. Everyone is sleeping, and the night is endless, with only the occasional feral cat keeping me company; Sandy will be dreaming doggy dreams, and I wish I could read a book or do something to make the time quickly. Gran had to leave unexpectedly and had left me alone. And I thought the village was boring when I was alive. Grrr! The church bell chimed at 2 a.m., shattering the silence. *Someone must have thought that was a good idea.* A fox barked in a nearby field. Stars twinkled in silence on an inky black backdrop, and I wondered how the Earth would develop when mankind finally discovered they were connected to the universe. As one lonely spirit with a small voice, I may not be able to change mankind's destiny, but I might be able to change one man's mind.

Norman Taylor was beginning to irritate me, so I decided to visit him. When I arrived, Norman was wheezing and snoring in bed. I wanted to throw a shoe to wake him but knew it wouldn't work. Tonight, even the sight of him made me anxious. How could he sleep at night after he'd snatched my life away before it had begun? I despised him and swore I'd make him pay for his crime. Gran reminded me many times to forgive him, to let it go and send him love. I can't do that, well, not until he is safely behind bars where he belongs. Frustration got the upper hand, and it seemed such a shame to do it, but I did it anyway.

"Norman! Wake up!" I yelled, surprised at how loud my voice was. He stopped snoring, but his eyes remained closed.

"Wake up, Norman!" I yelled again, but rather than wake up, he rolled onto his side, smacked his lips, and settled again. *Well, that didn't work.*

Desperate to attract his attention, I sat on his bed and pushed him, but my hand passed through his skinny torso.

"Norman, wake up. I want to talk to you. I heard you when you lied to the police, and now you're playing the victim to receive special treatment. It's time you grew up, took responsibility, and faced the consequences of your mistake."

Norman coughed and turned onto his other side. I found it impossible to wake him. Then, when I was about to leave, Norman switched the bedside light on and scanned the room with narrowed eyes.

"Ha! Fooled you, miss, 'I'm a ghost, and I'm gonna scare the hell out of you,' bloody Duval."

If Norman had one wish, he would wish to be loved. That special person would love him unconditionally to heal his scarred and blackened heart. My stomach churned when he sat up in bed and lit a cigarette. The room filled with smoke, and he had a smug grin. Instead of watching this despicable man, I left him to walk to Isabella's cottage.

When I walked into Isabella's bedroom, which felt intrusive, I noticed her innocence and soft features in the room's low light. I also noticed how shallow and quiet her breathing was. A bookcase was in the space where her oxygen bottle used to live, and on top was a framed photo of me with Sandy by my side. Her biggest wish was to lead a normal life and be given a second chance. Fortunately, a suitable heart became available when she most needed it. The ache of knowing we have no chance of ever growing up together struck me as I roamed her room.

"I miss you." I mused. "I miss singing with you while you played guitar." *I wish Norman Taylor had never been born.*

"I'll leave you to your sweet dreams. Have a wonderful life…" I said, remembering the film of the same name, "…and don't do anything I wouldn't do." I realised that out of the two of us, she was the least likely to get into any trouble. I was about to leave when she whispered something sounding remarkably like my name. *She knows I'm here.*

I left her sleeping and walked along the lonely, empty lane to our cottage. A tabby cat ran across my path but had nothing to do with me. Sandy was wide awake when I arrived, and his eyes seemed to follow me around the kitchen as I walked over to him. He shuffled forward and whined when I knelt in front of his basket.

"I wish you were able to talk," I whispered. "I was proud of you when you barked at Norman in the alley the other day. You did exactly as I asked and didn't harm him. You're such a good boy.

Go to sleep, and I'll see you in the morning." I said goodnight, and he seemed to watch as I left.

This is what happens when I'm bored. I go from one place to another, unfocused and irritable. I roamed the cemetery and lay on my memorial bench. While I was looking up at the stars, I remembered the legend of the homeless man, the one who died here one fateful night. A shooting star distracted me; then, I felt I was being watched. I sat up, and a shiver ran through me. A white-haired older man was standing by a graveside only a stone's throw away and appeared to be watching me. He saw me looking back at him and vanished. I searched the area, but he was gone. Perhaps the dead homeless man is a true story, after all.

FIFTY-FIVE

The room housing the Evidential Image Enhancement Department (EIED) was one floor up from the Media Room. Cunningham climbed the stairs and handed the valuable video cassette to the receptionist. He wrote down the time of the frames he required, and like the locket, he needed results yesterday.

To Cunningham's surprise, an email from EIED arrived that afternoon. He hurriedly opened the attachments, stared at them, and, with a hint of a smile, phoned DC Woodcroft.

"Hi, Woody. Where are you?"

"I'm in the cafeteria, Guv."

"Come back to the office when you're finished. I have something important to show you."

"Alright, Guv. I'll be there in five."

While he waited for DC Woodcroft, Cunningham examined the images closely. A voice at the door surprised Cunningham while deeply engrossed in the photos.

"What is it that you wanted to show me, Guv?" Woodcroft said, tossing a balled cake wrapper in the bin.

"It's all right for some, able to eat while the rest of us do all the work." He said jokingly. He swung the monitor to face Woody.

"Take a look."

"Wow! The date. That's the afternoon of Charlotte's attack."

"Correct. What are your thoughts?"

Woodcroft didn't need reminding that Norman Taylor maintained from day one that he'd stayed home the day Charlotte was attacked. Woody studied the three monochrome images and clucked his tongue.

"Incredible. Where did you get these?"

He printed copies of the photos, highlighted the date and time stamp in one corner, gave Woody a set and kept a set for himself. While Woodcroft studied the images, Cunningham relayed how the video player had landed at his feet while searching the shipping container. He also said that the same security camera (he pointed to the box) used to reside inside the Post Office.

The first image was of Charlotte leaving the shop with the fresh flowers tucked inside her jacket, and the second image showed a male hurrying past the Post Office moments later. The third image showed the same male running in the opposite direction around twenty minutes later, and there was no video evidence of Charlotte returning home that afternoon unless she walked a different route, but that didn't happen. Luckily, the machine stopped working that night. Otherwise, it may have been recorded over, and the images may have been lost forever.

"That's dynamite, Guv. That proves he's been economical on the truth." He said, stabbing the images with a finger. "This evidence can't be refuted. Oh! By the way, I've also received more evidence."

"And you kept this from me because…?"

"…because I received the message on my way here. Forensics have identified the woollen fibres discovered on Charlotte's clothing." Woodcroft said with a blank expression. Cunningham searched Woody's face.

"What else have you not told me?"

"I'm getting to that. As it said in the email from Professor Craig Marsden, forensics discovered tiny fibres from a drawer in Norman's bedroom. The kicker is that those fibres match perfectly, the fibres retrieved from Charlotte's clothing."

"Brilliant, Woody. Got him! I knew it. I'll arrange for an arrest warrant, and then we'll arrest the lying little weasel when he's least expecting it.

FIFTY-SIX

Because the night was growing old, I decided to make one final attempt at reasoning with Norman. I crept up the stairs, sat on the edge of his bed, and watched while he slept. When the time was right, I spoke to him outright.

"Hey, you! Wake up!" I yelled.

Norman shot up and leant on his elbows, heart galloping like a thoroughbred racehorse. Was it the strong coffee he drank in the night that woke him, or was it the ghostly voice in his room?

"'o's there? Show yer' self."

"It's me, Charlotte Duval."

"Nah! That's impossible. She's dead." He said, sitting up and drawing his knees to his chest.

"I am dead, no thanks to you. That's why you can't see me."

"I never killed yer." He said frivolously. "All right. I'll play yer little game. Whaddayawant?" He turned the bedside lamp on and glanced around the room. "Anyway. 'Oo do you think you are, coming 'ere in the middle o' the night and waking me up?"

"I already told you. I'm Charlotte Duval. You attacked me in the cemetery, not that you need reminding. Now that I have your attention, I want you to listen to me."

"I'm on'y awake 'cos a' you."

"Good. What else could I do? You've ignored me all week. Anyway, shut up and listen. In the morning, you will catch the train into Swynbourne, go to the Police Station and hand yourself in. Comprende? I'll be there to make sure you do."

"Yeah, no. I'm not gonna do that. You must be joking. Besides, you can't make me. Now, why don't you clear off and leave me alone?" He demanded, then threw himself back and buried his head under the pillow.

"This is no joking matter, Norman. You're right. I can't force you to do anything, but I can keep you awake all night and every night until you do as I ask."

"It's a good job you're dead, or I'd…"

"Or what? You can't hurt me any more than you already have."

"Pah! You're not real. Go away and annoy someone else."

"Of course, I'm real, but not in the true sense. I'm not going anywhere until you agree to do as I ask."

Norman turned out the light and tucked his pillow around his ears, trying to block my voice.

"Fer God's sake! Why don't yer leave me alone!"

"Stop pretending. I know you can still hear me. Oh, yes! Pretending. You're good at that, aren't you, Norman? You've been proclaiming your innocence and living a lie ever since the police questioned you. The time has come for you to be honest."

Norman muttered an incoherent remark through the pillow, so I sat in the chair by the window and began to talk nonstop. I must have been talking for half an hour when he sat bolt upright in bed and threw the pillow onto the floor.

"All right! All right! You win. 'ave it your way." He yelled, spittle flying into the air. He turned the bedside light back on. "I promise I'll 'and me-self into the police tomorrow if you shuddup and promise not to 'urt me."

"I won't hurt you, Norman. Why would I do that? Although it is tempting, I have to say. You promise to do as I ask?"

"Yeah! Yeah! I promise, but on'y if you promise to leave me alone. I'll be tired tomorrow, no thanks to you."

"Awe, poor thing. Got a busy day, have you? Another female to attack?" Norman huffed and tutted. *This could be fun if it weren't so serious.*

"That's not funny." He snarled and scanned the room with fear flaring his eyelids.

"You can't see me, so you may as well give up."

"Get stuffed." Norman spat.

I delayed going to the light to help arrest Norman. If he confesses tomorrow, my work on earth will be done, and I can go to the light, knowing I stayed for all the right reasons.

"Are you still 'ere?" He probed, then scanned the room again, eyes narrower than a paper cut. I kept quiet to fool him into thinking I had left. Norman retrieved his pillow from the floor and then laid back and relaxed.

"Thank God yer gone. Good riddance. Go to the police and confess…" he cackled and wheezed, "…some 'ope." He cackled again and triggered a coughing fit. His face turned crimson, his eyes bulged as he scrambled for breath, and the veins on his neck protruded like rubber hoses. *Don't you dare die on me, Norman Taylor. Not now.*

FIFTY-SEVEN

An approaching car burrowed through the early morning mist and stopped outside a neglected cottage. Two men stepped quietly from the car, then a neatly dressed, slim male crept down the side of a house, while the other, bigger-built male walked silently, other than the swishing of his unbuttoned coat, down the path to the cottage door. He banged on the door, making a dog bark in the distance.

Charlotte was grateful Norman had survived his coughing fit and was asleep when his reptilian brain alerted him of imminent danger. After glancing at the bedside clock, he donned his dressing gown, all the while wondering who was trying to break down his door at this hour. He peaked through a gap in the bedroom curtains, and his heart skipped a beat when he saw a large car parked in the lane. He fled to his parents' old bedroom, peered through the curtains, and saw a dark figure lurking in the shadowy backyard. Charlotte watched Norman shoot downstairs and freeze when he saw the shape of another shadowy figure through the opaque door glass. A second round of thumping on the door prompted a response.

"'old yer blinkin' 'orses. As if 'aving that kid talkin' and keeping me awake all night wasn't bad enough," he muttered, inching the door open to see who his caller was, through the narrow gap.

"What…" Before Norman finished his sentence, and with lightning speed, Cunningham thrust the arrest warrant through the gap and forced the door open, sending Norman sliding backwards across the hall floor.

"Norman Taylor, I'm arresting you on suspicion of the murder of Charlotte Duval. You do not have to say anything, but it may…"

Now awake and alert, using every ounce of his paltry strength, Norman ran at Cunningham and pushed him aside, then ran up the garden path and vanished in the mist. It took Cunningham a moment to gather his wits, and then he ran up the path after Norman, losing his hat on the way. Woodcroft sensed something wasn't right and ran to the front of the house. Cunningham was on his hands and knees, searching under his car.

"Did you drop your keys, Guv?"

"Hmph. If only it were that simple. The weasel gave me the slip." He whispered and clambered to his feet, letting out a grunt. "You go that way, and I'll wait here in case the maggot doubles back. He can't have gone far; he's no Usain Bolt."

Norman was young and rebellious when he first discovered cigarettes. That choice was now taking its toll. So, after dashing down the lane, wheezing and exhausted, he needed to rest and leaned against a wall to catch his breath. How he regretted those years of smoking. With his last reserve of strength and using his body weight, he pivoted over the wall and landed in an untidy heap in the confinement of a small backyard. Vulnerable and exposed, he fought for every breath, then crawled across the frost-covered concrete to conceal himself. In a twist of fate, the walls that cloaked him while he stalked Charlotte were now the walls in which he sought refuge. Once the hunter, now the hunted.

FIFTY-EIGHT

Inadequate street lighting barely penetrated the mist. Norman was grateful for the anonymity and made doubly sure he wouldn't be discovered by hiding behind a wheelie bin like a scared rabbit. Woodcroft searched every garden, nook, cranny, and passageway, crisscrossing the village like rat runs. It was both time-consuming and frustrating.

Running hadn't been such a good idea, and he stifled a cry of pain when his leg went into spasm. With no choice but to remain hidden and wearing only a dressing gown, he edged nearer to the wheelie bin and shivered in the bitterly cold night. His wheezing softened, allowing him to control his foggy breath, trying its hardest to betray him. Charlotte joined in the search, and it didn't take her long to discover Norman. She had the advantage of the ability to pass through walls to quicken her search. She wanted to call the detectives, then realised only Norman could hear her.

Cunningham used his phone to light the area while he waited for Woodcroft to return. A black cat darted across his path and ran behind a hedge; it, too, searched in the night. Woodcroft appeared through the mist while a plume of rising condensation caught Cunningham's attention. He put a finger to his lips, then pointed to a wheelie bin in a nearby yard. Woodcroft saw the rising mist and acknowledged with a nod. He leapt over the wall and landed silently in the yard, then crept towards the wheelie bin, yanked it to one side, and was surprised to find a domestic boiler outlet with steam rising into the air. He huffed and kicked the bin, sending it scooting across the yard. With gritted teeth, he scaled the wall back to Cunningham, shaking his head in disbelief.

"Why don't you make a bit more noise, Woody?" Whispered Cunningham sarcastically. "Taylor will know where we are now. The entire village will know where we are."

"Sorry, Guv. I thought we had him."

"Yeah, me too. Keep searching; the maggot can't have gone far."

Both detectives knew it was only a matter of time before Norman was found.

"You may as well give yourself up, Norman. Do it before you catch pneumonia." Charlotte said to Norman. Norman ignored her, and her constant bickering had made him doubly sure not to get caught. His flimsy dressing gown wasn't providing adequate protection from the cold, and he agreed with Charlotte that he could catch pneumonia. He cursed under his breath and prayed for the opportunity to run to the place he'd hidden when a youngster was found dead in the stream many years ago. The thought stirred a memory, but with more pressing matters on his mind, he let it go. Footsteps and whispering voices grew louder as minutes ticked by.

Their search led them to two rows of tiny cottages known as Narrow Lane. Cunningham stopped Woody with his hand and pointed to a walled yard. His keen eye had spotted another steam cloud swirling into the air. Woodcroft rolled his eyes.

"I'm not falling for that again, Guv," he whispered.

"Go over and check it out. We can't afford to miss an opportunity. Try not to make as much noise this time."

Cunningham mouthed, 'Go.' Instead of leaping heroically over the wall, Woodcroft opened the gate and crept towards the wheelie bin, identical to the one he'd kicked halfway across a yard earlier. Were they naked footprints in the frost, or was it a trick of the light? Unconvinced, Woody dragged the bin away from the wall and was shocked to find a shivering Norman Taylor curled into a tight ball next to a boiler chimney outlet. Woodcroft grabbed Norman's wrist. Tired and spent, Norman fell face down onto the cold and hard concrete.

"Don't 'it me," he pleaded and cowered on the ground.

"Stay where you are, and you won't get hurt. You're under arrest, Taylor."

Norman coughed and spat on the concrete.

"Dirty hound," Woodcroft remarked. In no mood for niceties, his patience was thinning. Unruffled by Norman's gaping dressing gown exposing him, Woodcroft gave him an order.

"On your feet. Hands behind your back!"

Cunningham joined them in the yard.

"Why 'are you arresting me? I ain't done nothin' wrong."

"Then why did you run?"

"I was scared," Norman said, then spat on the ground again and muttered something under his breath. The commotion woke the villagers, who came outside to film something they knew nothing about. Charlotte was elated. Her job was done, but would she finally be free to go to the light?

"Go back inside. Nothing to see here." Woodcroft advised onlookers. Cunningham cautioned Norman, then Woodcroft frogmarched him back to his house and propelled him through the open door. Norman stubbed his toe on the step.

"Ow!! Go easy. That was me damn toe." Norman complained, but his plaintive whimpers went ignored.

"Go upstairs, get dressed, and be quick about it. And don't even think about doing another runner. We've had enough of your shenanigans for one day. Next time, we might not be so gentle."

Woodcroft pushed Norman upstairs, and like a reluctant child dressing for school, he slowly pulled on a pair of jeans.

"It's your fault." Norman accused. Woodcroft raised an eyebrow.

"I beg your pardon?"

"Not you. I'm talking to 'er." Norman said, voice thicker than treacle.

"There's no one else here. Now get a move on; we haven't got all day."

"Whatever!" He said, waving a hand indifferently.

"Why was it my fault? I did nothing to provoke you." Charlotte said, in her defence.

"There you go again. Yap, yappity, yap. Clear off!"

Woodcroft scowled

"Who are you talking to?"

"Some kid. She kept me awake by talking all night, and now she's at it ag'en."

Woodcroft sighed wearily.

"It's all in your mind, Taylor. Nothing medication can't fix."

"I'll leave you alone once you're behind bars."

"Clear off. I don't wanna listen to your twaddle."

"That's enough," Woodcroft ordered and prodded Norman to get dressed. "I've had it up to here with your delaying tactics. Stop dawdling, and put your shoes on."

"Give us a chance. I'm knackered."

"You've had your chance; now get a move on!"

Woodcroft handcuffed Norman's hands behind his back when he was finally dressed.

"When was the last time you had a shower?"

"None o' your damn business." Norman sneered and muttered 'tosser' under his breath.

"That's DI Tosser to you, Taylor."

Villagers gathered in the lane to watch Norman being guided into the back seat of Cunningham's car. Woodcroft stared at the frost-covered windscreen and sighed as Norman leaned his head against the window and gazed at his house.

The investigation's progress had been slow initially but had gained exceptional momentum. Before returning to his car,

Cunningham closed Norman's door and retrieved his trilby from the garden.

The trio sat comfortably in the car as the engine sprang to life. While the windscreen was clearing, both detectives silently reflected on the morning's extraordinary events. The only sound above the heater blower was Norman's rattly chest.

Charlotte didn't want to miss out on one of the most critical interviews she would ever have witnessed and hitched a ride to Swynbourne Police Station in the back of Cunningham's car.

FIFTY-NINE

Interview.

Part 1.

Left waiting in a small holding cell for the duty solicitor, Norman's nicotine levels plummeted, and his anxiety increased. He nervously chewed on his paint-encrusted fingers. After weeks of stress and lies, he had reached the edge. Norman was smart enough to realise he was in deep trouble but not clever enough to wiggle out of it.

Dragged from a warm bed, alone in Interview Room 1, duty solicitor Sean O'Dowd examined paperwork while waiting for his client to be brought in. Norman was taken to the interview room and grunted when he saw the duty solicitor. O'Dowd continued to read paperwork while Norman sat, nervously tapping a foot.

Cunningham and Woodcroft's strategy was to keep Norman waiting and give him time to reflect on the trouble he was in. They finally arrived in the interview room and sat in chairs opposite O'Dowd and Taylor. Cunningham dropped a manila folder on the desk and opened the pages. O'Dowd shuffled papers and huffed. Charlotte read over Cunningham's shoulder, then leaned against the wall until Cunningham finished with formalities. Norman folded his arms and stared at them.

"In case you're in any doubt…" Cunningham said firmly, "…you are under arrest on suspicion of murder, and we're here to talk to you about the death of Charlotte Duval. I'll get straight to the point." As Cunningham flipped through the folder's pages, he could hear Norman's rapid, wheezy breathing.

"Let's start with the locket," Cunningham began, "A locket belonging to Charlotte Duval was recently found in Ashmarsh cemetery, and when tested, your DNA was detected. Explain to me how the locket came into your possession."

Cunningham began with a soft approach. His disarming method often put the accused at ease. Norman stroked his eyebrows while Cunningham attempted to penetrate Norman's multifaceted layers. Thoughts danced across Norman's brow as he searched the far recesses of his mind for a reply. If he told them he'd taken it from her after he'd jumped on her, he would undoubtedly go to prison. Thinking that Norman hadn't understood the question, Cunningham rephrased it.

"When did you hold Charlotte's locket?"

"I-I found it."

"Where did you find it?"

"On the village green, I think. I was gonna 'and it in, but l lost it." He said, shrugging his shoulders. Woodcroft stepped in.

"You *think* you found the locket on the village green? You don't sound too sure. Did you find the locket before or after you attacked Charlotte?" He accused. O'Dowd clicked his pen and settled his glasses with his finger.

"You don't have to say anything that might self-incriminate, Mr Taylor," O'Dowd advised.

"I'll rephrase the question. Did you take the locket from Charlotte while she lay unconscious?"

"You can answer with a no comment," O'Dowd said. "DC Woodcroft. You know better than to ask leading questions."

"I already told yer; I found it on the village green. If it was found in the cemetery, then that's where I must've lost it. What more can I say?"

"Now's the time to confess," Charlotte said, interrupting a shocked Norman. He glanced over his shoulder and scowled. "You promised me," she added.

"Gawd! Not you agen. Can't you leave me alone?" He mumbled.

"Pardon? I didn't quite catch that." Woodcroft said.

"It's that stupid kid talkin' to me ag'en." Norman glanced over his shoulder while the other three exchanged puzzled glances.

"What kid? The one you were talking to at your house?"

"Yeah. The one that kept me awake nearly all night."

"Don't call me stupid. I can hear you. If you don't confess, things may become awkward."

"GO AWAY!" He said, clenching his jaw.

"Confess now, and make it easier for yourself. Listen to them. No way will you walk away from this. I'll make sure of that."

O'Dowd stared at Norman over the top of his glasses, and the detectives looked at each other in amazement. Norman fidgeted.

"Giza fag." He demanded, holding his grubby left hand out like a beggar. Cunningham slammed his hand on the desk.

"Not this time, Taylor."

"Come on, Norman." Charlotte pleaded. "The situation is different now. It's time to admit your crime. How do you think my Mum and Dad feel? What if you'd drowned in the stream instead of that boy?" She tried to reason. "How do you think your Mum and Dad would have felt? Confess now, and it will end."

With the same piteous expression he'd used on Cunningham, Norman turned to O'Dowd and begged for a cigarette. O'Dowd shook his head and held his hands in an open palm gesture. Norman leapt to his feet.

"You can't deny me a smoke. I know me rights."

"SIT DOWN!" Bellowed Cunningham. "You'll have all the time in the world for a smoke by the time we finish with you. May I remind you that this is a murder inquiry? Show some respect."

Norman sneered and slouched in the chair, sulking like a chastised child. His lies weren't working, but because he was vague and evasive, the interview wasn't progressing, so Cunningham upped the game.

"OK. Stop playing games, Taylor. You wrote in a previous statement, and I quote, 'I was at home the weekend Charlotte was attacked because I had a cold.' Are you sticking to that story?"

"Yeh. Of course. I never went out all weekend."

"Liar!" Charlotte yelled. Norman jerked his head around, then turned to face the two detectives. Cunningham leaned in closer.

"Look at me when I'm talking to you. Are you sure you didn't go out?"

"Positive. Why?"

"Because we have evidence to prove otherwise. That's why."

"Pah! What evidence?"

Cunningham by name, cunning by nature. He drip-fed Norman, giving him plenty of time to ponder his situation and realise more evidence was stacked against him than he could imagine.

"We have photographic evidence of you walking past the Post Office on the afternoon of the attack and running in the opposite direction twenty-two minutes later."

"Allegedly," O'Dowd interjected. Norman smirked.

"What photographic evidence?"

"We have footage recovered from the Post Office surveillance camera."

Norman froze. His brow wrinkled, he scratched his head and fidgeted in the chair.

"That video, recorded on Saturday, November 25th, shows you wearing similar clothing to a person seen at the cemetery gates that afternoon." Norman turned to O'Dowd with a helpless expression of, 'why won't you say something,' written across his face."

"That alone proves you are lying. You did leave your house that Saturday afternoon, didn't you, Taylor?" Cunningham paused. "What have you got to say for yourself?"

"You're trying to trick me. Tell 'em." Norman said, addressing O'Dowd. "There was no camera in the Post Office; on'y a big mirror."

"There was a mirror. Yes. But there was also a camera pointing at the glass-panelled door." Cunningham pulled the photos from the folder and laid them neatly on the desk.

"Perhaps these will refresh your memory."

O'Dowd studied the photos. Norman waved a dismissive hand, then said, with a voice like a coughing cat. "I pass the shop loads of times. The time and date could 'of been set wrong. 'ow do you even know it was the right day?"

"The time and date are correct as we were able to ascertain the time and date using video verification techniques."

"Aw! There yer go ag'en with yer fancy words."

It was Woodcroft's turn.

"Never mind the fancy words. The morning newspapers are dropped off at the Post Office around the same time every morning. On the day in question, a clear shot of the front page was caught on camera when the driver carried the newspapers inside. We contacted the Daily Times, and they confirmed the time on the video corresponded to the correct date and approximate time of drop-off. That's how Norman." Woodcroft said, slamming a definitive hand on the desk. Charlotte spoke in the subsequent silence.

"You can't deny the facts, Norman. Evidence is stacking up against you, and it's time you told them the truth."

Norman waved off Charlotte's comments. O'Dowd examined the images in detail while repeatedly clicking his pen. He touched Norman on the arm.

"Remember, Mr Taylor. You have the right to remain silent."

"I know that." He barked and yanked his arm free. "That don't prove nothin'. Maybe I got me days mixed up."

"In that case, are you admitting you left your house on Saturday, November 25th?"

"I dunno. I forget. Anyway — that person looks nuffin' like me."

"That would be for a jury to decide. Those pictures prove you left your house and were near the Post Office when Charlotte called in to buy flowers." Woodcroft said, stabbing the date stamp on the images with a finger. "Facial recognition gave a ninety-five per cent probability match, despite most of the face being covered by a scarf.

"Let's go over the facts. One. A witness saw you outside the cemetery gates that afternoon. Two. Traces of your DNA were detected on Charlotte's locket. Three. And here's something you don't know. Samples of woollen fibres taken from your chest of drawers matched fibres recovered from Charlotte's clothing. That puts you at the scene, Taylor!" Woodcroft yelled, slamming a hand on the desk again. Norman jumped. "Let that sink in. We have you fair and square, Taylor, so you may as well admit your crime."

Beads of sweat clung to Norman's forehead, and his stench became unbearable. Cunningham quietly cleared his throat.

"The coroner's report said the bruising to Charlotte's throat was made by someone left-handed. You're a southpaw, aren't you?" Cunningham stated.

"Yes. I know what a southpaw is. There's loads of us left 'anded people."

"So, you admit that you're left-handed."

"Yeh. What difference does that make?"

"Let me spell it out to you. We have hard evidence to satisfy CPS of an unlawful killing. If you plead not guilty, and we go to trial, then we have enough evidence to satisfy a jury beyond all reasonable doubt. Think about that for a moment."

SIXTY

Interview.

Part 2

Cunningham allowed Norman to take a break before continuing with the interview.

After their break, they sat around the table, and there was an awkward silence before the interview resumed.

"I hope you've had time to consider your situation during the break," was Cunningham's opening line.

A confused and frightened Norman fidgeted in the chair, and as frenzied expressions darted across his face, Charlotte rolled her eyes while she rested against the back wall. Norman slumped forward and covered his head to escape the world. He tapped his foot rhythmically and drummed his fingers like a frantic piano player. O'Dowd clicked his pen to the point of annoyance, and Cunningham and Woodcroft glared at Norman, now burying his face. Charlotte launched herself off the wall.

"Right, Norman! It's time to face your responsibilities, and I mean it!"

Norman uncovered his ears.

"Leave — me — alone!" He growled.

"End this now, Norman." She demanded. "You and I know your attack led to my death, and Cunningham can prove it. Admit your guilt, and I'm sure the judge will consider the fact that you didn't intend to harm me." She breathed a deep, juddering breath as memories of that ill-fated afternoon washed over her.

"If only you could see how your actions have affected me, even in spirit." She inched closer. "I'm so sorry you had a terrible upbringing. Even if kids did call you names, that's no excuse for your behaviour as an adult. I'm sorry your parents are no longer with you and left you to cope alone. I'm sure they would plead with you to accept your responsibilities if they were here." She paused, giving him time to reflect.

His actions were like ripples in a pond, and her death changed the lives of everyone she knew.

After his unscheduled dash for freedom, sleep deprivation, and nicotine withdrawal, Norman had taken on the appearance of an old goblin. Tired and weary due to Charlotte's incessant heckling, he sat up, jaw tighter than a crossbow. Charlotte was relentless.

"Norman. I know you're ignoring me. You can't see me but listen. I'm on my knees, begging you to tell the truth."

"What have you got to say for yourself, Norman?" Cunningham said in a nurturing tone. "Perhaps I haven't made myself clear. Here's the situation. You maintained you stayed home that weekend, but we have evidence to prove you left your home at least once. Your DNA was detected on Charlotte's locket. Fibres from your bedroom drawer matched fibres on Charlotte's clothing, and we have video footage of you outside the Post Office before Charlotte was attacked." Cunningham said, then leant forward. "You are in serious trouble. Do you understand?"

Norman closed his eyes and began to rock and hum.

"A jury will find you guilty, and the judge will take a dim view that you denied your connection with Charlotte's attack. Think about it." Cunningham said, then relaxed back in the chair. His cold stare drilled into Norman. Charlotte continued to plead with Norman.

"Do you think I'm enjoying being in the same room as you? It was bad enough sitting next to you in Cunningham's car. All you have done is lie. Evidence is stacked against you, Norman, and you still won't tell the truth. I can't tell you how much pain and misery you've caused. I hope you're feeling pleased with yourself."

Norman glanced over his shoulder, then cleared his throat.

"Fer goodness' sake, leave it out, will yer before you drive me nuts."

"You'd better not be talking to me!" Cunningham said. The other three exchanged glances while Norman spoke to himself. The atmosphere grew tense when Norman leapt up from the chair, leaned across the desk, and stared at Cunningham. Woodcroft raised a hand to the camera, signalling assistance to wait. Eyes bulging and face redder than a post box, he glowered at Cunningham for ten seconds, then…

"All right! All right!" He yelled and stepped away from the desk.

"It was me. I did it, but I never meant to 'arm 'er. It was an accident."

O'Dowd stopped clicking his pen. The two detectives froze. Charlotte palmed her mouth, and the room fell deathly silent.

"Oh My God, Norman." She said and touched his shoulder. He turned.

"I 'ope yer satisfied?" He yelled, angrier than a provoked dog. "Maybe you'll leave me alone now."

O'Dowd tried to stop Norman from saying anything that might incriminate him further. Cunningham and Woodcroft exchanged glances. O'Dowd stood.

"I'd like to speak with my client alone."

"Too late," Woodcroft said. O'Dowd settled down while Cunningham and Woodcroft stared at Norman with relief.

At that moment, everything came together like an implosion. They now had answers to all the questions that had troubled them from the start of their investigation.

SIXTY-ONE

For weeks, Norman's explosive admission dissolved the burden of guilt that had hung over his head like a dark cloud. Guilt affects the physical body, and shame is a close companion. If neither are dealt with and dispelled, a person may unwittingly shackle themselves to a lifetime of chronic pain and misery. Due to a complex childhood, Norman's guilt was eased temporarily when he burned his clothing in his back garden. He had been shackled by guilt ever since that ill-fated afternoon when he made a bad choice, but today's confession set him emotionally free.

Norman explained to the detectives how he waited in his bay window for Charlotte to walk past, then followed her to the cemetery without her knowledge. The decision to leap out and surprise her was part of his game. Close enough to smell her perfume, he panicked and pushed her away. He had no idea why he pounced on her and pinned her to the ground, but Charlotte struggled and fought him when he tried to touch her exposed skin. For the first time in his life, he felt in control. Unfortunately, she screamed, and he clamped a hand over her mouth to silence her. The more she struggled, the harder he pressed. He kept her locket for personal reasons and was devastated when he lost it.

He signed a statement, and dragging the combination of relief and fear behind him, Norman was led downstairs, then along a corridor to a gloomy cell.

With only his thoughts for company, Norman had ample time to reflect on his actions and to contemplate his future. Que sera, sera. (What will be, will be.)

He lay in the foetal position as ruthless visions soured his dreams through the night. These were the same horrors and nightmares he experienced as a child. After a sleepless night, an unyielding mattress, and a narrow strip of light streaming in from under the door, he sat up and swung his legs to the floor. Reality hit him hard, and he soon realised that his liberty had been snatched away faster than a swipe from the back of his mother's hand. His childhood perceptions of confinement, true or false, were nothing compared to last night. Every unfamiliar sound reverberated in the featureless cell and triggered anxiety. How could he improve his miserable life if he was to be imprisoned at Her Majesty's pleasure for decades? What had he achieved in his life? How did he sleep on a pillow so hard he could hear his heartbeat in his ear? His game had ended in tragedy. How could it have gone so wrong? Last night was far worse than Charlotte's night-long torment. A child who failed to reach cognitive development milestones was finding it impossible to cope in an adult world. A boy trapped in a man's body, he loathed his deceased mother while, at the same time, longing to be in the comfort of her arms.

"Are you there?" He called quietly. "Charlotte? Are you in there? If you can 'ear me, I want you to know I never meant to 'arm yer. I didn't mean to push you so 'ard. I panicked. I've never been that close to a female before. I'm sorry you died. Will you forgive me?" Norman had no way of knowing whether Charlotte heard his plea or not.

Thrown to the wolves in a dog-eat-dog world ruled by hardened criminals lacking empathy, their warped principles were created for one purpose only — survival. He would be eaten alive in prison and was about to be punished for wanting to be loved and needed, making him no different from any other male.

His mother's hatred for him may have been out of fear of having another mouth to feed, of never having enough. They struggled financially after Norman was born, and his mother begrudged every penny spent on his upbringing. Had Norman been an unplanned pregnancy they couldn't afford? Right or wrong, he took the blame for her problems.

Charlotte deeply regretted the name-calling directed at Norman when she was too young to know better. Today, she felt nothing but empathy for him, especially after he had admitted his crime. She'd worked hard to bring him to justice, but her ultimate concern was his mental state.

In a matter of hours, Charlotte's parents would learn the truth; a bittersweet truth Sweet — the relief of knowing their daughter's killer had been caught. And bitter — because the culprit was a neighbour, someone they had given nothing but friendship and compassion.

SIXTY-TWO

The Chrysler's headlights frightened a feral cat, which ran for cover. Katrina saw the car lights from the kitchen window and hurried to greet Cunningham at the door. She invited him in, took him to the kitchen, and offered him a seat.

Unearthing the truth from Norman was like shelling winkles, and indicative of a long and tedious past forty-eight hours, he had dark circles under his eyes. Philippe, dressed in an old pair of jeans and floppy jumper, joined them in the kitchen.

"I thought I heard voices. Hi Tim. Wow! You look tired."

"That's an understatement. I've had a couple of demanding days. Anyway. I'm glad you're both here. I was on my way home and wanted to give you the news before it went to air. We've had a breakthrough with Charlotte's case."

Philippe held Katrina's hand at the kitchen table, expecting it to be bad news.

"What kind of breakthrough?" Asked Katrina, eager to know.

"We arrested a male early yesterday morning on suspicion of Charlotte's murder. He initially denied the charge, but when questioned at length, and with evidence stacked against him, he finally admitted the charge."

Katrina was left speechless as the phrase, 'Charlotte's murder,' hit her with the speed of a striking snake. Her head was in a whirl as the kitchen walls collapsed in on her, trapping her in a tiny, suffocating cube. Although she'd longed for the news, the impact hit her hard, and she struggled to catch her breath until the kitchen walls expanded again.

"Is he local?" Philippe enquired. Tim stared long and hard. What effect will it have when he tells them?

"It will sound better coming from me. You'll find out soon enough, anyway. He is local and lives down the lane."

"What? In our village? Do we know him?"

"Yes. He's well known." Tim paused before dropping the bombshell. "Norman Taylor."

"Norman Taylor?" Katrina echoed, palming her mouth.

"Yes." He said, glancing at the photo of Charlotte on the Welsh dresser. "He lives in the same street..." Tim's voice trailed off as Katrina and Philippe stared vacantly at the table, creating a mental image of Charlotte.
"Norman Taylor, from number eleven? How could he do such a terrible thing to our daughter? We offered help when his parents died, and he does this in return."

Tim toyed with the brim of his trilby. "We thought we would have to take it to trial until he finally admitted the attack."

"Why? — Why? Charlotte wouldn't harm anyone. She didn't have a nasty bone in her body. Did he offer an explanation?"

"Indirectly. The attack wasn't pre-meditated, and he said her fall was an accident."

"Accident? As if that makes it okay. He's only saying that to save his own skin."

"Don't, Katrina," Philippe said. "It's over now." He squeezed Katrina's hand, then looked up at Tim. "Why did it take him so long to admit it?"

"He thought we didn't have enough evidence to convict him, so he tried to lie his way out of it. Unfortunately for him, his DNA was on Charlotte's locket, which he couldn't deny. He said he took the locket because it was shiny and belonged to Charlotte. Then he lost it somewhere, and you know the rest of that story."

Katrina recalled the moment she discovered the locket and earring in the cemetery. The locket belonged to her grandmother, which meant a great deal to her when her mother gave it to her on her thirteenth birthday. She kept it around her neck until the day came for her to gift it to Charlotte on her thirteenth birthday. She unconsciously felt for her neckline. *Will I ever see the locket again?'* She returned to the now.

"Was the amount of his DNA on the locket sufficient evidence to charge him?"

"It was one of the reasons why he confessed. But we uncovered other, rather unexpected evidence."

Tim explained how he had accidentally discovered the security tape in the shipping container.

"The camera pointed to the shop doorway. Do you remember, Katrina?" Philippe interjected. Katrina gave him a hard stare, and he stopped talking, allowing Tim to continue.

"I spoke to Ernest Barnes about the CCTV recorder, and he remembered it stopped working in November. Rather than have it repaired, he unplugged it, left it in the back room where it became buried beneath clutter and forgotten."

"What was on the security tape that was so important?" Katrina asked.

Tim relayed the story of the video footage and how critical it was in solving the crime. "Additionally, his clothes matched the description of a person seen outside the cemetery gates late that afternoon, the same clothes the person wore in the video footage."

"Amazing. The video may have remained lost for years if the shop hadn't been sold recently." Katrina remarked.

"It would have surfaced eventually but may have been too late for our investigation. And the camera was taken for granted, I suppose. It was a vital clue that never occurred until I found the video recorder in the shipping container. I wouldn't have found it if I had turned right instead of left from your driveway that day."

"It was as though you were guided to that shipping container. Synchronicity, or St Anthony." Katrina remarked.

"St Anthony?" Tim queried.

"Yes. The patron Saint of finding lost and stolen articles."

Tim was puzzled. *Why had he never heard of St Anthony?*

"Thank goodness for Saints and modern technology. He couldn't deny it with the evidence you had against him. So, what happened next?" Philippe asked.

"I will sit if you don't mind," Cunningham said, pulling a chair out from under the table.

"Fibres taken from a chest of drawers in Norman's bedroom matched foreign fibres discovered on Charlotte's clothing. With that, we had evidence to present to CPS and enough to convince a jury beyond all reasonable doubt if Norman had pleaded not guilty. But he admitted the crime, so we don't need to take the case to trial."

Philippe and Katrina stared at each other with meaningful expressions. No words were necessary.

"There is one more thing, and I shouldn't be telling you this, but as parents, you have the right to know."

"It won't go any further, Tim," Philippe said.

"On several occasions during the interview, Norman claimed a female was hounding him. There was no female in the room. No one else in the room saw or heard anyone, so we assumed he was having a mental breakdown. He said the voice pleaded with him to confess and had been harassing him all night. It drove him crazy, and he eventually gave in to her taunts."

"A voice badgered him into confessing? How strange?" Katrina said, eyes wide with interest.

"It was very odd to witness, and in all my years at the job, I've never experienced anything like it. This may sound crazy. I wouldn't normally mention anything like this to grieving parents, but Norman said the girl claimed her name was Charlotte and said to repeat the words Elephant Juice and the name Beatrice to her parents."

Katrina stared at Philippe with her mouth wide open.

"I told you Charlotte was still with us, didn't I, Philippe? Elephant Juice was our private joke. It must be her because Norman couldn't possibly know Charlotte's middle name. Now, do you believe me, Philippe?"

"Charlotte's full name was on her Order of Service leaflet." He argued.

"Norman wasn't at Charlotte's funeral so he couldn't have seen the Order of Service leaflet. I doubt she ever told him her middle name or ever mentioned Elephant Juice, for that matter. I don't think she ever spoke to him, so how could that be possible?" She claimed.

Philippe wasn't convinced about the afterlife, but rubbed Katrina's shoulder in acknowledgement. She glanced at Charlotte's photo on the Welsh dresser and mouthed, 'Elephant Juice.' Sandy clambered from his basket and, with pinpoint accuracy, sat between Katrina's feet and gazed at her with hopeful eyes.

"Who's a clever boy then?" Katrina said, cradling his muzzle. "You were trying to tell me it was Norman when you barked and snarled at him, weren't you, a-a-a-y? It would have saved

Tim a lot of time if you could speak. Who's a clever boy then, a-a-a-y?"

"It's a tremendous relief, knowing that Charlotte's attacker has been apprehended. You had your suspicions about him all along, Tim. We can't thank you enough. You've done a great job, not only as a detective but as a friend." Philippe said.

"I can't take the credit. It was a team effort." Cunningham glanced at his watch, stood, and edged towards the door. "Listen. I know it's a lot to take in, and I wish I could stay longer, but I must get home. The boys will have forgotten what I look like," He joked.

"Incidentally. Norman will appear in court tomorrow, and because he pleaded guilty, I expect he'll receive a lesser sentence. Involuntary manslaughter would be my guess."

After hearing the news, Philippe turned to Katrina, who could no longer hold back her emotions. Her chin dimpled, and her expression of relief was not wailing or screaming but a sorrowful, rolling, boiling emotion. Philippe cradled her in his arms.

"Taylor's fingerprints weren't found at the scene because his fingers are coated in paint. Despite the lack of fingerprints, forensics did an amazing job. It's them you should be thanking, not me." Cunningham half smiled and turned to leave. "Hopefully, the news will bring you closure."

"Will we have to appear in court?" Philippe asked.

"No, but you can view from the public gallery. One other thing. TV crews will be waiting outside the court, and I expect they'll be at your gate before long."

"Thanks, Tim. Thanks for all your hard work — you and your team." Katrina said, dabbing her tears.

"Wouldn't that prove the attack was premeditated if he deliberately covered his fingers in paint?"

"Sounds plausible. But the truth is, when we searched Taylor's house a second time, we found a concealed door leading to Norman's art studio. Inside the studio were dozens of paintings, mostly of Charlotte. Some wouldn't look out of place in an art gallery. We believe he was obsessed with Charlotte and had no real intention of harming her."

"How creepy. So, he told the truth in the end." Katrina commented.

"Yes. He wasn't trying to conceal his fingerprints; he rarely cleaned the paint from his hands. Our investigations would have been much easier had we found his prints at the scene." Cunningham said sadly. "I hope you're not too upset with the news. I'm relieved, too. I expect it'll come as a shock to Celine; she doesn't know yet. I'd better go. I'll call you later." He said, opening the front door. "…and don't forget to watch out for the media invasion."

"Thanks for the reminder, Tim," Philippe said, closing the front door with agony indelibly imprinted across his forehead. He leaned against the door, looked up at the ceiling and whispered a prayer.

Katrina had her back turned when he returned to the kitchen, and a photo of Charlotte was in her hand. She shuddered when Philippe pulled her close.

🐘

The recent news about Norman Taylor hit Katrina at the speed of light. Philippe turned her around slowly and kissed her salty tears.

As a child, Charlotte ran around the cottage like a whirling dervish. She fell, seamlessly climbed to her feet, and ran off again. Katrina remembered that. After Charlotte had uttered her first words, she talked constantly, even when no one was listening. She remembered that. Katrina's grandmother was clairvoyant, and it didn't faze Katrina when Charlotte spoke about seeing a lady in a white lacy dress. She said the lady always wore a cream bonnet with pink roses, white lace-up shoes, a frilly parasol, and a matching purse. She remembered that, too. Charlotte saw a girl with curly hair on TV and wanted her hair to be like that. She twisted her hair around her fingers to make it curl. She remembered that, too. It was as though all of Charlotte's birthdays were only yesterday. Her most vivid recollection was of Charlotte's twelfth birthday when Sandy was welcomed into the family. Charlotte always knew when Christmas was near. Dad sat the fairy on top of the tree in the front garden, and from that night on, she searched the sky for Santa and his reindeer before being tucked into bed with a goodnight kiss. She remembered that, too. She smiled at the memories of Charlotte's childhood and was glad they of the sixteen wonderful years filled with treasured memories.

SIXTY-THREE

Clunks, bangs, and voices in the lane woke Philippe from a deep slumber. He checked the time: It was five-thirty. Disturbances in a sleepy village at this hour were unacceptable. He slid out of bed and peered through a gap in the curtains to see where the noise came from. Annoyed by what he saw from the window, Philippe stormed back to bed and unintentionally disturbed Katrina.

"Sorry. Did I wake you?"

"No. I heard noises. I thought I was dreaming."

"It's the media. They're setting up camp in the lane. Tim was right. How dare they disturb the entire neighbourhood at this hour? All they want is a punchy headline and a sensational storyline. It's just a game to them." He huffed. "Have they no compassion? I'm in two minds whether to go outside and ask them to leave."

"What, in your boxers?" Katrina said, then playfully elbowed him in the ribs. "That would give them a punchy headline."

"Ha, ha. Very funny."

"They will hound you for a story if you go outside. Ignore them. They'll leave if they think we're not at home."

"I have to go to work."

"Take the day off. I'm sure work can cope without you for one day. You deserve a day off after yesterday's bombshell. They'll provoke you until you react if you speak to them. Remember how the media hounded Diana?"

"I don't think we're in that category. They can't talk to me when I'm in the car."

"Don't bet on it. They'll stop you from leaving until they get what they want."

"Maybe you're right. With any luck, they'll leave when they realise they're wasting their time."

"We might be away on holiday for all they know. Don't turn the lights on, and stay away from the window." Katrina said, then giggled like a child playing a game of hide-and-seek.

"Better still. I'll ring Alistair?" He said, reaching for the bedside phone.

"Morning, Alistair. Sorry to disturb you this early in the morning…"

🐘

Sandy barked when Alistair's Jaguar XE drove into the drive. Philippe let Alistair in via the front door, and he shielded his face from bright lights, microphones and cameras aimed in his direction.

"Have you anything to say about Norman Taylor?" A reporter shouted.

"Mr Duval. What are your feelings on Norman Taylor's arrest?" Shouted another.

"How do you feel, knowing that a neighbour caused your daughter's death?"

Philippe took Alistair into the kitchen, and Alistair handed him a previously prepared statement. He read it and gave Alistair the thumbs up, and then Alistair went outside to read the statement to the media. Satisfied with a story, they packed away and were gone within half an hour.

Today's Media is not about news but money and disinformation. It's about being the first to get the money shot or vox pop to swell their ratings and bank balance. Mainstream Media lack empathy, and people's lives mean nothing to them. All they care about is receiving a fat paycheque for their efforts. To have your private life thrust into the public eye is the ultimate betrayal. Philippe and Katrina were their victims, and to have a story flashed around the globe via satellite and social media was too fast, too soon.

There were many obstacles to overcome; now they knew a neighbour had contributed to their daughter's death. They will eventually come to terms with the knowledge and acceptance is a strange companion. It was hard to comprehend why a man known to them, a love-starved husk of a man, attacked their daughter and caused her death. They will forgive Norman Taylor over time, but will they ever forget?

SIXTY-FOUR

If Philippe had gone to work that morning, he would have heard the bells of Swynbourne Cathedral chime the hour of twelve. He would have witnessed people rushing across the city square, carrying coffee cups in cardboard trays, unaware of Norman Taylor's incarceration, mere yards below their feet.

With his body in constant fight/flight mode, Norman's heart rate soared with every unfamiliar sound. Throughout his life, Norman believed everyone was trying to deceive him, and he always overreacted. He exploded when criticised, however intended, and wouldn't accept responsibility. He defended his ego by putting the blame squarely on the shoulders of others.

He lay on the bed with his legs crossed, contemplating the prospects of a lengthy prison term. Confined within four walls, Norman wept. Was he feeling sorry for himself or remorse for what he'd done to Charlotte? A dark cloud hung over his head. — Consequences: He hadn't thought of those while he pinned Charlotte to the ground with his knees.

Mid-afternoon, Norman was handcuffed and escorted to a waiting security van. The van then took him to Swynbourne Magistrates Court, where the media aimed cameras at darkened windows as it drove through the brick archway. Inside the echoey, wood-panelled courtroom, Norman stood beside O'Dowd, hands clasped in front as the judge read out the charge.

Norman pleaded guilty, and the judge remarked that it was a motiveless crime and his dysfunctional childhood was no excuse to take the life of an innocent teenager, whether intentional or not. The judge took into consideration the fact that the attack wasn't pre-meditated, and Charlotte's death was the result of an unfortunate accident. Norman was detained under the Mental Health Act for psychiatric assessment, and an officer led him down a wooden staircase to the cells below.

SIXTY-FIVE

I had heckled Norman for almost nine hours, draining my spiritual energy. I needed to recharge, much like my old mobile phone.

Before Gran died, she taught me about ley lines and how they connect the planet to the universe. 'They possess tremendous healing powers,' she said. She also told me two ley lines intersected at the Celtic Cross on our village green. *Those Celts knew their stuff.* She sensed my low energy and suggested we walk to the Celtic Cross.

I sat on the plinth and looked at Gran.

"Why are we here, of all places?"

"We're here to replenish your energy. You will learn how to conserve your energy in Paradise, but until then, I'll show you a little trick I learned. Remember how I told you that two ley lines intersect at this point?"

"Yes. I remember, but what has it got to do with me?"

"I'll explain. Come with me to the cemetery; it's quieter there." She said and took me to the memorial bench bearing my name. I ran my fingers along its wooden slats. Willing to share its secrets, the bench showed me images of those who'd rested here or had recently passed. The bench stored memories, much like a computer hard drive, secrets for the minds of higher spirits. I saw images of Mum and counted the times she'd visited the bench. Was she recalling happier times, or was she grieving?

Gran told me that ley lines are our saviour. She explained how they help us align with the universe and restore our energy by raising our vibration. We returned to the Celtic Cross after my education, and when I sat on its base, I immediately became surrounded by a warm, vibrant, crystalline rainbow of light. I had ringing in my ears, and then an irresistible force drew me into another realm. Then, in seconds, I was floating effortlessly through myriad multidimensional spiral universes. My essence shot through time and space, never finding a beginning, never reaching the end. Stars streaked by, swifter than the speediest thought, and their silvery ribbons of light were my guide. An open-hearted field of energy raised me to a higher consciousness and vibration, and there was an infinite awareness of all-knowing knowledge. I wasn't drifting amongst the galaxies and stars; I was the galaxies and stars. Now I understand what Gran meant by ubiquitous. If Paradise is like this, then I can't wait.

Thirty minutes had passed, according to the church clock, but to me, it was only a few short moments. My frequency was raised and realigned, and I tingled from head to toe with zing and vitality.

"Welcome back. How was your journey?"

"Wonderful. What an amazing experience. I feel so revitalised."

"Would you like to go somewhere special now that your energy has been restored?"

I gave it some thought; then, without giving her an answer, I took hold of her hand.

"Come with me."

My earliest recollection of the Post Office was a tired and neglected building desperately needing repair. We stood on the opposite side of the road and couldn't believe our eyes. The old Post Office had been transformed and looked new but retained the pretence of a bygone era. The spalling brickwork had been cleaned, the peeling fascia gleamed in the sunlight, as did the windows, and the words, 'Gran's Tearoom,' were handwritten in gold letters above the forest-green frontage. Below, it said 'Proprietor, Katrina Duval, and an eye-catching sign displayed across the window said, OPENING SOON. The sight filled my heart with pride. I turned to Gran.

"Mum's scones recipe will be useful in the tearoom," I commented.

"My recipe, if you don't mind."

"I know. I was only kidding. Now the whole village will know who owns the building."

Norman was the last person on my mind as I looked at the tearoom with pride. I overheard Cunningham saying that Norman pleaded guilty to a charge of involuntary manslaughter through gross negligence, and sentencing was delayed for further reports.

Well, that was it. My time on earth is done, and I can go to the light. I'm ready, but first, I must say goodbye to everyone.

The Post Office side of the business closed over two years ago, but the shop had always affectionately been known as 'the Post Office.' Habit, I suppose. But I'm sure that will change over time. Gran stood in the doorway and smiled, proud of her daughter's achievement.

I said goodbye to as many friends as possible, then returned to the Post Office; sorry, I meant Gran's Tea Room to say goodbye to Mum and Dad. Gran sensed my eyes were upon her. She turned and then beckoned me.

I had said my goodbyes and promised everyone I'd return soon. She rested a hand on my shoulder.

"It's time."

"Yes, and I'm ready. Although excited, I'm a little apprehensive. I'm going to miss everyone. Will I be able to return? I promised I would."

"Of course you can return, Lottie. But not until you've undergone a healing process."

"Healing? What do you mean?"

"Emotional healing, tailored specifically for you. It's difficult to explain, but you'll understand once you're there. There's no reason to be afraid. I'll be with you every step of the way. Ubiquity, remember?"

Mum and Dad were setting tables, so I mouthed 'Elephant Juice' one last time and cried with mixed emotions.

"It's a wonderful life," I sobbed, remembering the film. See you soon..." I said, my voice trailing to a whisper.

Gran said it would be fun in spirit, but for some reason, my sense of humour eluded me at times. I thought aggravating Norman would be fun, and initially, it was, but I got bored until I got a result. Because of him, I was in spirit, which is why I needed to stay longer.

I was reluctant to leave Mum, Dad, and my friends, especially Isabella and Abigail. Look at Isabella now — how healthy she looks. With a new business venture to occupy Mum, her life will move forward with no regrets.

My extra time on Earth was an education, and I learned so much, especially from Gran. It was rewarding to watch them come to terms with my loss, to come through smiling despite their sorrow. At first, I thought that running Gran's Tea Room was a distraction for Mum to hide her grief. But I was wrong. She runs Gran's Tea Shop in honour of her mother and me, her only daughter.

We achieve personal goals using tenacity and strength. I'd achieved my goal in spirit, and when I stood with Gran, there was a knowing, an awareness not to be resisted. She held her hands like a beckoning Angel, eyes glistening with the warmth, affection, and unconditional love only a grandma can have. I hesitated, but having accomplished my task, I knew it was time. The heavenly aroma of Sandalwood and Lavender surrounded me like a warm-scented breeze. As light from above intensified, love slipped over me like a silken cape and entered my soul as if by invitation.

"It's time." She whispered.

"I'm ready," I replied.

The white light surrounding us felt softer than an Angel's kiss. The air crackled as speckled light shimmered and cascaded like a silky-smooth waterfall. Every cell of my being warmed, and I glanced heavenwards as the light grew in intensity. A gentle breeze tossed my hair, fluting it. Beckoned by the tunnel of True Divine Light, the ground fell away as we slowly ascended through the shimmering tunnel leading to Paradise.

SIXTY-SIX

Time passed quickly in Paradise, but since I learned I could visit Ashmarsh, it began to drag as I waited for that day. This will be my first visit to Earth since going to the light, and it is like going on holiday, minus a suitcase. I'd spent three of our months in the hospital, healing and learning the intricacies of spirit life. I've grown and matured so much since then, and come that day, I will be free to visit family and friends whenever I choose.

Dizzy with excitement, the trip back to 3D Earth took only a moment, and when I arrived at the cottage, I instantly regretted not bringing a suitcase filled with souvenirs. *It's a ridiculous idea, I know.*

Three earth years have passed, and there have been many changes. Gran's Tea Room was enormously successful, and Ashmarsh was voted the prettiest village for two consecutive years. The council were shamed into upgrading the streetlights and even provided dainty flower boxes throughout the village. Other than that, everything seemed familiar.

Sandy was in the back garden, sunning himself by the gazebo. His fur showed grey specks, and he'd become slightly podgy.

"Hello, Sandy," I said, excited to see him. "C'mere. I've missed you so much." I said, out of habit and believing he could hear me. He raised his head and stared at me, then whined and rested his head between his paws.

Dad was clearing tables, and Mum was serving behind the counter when I joined them. I told Mum and Dad how proud I was and promised to join them at the cottage later. I knew they weren't aware of my presence, but talking to them felt normal.

A young couple bought and moved into Norman Taylor's old house, and with a new baby, I prayed they would give that child all the unconditional love it deserved.

There was so much gossip to catch up on in the village. In one conversation, I learned a few interesting facts about Norman Taylor. Two old ladies were saying that he had completely turned his life around after spending two and a half years in prison, followed by six months in a Psychiatric Rehabilitation Facility. He works in London as an accomplished artist for a well-known art studio. The outcome was better than I imagined, and I'm pleased his life wasn't wasted in prison. He contributed to my death, but I forgave him long ago. Everyone deserves a second chance.

Although she says it's purely platonic, Isabella juggled her life between studies and her hot, new boyfriend, Jacob. With her parents' blessing, she rents the flat above Gran's Tea Room and works in the Tea Room on Sundays to help with the bills. She plans to work full-time in the kitchen after studying catering at Swynbourne University, which is a complete change in direction. She has grown into a confident young lady, and you would never guess she'd undergone heart transplant surgery unless she told you. Mum and Isabella were closer than ever. They are more like sisters, and I must admit, I am a teeny bit jealous.

My next stop was the memorial bench dedicated to me. Gran had also made the trip to Earth without my knowledge and joined me as I slipped through the familiar iron gates. And there it was, silhouetted against the blue sky like a modern art sculpture. When we sat, the bench told me how well-loved and perfectly placed it was, flanked by rose bushes on either side. I read the nameplate quietly and dearly hoped I was not forgotten.

The view from the bench was striking, set beneath overhanging branches offering shade on sunny days, shelter on rainy days, and an unblemished view of the church and Table Mountain in the background. How many had shared the view from the bench with thoughts of past loved ones and talking to them as though they were present?

"I'm proud of this bench, and I'll spend as much time here as possible. Reading my name on the brass plate has given me a sense of pride, and I know I will never be forgotten." I said to Gran.

"The bench will be here for many generations, and you'll get used to seeing your name." She replied.

"I expect it was expensive. I hope I was worth it." I said, chewing my cheek.

"I don't suppose anyone begrudged a single penny."

I ran my fingers along the smooth-grained oak slats.

"It's a shame my life ended so soon." Gran clasped my hand, and I turned to face her.

"Do you remember the day I was born?"

"As if it were only yesterday." She said, eyes sparkling with memories. "I was with your mother when you came into this world. Your father was working away and couldn't be there. You were in a hurry to make your presence known, and I knew you were special from that moment on."

"Special?"

"Yes. I sensed you were an earth Angel from the moment you were born. Your parents adored you, but our bond was undeniable."

"I felt it too, Gran. I love you, and I'm glad I'm with you, although I didn't expect it to happen like it did and so soon."

"Human lives don't always go as planned. Souls choose their spiritual path before they're born. They may stray from their chosen path but will always return."

"Are you saying I chose to die at a young age before I was even born?" Gran held my hand tightly and smiled.

"It's not that simple. Our earth experience involves many connected souls. Those souls may choose to take a human life. As light beings, we decide the earth experiences we need to evolve and ascend to a higher frequency when we leave our mortal bodies. Spirits have a higher frequency, so your Mum and Dad can't see or hear you."

"Then why was Norman Taylor able to hear me?"

"That's an excellent question. Clairaudience involves an increased ability to hear sounds, voices, or messages beyond the normal range of human auditory perception. Norman possessed that ability, a residual memory bleeding through from the spiritual realm."

"Mmm. I remembered everything when I entered Paradise. Our memories are wiped when we are born."

"Correct. For obvious reasons our memories are wiped before we enter the 3-D world. There wouldn't be any point in us having an earth experience if they weren't."

I thought about her words. She's so wise, and I ached to ask her a question that had been bothering me since my first day in spirit. We discussed our earth experiences, so I thought now was the right time to ask.

"Was I a good person on earth, in your opinion?"

"Oh, my goodness. Why do you even have to ask? I'm in no position to judge. You chose your path and lived to the best of your abilities."

"Well. I asked because I had close friends but didn't connect with them."

"That's not true. You were a beautiful person on earth. People loved you, but you were always too distracted to notice."

"You're right. I did keep myself busy, didn't I? I have self-doubts, and I'm asking for reassurance." I said, then dropped my gaze.

"Seeking reassurance is a waste of energy. Believe in yourself, Charlie."

"Charlie? Where did that come from?"

"Your friends called you Charlie. I like it. It has a certain ring to it."

"I suppose it does. I haven't been called Charlie in ages." I needed more and probed a little deeper.

"Did you watch over me after you'd passed?"

"I did. I made sure you were safe by observing you when you were with your friends. I didn't judge or spy on you. I saw the looks your friends gave you and heard their kind words when you weren't with them. It's a shame because most don't know they're loved until it's too late. If you chose to live longer, perhaps you would have made your way in the world and found your purpose. Of course, it all changed when your life ended suddenly. But that's no longer important. Release your fears. Hand them to God, and let Him take care of them."

My concerns were lessened, but that didn't stop me from shedding a tear. It was as though a veil had been lifted from me, and I was grateful for the warm sun, the beautiful trees, the gorgeous flowers, the sweet melodies of a songbird — all God's wonderful creations.

It may seem odd to cry in spirit, but tears serve a purpose. Their cleansing washed away my doubts about myself during my time on Earth.

"Thank you. I regret never being able to share special moments with my friends again. I wish I'd paid them more attention."

"Shhh. Don't berate yourself. It's better to regret what we've done than to regret what we haven't."

"Yes, but…"

"…no, buts." Gran insisted. "It wasn't your fault. It was no one's fault. It was the way."

"If only I had your wisdom. I was healed in the hospital, but returning to earth has reopened my wounds. Will it always be this way?"

"I feel your pain, but it will ease over time."

"You make it sound easy."

I yearned to be with Gran shortly after her death, but I didn't expect to join her so soon; I was too much of a fan of living. My regrets were free falling. If I'd gone into Swynbourne with my parents that day, then the attack wouldn't have taken place. If they hadn't taken Sandy, I would have had him with me at the cemetery, and maybe Norman wouldn't have followed me. There were too many ifs and buts, and it's hard not to torture myself after my traumatic experience. Gran was right, though. She said I would find it difficult to understand, and 'what might have been' no longer mattered.

What kills you makes you stronger.

SIXTY-SEVEN

Mum and Dad were discussing the Tea Room over dinner. Dad was proud of her achievement regarding Gran's Tea Shop. I sat in an easy chair and hugged my knees while Mum talked about the anniversary of my death and the miracle of Isabella's heart transplant operation, all in the same sentence. I gave them my full attention.

"I'm pleased Charlotte carried an NHS Organ Donor Card with her so that her organs would be donated upon her death. Her thoughtfulness has made an enormous difference in other people's lives. I am eternally grateful knowing that Charlotte's heart wasn't wasted and was used to save Isabella's life." She said, raising a glass to my portrait above the fireplace. "I'm so happy that Isabella is keeping the memory of our daughter alive."

"Isabella is a constant reminder," Dad said, raising his glass. "They were like sisters, and now, I swear Isabella has developed some of Charlotte's characteristics."

Mum raised the gold locket around her neck and touched it to her lips.

"She does have similar tastes in food and clothing since the operation, although, unlike Charlotte, whose intention was to study

Law, she's studying catering. I agree with what you're saying about Isabella, but there are differences."

"I know, but I can't help seeing the likeness."

He didn't reply. Instead, he sipped his wine and formed a mental picture of me shaking my hair from my face, the way Isabella now does.

The news came as an enormous shock. To learn Isabella had received my heart was monumental, and I needed time to process the information. All the loose ends were coming together at last, and it dawned on me that we were in hospital at the same time she received a heart. How fortunate. Synchronicity. Doctors performed a tissue-type test and agreed that my heart matched perfectly. Perhaps my sole purpose on earth was to save Isabela's life. If that was the case, I have no regrets: not one.

How did Mum and Dad find out about my heart recipient? The truth would be highly upsetting for Isabella, so I doubt she knows. To learn you have received your bestie's heart would be too big a burden for any young lady to carry.

Cunningham removed my NHS Donor Organ Card from my jeans pocket before he bagged my clothing and took them away for analysis. They didn't know it at the time, but by carrying out my wish to donate my organs, Mum and Dad had unwittingly saved Isabella's life. Was the timing perfect, or was it synchronicity? Confronted with the heart-rending decision to turn off my life support or not, that decision was made for them.

Isabella benefited from my death, and my love for her has grown with every passing day. Do you know that gap-filling foam, which expands to many times its size when exposed to air? Well, that's how my love feels for her. We were besties when I was a living soul, but now we're closer than ever, and our commonality will keep us together. Pour l'éternité. For all eternity. *Besties forever.*

The End

SIXTY-EIGHT

The steamy bathroom mirror caught Katrina's attention as she stepped out of the shower. With a fleecy towel around her waist and a puzzled frown, she stared at the mystery on the mirror. Was it one of Philippe's silly jokes? She called his name but was met with silence. What she didn't hear, was Philippe's assurance that it was a joke, and not meant to frighten her. Denied her assurance, gripped by alarm, she stared in puzzlement at the mirror, then read the short sentence inscribed in the steam. Katrina covered her mouth and took a sharp breath, sending the towel sliding to the floor. The two words jumped out from the mirror as she reread them. By now, she knew it wasn't her imagination playing tricks. She stared silently at the mirror to affirm her thoughts, and love allayed her fears as she mouthed the two sacred words. She reached for the locket on the wash basin and held it to her lips as falling tears mimicked the water beads tracking down the mirror. Each cursive letter slowly turned into meaningless streaks. But that was irrelevant because she knew. Her sorrow turned to joy, and a smile played upon her lips as the words ELEPHANT JUICE slowly dissolved.

The End

Also, from Stephen J Cherrill.

The sequel to **ELEPHANT JIUCE**

ISBN 9 780648 623526   **amazon.com**

Once again, the village of Ashmarsh is shaken by the sudden death of a young female.

The coroner's report recorded death by misadventure, but DCI Cunningham's uncanny knack for probing deeper takes things to the next level. He embarks on a secret operation into the young female's death with the aid of a new teammate, DS Greg Armstrong.

That next level is soon achieved when Cunningham uncovers a serious clerical error. He presents the new evidence to the Chief Superintendent, who officially begins the investigation.

Follow the intricate journey of two detectives with opposing views as they embark on a complex journey into an unnecessary loss of life.